D0112871

In Everything Give Thanks

**Compliments of
The Jerry B. Jenkins
Christian Writers Guild**

ChristianWritersGuild.com

IN EVERYTHING
GIVE THANKS

TERRY BARNES

Tyndale House Publishers, Inc.

CAROL STREAM, ILLINOIS

Visit Tyndale's exciting Web site at www.tyndale.com

TYNDALE and Tyndale's quill logo are registered trademarks of Tyndale House Publishers, Inc.

In Everything Give Thanks

Copyright © 2007 by Terry Barnes. All rights reserved.

Cover photograph of shoes copyright © by Siede Preis/Getty Images. All rights reserved.

Cover photograph of buildings copyright © by Photos.com. All rights reserved.

Cover photograph of gravel road copyright © by Bruce Bean/iStockphoto. All rights reserved.

Author photo copyright © 2006 by Katie Schwyhart. All rights reserved.

Designed by Ron Kaufmann

Scripture quotations are taken from the *Holy Bible*, King James Version.

Some Scripture taken from the New King James Version®. Copyright © 1982 by Thomas Nelson, Inc. Used by permission. All rights reserved.

This novel is a work of fiction. Names, characters, places, and incidents either are the product of the author's imagination or are used fictitiously. Any resemblance to actual events, locales, organizations, or persons living or dead is entirely coincidental and beyond the intent of either the author or publisher.

Library of Congress Cataloging-in-Publication Data

Barnes, Terry.
  In everything give thanks / Terry Barnes.
    p. cm.
  ISBN-13: 978-1-4143-1301-6 (pbk.)
  ISBN-10: 1-4143-1301-2 (pbk.)
    1. Boys—Fiction. 2. Fathers—Death—Fiction. 3. Nineteen sixties—
Fiction. I. Title.
  PS3602.A77565I55 2007
  813'.6—dc22   2006100943

Printed in the United States of America

13 12 11 10 09 08 07
 7   6   5   4   3   2   1

. . . to the wife of my youth
and to the children that she bore me.

I would like to briefly acknowledge Jerry Jenkins, those at the Christian Writers Guild, and also the many faithful at Tyndale House. I am keenly aware that your collective vision, dedication, and skill made this novel possible.

Thanks.

ONE

The race set before us began at the hedge corner post, ran the entire length of the dirt road, and concluded at the drainage tube at the south end. Ditches and fences lined the road, and an intermittent tree line followed the fences, with pastures and gently rolling fields beyond the trees. Wheat grew in some of the fields, and in the summer we would sometimes watch combines cut huge swaths in the grain, then throw chaff and dust into the air. Grain trucks lumbering along the dirt road stirred up dust too, and this dust hovered above the road before slowly drifting through the trees and settling over the fields. Traffic rarely used the road, and only then when someone desired a shortcut between the two gravel county roads located at either end.

"On your mark!"

But he did not die on a dirt road.

He had been killed on the two-lane blacktop highway just east of Bethel. The race set before him had abruptly ended on a muggy July night after he had finished the late shift at the plant. He had been driving home at one o'clock in the morning when a drunk driver hit him head-on, killing them both instantly.

He had been a soldier of the Fourth Marine Division in the war and had been wounded on Iwo Jima. As a direct result of that horrible experience, he had received Jesus Christ as his Savior and had served his Lord ever since. He had been the chairman of the deacon board at Bethel Baptist Church, and everyone who knew him affectionately called him Tommy.

I called him Dad.

"*Get set!*" Squareface bellowed the commands in his usual raucous manner.

We would often sprint down the dirt road because the footing was surer than loose gravel on county roads and the gentle grades were of little consequence. We would try to race in the mornings to avoid the heat, but sometimes we raced in the afternoons, for we were young then and strong.

The hot August sun punished everything that lived and breathed, and it even bleached the dirt road. Thinking too hard caused perspiration in the sweltering heat. We wiped sweat from our brows.

"*Go!*"

The race began.

Squareface pedaled his bicycle past us so he would arrive at the finish line first and could officially declare the winner. His effort was quite unnecessary. There was no question who would win this race.

Colby would.

Stanley Colby always outran me. He was six months older and a half inch taller. We had always been best friends, a result of sitting next to each other in school during the early years. *Colby* invariably sat in front of *Collins* in a school district bent on seating children in alphabetical order.

We ran down the gentle slope for nearly a quarter mile to the culvert that fed the pond where the willow trees grew. Squareface rode ahead of us, and we pounded after him like dogs chasing a mechanical rabbit.

Grasses and weeds grew in the ditches, and there were some sunflowers, too, lost and forgotten. Cicadas, defying the heat, sang their monotonous, droning song. Colby took the lead and ran in the left wheel path while I took the right. He set the pace. It was too fast.

Colby breathed easily. I puffed in agony.

By the time we reached the willow trees, sweat poured off us, stinging our eyes and dripping to the ground, only to be devoured by the parched dust of the road.

Life had forever changed on that horrible July night. The highway patrol came to the house, and Mom and I ended up at the funeral home to identify the body. Dad had survived a world war, an awful campaign on that horrendous island, and even a Japanese bullet, just to be killed by one of his own countrymen eighteen years later. And a drunk countryman at that. Dad was only thirty-nine.

On we ran.

I knew I could not catch Colby, for I had never beaten him in my life.

A dead cat, partially decomposed and swarming with maggots, lay in the grassy center strip beyond the shade of the willow trees. Flies buzzed around the cat, and there was an odor, deep and rank and intensified by the heat. We each covered our nose and mouth the best we could with our hands as we ran by. We ran and tried to hold our breath, though we were panting by now.

Death comes to all things. Even dreams.

Sometimes faith.

I gasped and tried to regain my breath.

Colby increased his lead slightly as we ran up the gentle incline toward the woven fence line. The fence followed a truck path that separated fields, and this marked the halfway point. The sun beat upon us, and we felt no breeze except what we stirred by running.

Dad had loved God. He said as much. Everybody knew it. His actions proved his words. Dad would attend church every time the doors opened for any reason. He served God faithfully. For his reward, he died in a horrible crash with a stupid drunk while God idly stood by and watched.

Some reward.

I would not make that foolish mistake.

McLean's section, located on the east side of the dirt road, contained the large pond, and he often let us fish there. Sparse trees encompassed the pond, and there were cattails, too, growing out of the murk along the west edge. South of the pond stood his cornfield, tall ripening stalks about ready for harvest. The dirt road bordered the entire length of McLean's section, a distance we arbitrarily agreed to be one mile.

Other people owned the land on the west side of the

road. One field of wheat had been cut earlier in the summer, and the woven fence line divided a field of beans from Zimmerman's pasture. Holsteins lazily grazed in the pasture, and several of them were lying down in the meager shade, paying us no mind. The dirt road became mostly level here and continued between mulberry trees for nearly half a mile until ending at the gravel road.

God betrayed us on that terrible July night. We somehow believed He took care of those who loved Him, but this obviously was not true. It had been a violent shock to realize how unfair God could be. A very violent shock.

Mom took it hard.

She wailed that night and fainted once, then cried all through the funeral. Now after five weeks she still cried in the night, pitiful wailing that painfully stabbed the heart. Though my bedroom was located at the other end of the house in what was once the garage, I could hear her soul-wrenching sobs. Her bedroom door would be closed, and I would close mine, too. That stopped the sound, but it was still no good, for I knew she was crying.

Then there was Debbie, my kid sister. We were real close. Deb had tried so hard not to cry, especially at the funeral, but she did and she cried a lot afterward too. She would bite her lower lip and try so hard to be brave, then melt in a flood of tears.

"Come on, Matt!" Colby called.

I'm coming. Though I tried, my legs could not move any faster. They complained instead, along with the rest of my body.

Squareface reached the county road and was waiting while we approached. I watched Colby pound onward, his lead increasing. In this final stretch, the mulberry trees afforded us some shade, and the shade provided us some relief.

I did not cry at the funeral.

Nor afterward.

I vowed to never cry again. Though I did love Mom and Deb, I would never love anybody else. If you loved, you got hurt because God would take your loved one away from you. Nothing was worth such pain. Nothing.

Colby reached the gravel road and finished first, maybe twelve seconds ahead of me.

I crossed the drainage tube that ran under the dirt road and clicked my stopwatch. I bent over and gulped for air.

"How fast?" Colby asked.

I stood straight, stared at the watch, and fought for breath. "Five fifty-eight."

"Not bad for this heat," he said.

"I've done better."

"Coach Garrett thinks we'll break five minutes this year."

"Coach Garrett thinks *you'll* break five minutes," I said.

"He didn't say me. He said he expected one of us." Colby smiled. He was taller than average, well proportioned, strong, and devoid of any physical flaw. He had brown eyes, short brown hair, and an engaging smile that would win anyone over to his side.

I had often invited him to church, and he had even come two or three times. He finally said church was not for him. I never pressed the issue.

Colby had always been a faster runner, but I had always received better grades. I assumed I was smarter. This assumption had been incorrect. Colby was much smarter. He knew enough to leave God alone. This was sound thinking. If a fifteen-year-old could be called a complete man, Colby deserved the title.

"Haven't seen you at cross-country practice," he said. "Didn't you get your notice?"

"Yes."

"Aren't you going out this year?" he asked.

"Nope."

"You're not going out?" Squareface exploded from behind us.

We both turned and looked at him, having momentarily forgotten he was there. His name was Ronnie Kindle, but with his square jaw and flattop haircut, the nickname fit. He followed Colby around like a puppy dog.

"We're not talking to you," Colby said.

Squareface instantly became stiff at the rebuke.

Colby then turned and winked at me. "Don't pay him no mind. If you don't want to run cross-country, you don't have to run cross-country. And you don't have to worry none what nobody says."

"But everybody expects you to run," Squareface said. "Both of you are so fast. The fastest in our class."

I shrugged. "Not going out for cross-country."

"But—"

"Why don't you just ride on home," Colby said to Squareface. "Me and Matt will walk on back. Alone."

Squareface silently opened and closed his mouth while giving me an ugly look.

Yeah, just go.

He stomped the left pedal of his bike, briefly spun the rear wheel, flinging dirt, and sped away.

We watched him ride off beyond the lingering dust of his tantrum. Colby and I began our walk back.

"Squareface sure left in a huff," I said.

"Oh, he's okay."

"If looks could kill . . ."

"Squareface is okay. Besides, he knows how to have fun. That's what I like about him."

"I suppose."

"Matt, that's the problem with you. You're too serious. You need to loosen up. Have some fun. That's what you need."

"Fun? What I need is water." We were hot, and our shirts and shorts were completely soaked; we desperately wished for even a hint of breeze.

"Matt, my boy," he said, "I hope you realize Coach Garrett'll be ticked. He's got high hopes for you on the junior varsity team."

"I guess he won't be pleased. But you understand."

"Yeah, I guess." Colby shrugged.

"I knew you would. Friends understand such things."

I would have given anything to be him or at least be like him. That was now my goal—to be like Colby.

Colby was wise because he had nothing to do with God. I would be wise too and have nothing to do with God.

I became a Christian when I was eight. Then just four months ago, back in April, I had gone forward during a Sunday evening service at Bethel Baptist Church and told the congregation that I firmly believed God had called me to preach. Dad and Mom had been very proud.

That decision had been a terrible, terrible mistake. I now regretted everything.

"But you're making a big mistake by not running," he said.

"How's that?"

"Think of the glory."

"What glory?"

"You know. Everybody will notice you. Even girls. Know what I mean?"

"I suppose." I really didn't.

"You should reconsider."

We jogged past the dead cat to escape the horrid stench. Once clear, we stopped and looked at the stubble that was once a beautiful field of wheat. Several defiant stalks remained at each corner of the field, ignored by the combines, but now their proud heads drooped, having lost their overripe grain to the ground.

Back in July there had been a panic to harvest the golden grain because a storm was brewing. It was late and dark, and you could see the faraway lights in the field as well as the angry clouds when the lightning flashed in the black sky. There was the muffled droning of machinery spiked with the crack and rumble of thunder; then suddenly it became real cool, and there was the clean smell of approaching rain. The wind became strong, and the rain began to fall hard, and there was hail that bounced off houses and cars and drives. The men left the combines in the fields and drove away in the grain trucks, and later we saw deep ruts left behind by the trucks that disfigured the road.

"That was a lifetime ago."

"What did you say?" Colby asked.

"Nothing."

"Matt? You okay?"

I looked across the stubble at the neglected stalks. "Yeah, I'm okay."

"Come on," he said. "Let's go to your house."

"Sure."

"We need some water."

"Yeah."

"What we really need's a change of weather. This heat's awful. We need a change."

We started again toward my house.

No, I would not preach. I would have nothing to do with God. Never. I made a deal with Him. An agreement. I would leave Him alone, and He would leave me alone.

We would stay out of each other's way. I would live without His help, thank you.

I fully intended to keep my half of the bargain.

Colby got his wish. The next day the weather did change. On the Friday before the beginning of our tenth-grade year at Bethel High School, a cold front came down from the north, causing cloudy skies and cooler temperatures. The day brought a touch of fall to the air, and everybody said we might have an early one. Later I even noticed that old Wilmer McLean was scrambling to prepare an east field so he could drill winter wheat while he still had the chance.

Not only did the weather change, but other things changed as well. On that cool, unusual Friday, they moved in next door, and he intruded into my life.

TWO

That year we lived in a little gray house on Church Street on the southwest edge of Bethel. Fields surrounded the town, and there were also fields west of the house and south across the street. Two large pin oaks dominated the front yard, and over the years we would often sit under those trees and watch the sparse traffic enter town from the gravel road. Church Street became that gravel county road about a hundred feet west of our property line. Sometimes while we were sitting under the trees and a car came racing into town, if it had been dry and there was a breeze from the south, there would be a cloud of dust that followed the car and would drift our way and settle over the yard and dust the little gray house. Our little dusty house was painted two shades of gray on the outside and several shades of despair on the inside.

"Where you going, Matt?" Debbie asked.

It was early afternoon, and we were sitting outside under one of the tall oaks. I had just stood up and stretched.

"Inside."

"Aren't you going to wait for our new neighbors?" she asked.

"No."

"But . . ."

The day was very pleasant, and it was a joy to be outside for once and not to be frying like eggs. Yet regardless of the weather, I started walking toward the house.

". . . but Mom said that they are supposed to come today," she said.

I entered the house without answering. I walked to my room, flopped crossways on my bed, and began reading a novel as it rested on the floor. Unfortunately, within just a few minutes, I heard the sound of a truck. I kept reading.

It seemed like it was no time before Debbie skipped into my room. "They're here."

"So?"

"Mom said we should help when they come."

"So?"

"Matt!"

I left the novel on the floor, rolled over on the bed, and sat up.

"Come see," she said.

I followed her as she bounced to her bedroom at the other end of the house. We went to her east window, and I looked over her shoulder at the house next door. There was a rental truck parked near the front porch, and we watched as an older man climbed into the back of the truck.

Debbie gave a little hop. "Let's go," she said.

"You go ahead."

"You need to come too."

"Naw. I'll stay here."

"But Mom—"

"I'm busy."

"But aren't you even curious about them?" she asked.

Though I'd have rather returned to my book and solitude, I *was* curious about them—at least a little—their being our new neighbors and all. "No. I'm not curious."

"Matt!" She stomped her foot.

I was getting a big kick out of irritating Debbie.

"We have to go. Mom said. Please?!"

I shrugged and followed her outside.

We walked into the neighbors' yard toward the truck. The day was not cool enough to wear a jacket but cool enough to make you think about wearing one. The feeling of fall filled the air, and this was a dramatic change from the preceding day. We walked up to the back of the truck at about the same time the older man we had seen earlier jumped out.

"Hi," I said.

"Well, howdy," he said. He spoke with a drawl.

"I'm Matthew Collins. This is my sister, Debbie. We live next door."

Debbie smiled and nodded.

"Well, glad to meet you, Matthew and Debbie." He gave us each a hearty handshake, and he had a warm smile. "I'm Arthur Scott. My wife, Elaine, is inside, and so is Wade, our boy."

Mr. Scott was an older man with short gray hair and

deep lines across his forehead and on his face. His kind gray eyes had a sad look to them. Though of average height, he was big and bulky. Not fat, just muscular and stocky. He looked like he could lift up the truck with one hand if he had a mind to. At least the front end. He wore blue jeans and a blue long-sleeved work shirt that was rolled up to his elbows.

"Come inside and meet everybody," he said. "You'll need to meet Wade. What grade will you be in, Matthew?"

"Everybody calls me Matt."

"Well, Matt it is. What grade will you be in, Matt?"

"Tenth."

"Sophomore, eh? Well, so is Wade. You two will be classmates."

"I'll be in fifth grade," Debbie said.

"I see." He smiled at her.

We followed him up the porch steps and inside the house into the living room. The room was empty except for a few scattered boxes.

"Elaine! Wade! Come meet our neighbors!"

We neither saw nor heard anybody.

"Wade's probably in his bedroom," he said. "Why don't you two go meet him? I'll find Elaine."

The house had the same floor plan as ours, so Debbie and I walked toward the two bedrooms on the east end. The wood floor needed waxing, but the plaster walls had a fresh coat of creamy white paint. We entered a bedroom, where several boxes were stacked in the center; an open Bible rested on one of the boxes.

We also saw Wade standing near the window. He was a little taller than me and heavier, too, but his body looked mushy and soft. He had a pale color that you'd expect from somebody who never went outside. His hair was dark and plastered down on his head, and he wore thick, black-rimmed glasses.

"Ch-charge!" he said. He held a toy sword in one hand and its sheath in the other, and he swung and jabbed them wildly into the air. He bobbed in some strange dance, wild and contorted.

He whirled around and saw us. "G-get back, you Y-Yankees," he stuttered while swinging the sword over his head. "I-I follow General L-Lee."

He continued swinging wildly, his movements awkward and uncoordinated. He struck the sword on a box, jabbed wildly in the air, then swung with a spasmodic movement behind him.

"He's nuts," I said. I pushed Debbie back a couple of steps, and we stood in the doorway.

"Did we make him mad?" she asked.

Wade thrust the sword in our direction, though we were well out of reach, and swung it over his head. The sword looked like it might have been purchased at any toy department. Though rounded on the end, it was still metal and would probably hurt if it hit someone.

"Maybe we should leave," Debbie said.

He pointed the sword directly at me. "Ch-charge!"

"If he charges me, I'll wrap that thing around his neck," I told Debbie.

I don't think he heard.

"What's wrong with him?" she asked.

"Who knows? But I agree with you. Let's leave."

We turned toward the hall.

"Before he hurts someone," I added.

"W-wait," Wade said.

We turned around and faced him.

He lowered his toy and moved toward us in a shuffling, pigeon-toed walk. He tried to insert his sword in its sheath, but this took several attempts before he finally succeeded. While standing in front of us, he made an exaggerated bow, nearly losing his balance. "W-Wade Hampton S-Scott at your s-service," he said with some spit.

I looked him over. "Matt Collins. This is Debbie."

"P-pleased to m-meet you." His stammering voice had a softness to it, much like the looks of his spongy body. He looked older than a sophomore. His hands were curled slightly, and he held them forward from his elbows. He attempted to hold out a curved hand toward me.

I ignored his gesture.

"Pleased to meet you, Wade," Debbie said. She shrugged at me.

"I-I am a famous g-general," he said. "Yes-sir-ee. F-famous general."

Sure. And I'm Mickey Mouse, and this is my sister, Daffy Duck. Two can play this nutty game.

"W-Wade Hampton from South Carolina rode with General L-Lee."

I may have not been up on General Lee, but I did know that Bethel was at least twelve hundred miles from

Charleston and many miles north of the Mason-Dixon Line. I wondered if Wade even knew what part of the Union he was in.

"I-I so thankful to be h-here," he said.

"Nice to meet you," I lied. "Come on, Debbie. Let's go help Mr. Scott." I turned back to the hall, and she followed after a second. We retreated toward the living room.

"M-Matt?"

"He's calling you," she said.

"So?"

"Aren't you going to answer?"

"Look. He's crazy or retarded or both. Swinging that sword at us!"

"I don't think he meant anything by it."

"Doesn't matter. I don't have to be threatened by a retard."

So much for our new neighbors. Oh, well. . . .

"But he called you," she said.

"So?"

"Aren't you being rude?"

"He swings a sword at us, and I'm being rude?"

We walked through the living room and through the archway into the dining room.

"Look," I continued. "He's nuts. That's obvious. What if I acted like that? I can see he will be no help to Mr. Scott. It's all up to us to help."

From the dining room, we walked into the kitchen, looking for Mr. Scott. We found Mrs. Scott standing at the sink.

She turned toward us; her eyes and smile had the same sad look as her husband's but were equally kind. About the same age as her husband, she did not look dainty like Mom used to but rather had a rugged look that work and time had given her. She wore a light blue dress.

Mr. Scott entered the kitchen from the basement stairs. "Elaine," he said, "these are our neighbors Matt and Debbie Collins."

"Hi," I said.

"Pleased to meet you," Mrs. Scott said. She smiled and came over and squeezed each of our hands. "Have you met Wade yet?"

I took a deep breath. "Yes, ma'am," I said.

"What's wrong with him?" Debbie asked.

I tried to elbow her, but she was just out of reach. *Who's being rude now?*

"He was injured as a tiny baby, dear," she said. "He really has made great progress though. He can even keep up in school."

Injured? As in losing his brain?

"Oh," Debbie said.

"He's really a very sweet boy," she said.

Sweet? Does he threaten everybody?

"We've come to help," Debbie said.

"Why, thank you," she said. "That is sure thoughtful of you two."

"Need some help, sir?" I asked Mr. Scott.

"Could use a little with the heavy stuff," he said.

We walked outside to the truck, and Debbie followed.

The move-yourself rental truck looked to be about twenty-four feet with dual rear wheels and a storage area over the cab. There was a dolly and a ramp that Mr. Scott had extended from the back of the truck to the front porch, where the iron railing had been removed. There were many boxes still in the truck—some stacked to the top and in the area over the cab—along with furniture covered with blankets.

"Wade is sure looking forward to meeting some new friends," Mr. Scott said.

I can tell.

I stood on the sidewalk beside the ramp and pulled a brown box from off the edge of the truck. It was light, so I handed it to Debbie to carry inside.

"We certainly live on the edge of town," he said.

"We live on the edge of the world," I replied.

"On the edge of the world?" He laughed, and his laugh was deep and hearty.

Dad had always said we lived on the edge of the world, and I thought it was a very good line. "Yes, sir. But I don't know whether the real world is made of paved streets, city blocks, and houses or whether it is made of rolling fields, gravel roads, and tree lines." Dad had also said that, and I always found it amusing.

"I see." Mr. Scott's eyes sparkled, and I could tell he thought it was funny too.

"We live on the edge of the world," I continued, "but I don't know whether we live in the world or outside the world."

"That's pretty good."

"We like living here," I concluded.

"We think we will too," he said. "Let's get a few of these boxes out of the way; then we can move the heavy stuff."

We strapped the refrigerator to the dolly, but we just two-manned most of the furniture. Mr. Scott was so strong I questioned whether I was really of any help. Moving seemed easy to him, natural-like. Debbie helped Mrs. Scott unpack boxes in the kitchen.

We carried the table into the house and maneuvered it to its place in the kitchen.

"So what all do you do in high school?" Mr. Scott asked.

"Matt runs," Debbie chimed in.

"You run?" he asked.

I glanced at Debbie and sighed. "I have in the past," I said. "I'm not sure if I will this year."

"Well, President Kennedy will be pleased with you."

"Sir?"

"The president—he would be pleased. You know, all of this physical fitness stuff the administration has been talking about."

"Oh." I had no idea the president was talking about physical fitness. I paid very little attention to politics.

We worked steadily into the afternoon, for the cool day made everything pleasant. In truth, I did not mind the effort. It was a very good day to work. Wade shuffled around us, sometimes adding comments and spit but never offering to help. The latch on the storm door was broken, but Wade did not even bother to hold it open for us, which would have actually been a help.

"I-I so thankful to have M-Matt next door," he said.

I just ignored him.

"We've been praying for good neighbors," Mr. Scott said.

We finished unloading by midafternoon. We sat on some boxes in the living room for a minute and rested. A slight breeze drifted through the picture window. A brick fireplace stood against the west wall, and Mrs. Scott sat on a dining room chair under the large archway that divided the living and dining rooms. Wade sat down on a box like the rest of us. No doubt he was exhausted.

"D-did your dad just d-die?" he asked me.

A cold chill ran up my spine. I forgot how to breathe. Everything became quiet; the room zoomed out of focus.

"Wade!" Mrs. Scott stood up. "You don't need to talk about it!"

"*Mrs. Collins, there has been a terrible accident. You'll need to come with us.*"

"M-must have been real b-bad."

"Wade! I'm surprised at you! Don't be rude!" Mrs. Scott's face was red.

"*Matt! I need you!*"

I exhaled. Slowly. The room zoomed back into focus.

"I'm sorry," she said to Debbie and me. "The Realtor told us a little about it. If there's anything we can do, please tell us." Mrs. Scott sat back down.

I began to breathe again.

"We're okay," Debbie said. She then shrugged. "Right, Matt?"

"*I'm sorry, Mrs. Collins, but your husband is—*"

"Matt?"

I glared at Wade. "Yeah," I said. "We're okay."

"Wade," Mr. Scott said while reaching into his pocket, "why don't you take our new neighbors up to that store we saw in town and buy them some pop?"

Wade stood and shuffled over to his dad to receive the change. "Th-thanks, Dad."

"That's not necessary." I stood up. "We really need to be going."

"Please. I insist. You both have been great help. It's the least I can do."

"L-let's go." Wade ambled out the front door and negotiated the steps.

"Yippee," Debbie cheered. She leaped to her feet and bolted out the door like a flash. She'd do anything for pop.

"Debbie!"

She was already gone.

Trapped, I could only follow.

The Bethel Superette was four blocks up and three blocks over and sat on Main Street across from the First State Bank. The two-lane, blacktop highway became Main Street as it entered Bethel, and in town the speed limit was 20 mph. Bethel employed only two full-time policemen, and they spent much of their time catching speeders who refused to slow down in town. These efforts brought much money into the municipal coffers of Bethel.

We walked up Tenth Street and crossed Delaware, Shawnee, Walnut, then Main, walking on the redbrick sidewalks. Wade obviously knew where he was going. Debbie walked beside him on the sidewalk, and I sullenly followed.

Wade waddled along in his pigeon-toed gait with his curled hands hanging forward and swinging gently. He had the grace and coordination of a hot air balloon in a variable wind, and his shuffling mode of transportation was almost comical. He hummed an unrecognizable tune in some dreamworld of his own.

We reached the Bethel Superette, a redbrick building erected many years ago, probably when Main Street itself was surfaced with bricks. The pop machine stood just outside the large glass door of the store. Wade handed the dimes to Debbie without comment, and she operated the machine with great efficiency.

"W-what's g-good?" he asked.

"Everything," Debbie replied.

"Root beer," I ordered. "Everything else is nasty."

"Root beer is all right," Debbie said. "Everything is all right, but orange is the best."

"I w-will have root beer with my f-friend. Yes-sir-ee."

Friend?

Debbie distributed the bottles. They sat on a wooden bench outside the store, and I stood next to the machine as far away from Wade as possible. The day was cloudy and cool, and we drank out of the cold bottles and watched the cars and people along Main Street.

"Feels like fall," Debbie said and shivered.

Wade nodded. He drank his root beer, and some of it ran down the corner of his mouth to his shirt. He made an unsuccessful attempt to wipe his mouth.

I concentrated on the sporadic traffic along Main Street.

"W-what grade y-you in?" Wade asked.

I watched a gray phone-company truck creep eastward on Main Street. The pickup had a toolbox built into the bed and an extension ladder secured to a bracket on top of the box.

"Matt, Wade's talking to you," Debbie said.

If he speeds, who pays for the ticket? The driver or the phone company?

"Matt!"

"W-what grade you in?"

I took a long swallow of root beer. "Tenth."

"M-me too! W-we'll be classmates."

"I guess."

"W-we can be best f-friends."

"D-did your dad just d-die?"

Some friend you are.

"B-best friends w-we are."

"Now look—"

"Mom works there," Debbie said, pointing at the bank.

"Sh-she does?"

The First State Bank, a stately new structure built

of adobe-colored brick, beckoned us from across Main Street.

Or at least beckoned Debbie.

"Let's go see her," she said.

"No, Debbie. Let her work."

"Let's go see her and introduce her to Wade."

"No. We might get her in trouble."

"No, we won't." She confidently got up, placed her empty bottle in the rack against the machine, and walked across the street.

Wade followed suit.

"Debbie!"

She ignored me.

I finished the root beer and tagged along.

The plush bank smelled new. A large marble counter dominated the lobby, and the teller windows stood off to one side. Mom had worked at the bank for only two weeks, and we were very thankful for the job, even if it didn't pay much. She counted money, helped customers, and even managed to smile at a few of them. Mom's window was the only one open, but luckily there were no customers at the moment.

Debbie hurried Wade over to the window. "This is our new neighbor," she announced.

Mom stood an inch over five feet tall and was rather thin and frail-looking. She must have aged ten years in the past five weeks. Now she stooped slightly and usually had a faraway look.

"W-Wade Hampton S-Scott at your s-service," he said.

"Pleased to meet you." She smiled.

Wade gave a half bow.

"Are you two helping them get moved in?" she asked.

"We sure are," Debbie said. "And Wade just bought us some pop."

Mom looked at me and I shrugged. "Mr. Scott really did," I said.

"Well, Wade treated us," Debbie said.

"We need to be going," I said to them. I did not want to get Mom into any trouble.

"Thanks for stopping by," Mom said.

Without argument, we all said good-bye and left the bank and reentered the outside world, Wade lagging behind us.

"Y-you C-Christians?" Wade asked.

I stopped and snapped my gaze back at his soft countenance.

"Yes, we are," Debbie said.

Debbie! Just please shut up!

We were stalled on the sidewalk just outside the bank.

"S-so am I," Wade said.

That figures.

"I-I've been called to p-preach."

Preach? Where? At a circus? Or a freak show?

"That's great. Matt has too; haven't you, Matt?"

An empty lumber truck rolled east along Main Street toward the lumberyard and hardware store on that end of town.

"I don't really know, Deb," I answered. Preaching was not a good topic at the moment.

"G-great. I'm excited 'bout p-preaching."

So will everyone who hears you, I'm sure.

"I-I'll tell people they need to p-pray."

"Neat," Debbie said.

"Y-you pray?" he asked me.

Don't preach at me.

"We sure do," she said.

"We all n-need to t-talk to God."

I don't. Me and God have not been getting along too well lately.

"God is g-good."

Don't talk to me about God.

"That's neat," she said. "You need to come to church with us."

Things were now getting way out of hand. "Deb, we need to hurry back home. You've done enough for one day."

She looked at me questioningly as if she had no idea what she had done or was doing.

"M-maybe we can come to your ch-church."

Great. That's all I need. Him next to me, hounding me about God.

"We go to Bethel Baptist Church, just down the road from us," she said.

I glowered at her. She ignored me.

We started up again, back toward home the same way we had come. This time I kept in the lead, hoping to speed things along.

*Why couldn't we have gotten good neighbors? Instead
we've got this . . . this retard. Worse still, he's going to
preach God at us. And probably all the time.*

Unfortunately, the only result of my lead taking was
leaving Wade many steps behind. Debbie hung back to
stay with him.

So Wade was going to preach. That was great. I
certainly wasn't. If God wanted me to preach, well, He
blew that chance. Just another one of those things that
are now forever gone.

But if Wade wanted to preach and tell people to pray
and talk to God, that was fine with me. He could preach
till he turned blue in the face and talk to God till he
dropped dead. I certainly didn't care. It was obvious that
God was getting desperate if he needed Wade to preach
for Him. Of course, that was understandable when you
considered the way God treated people who showed any
interest in serving Him.

God and Wade. God and Wade. A perfect match.

The way I saw things, they deserved each other. Like
two peas in a pod.

They just both needed to stay out of my way.

THREE

On Sunday we walked the five blocks to Bethel Baptist Church, an old, wooden structure that stood on the northwest corner of Church and Fifth streets. The church was white with board siding, and there was a steeple, too, tall and proud. The church was probably as old as the massive elm that towered in front and provided shade for the church and yard. A white bench under the elm faced the church and provided outside comfort for the saints, and there was a large sign built on the back of the bench that faced Church Street and proudly identified to the entire world:

> Bethel Baptist Church
> Greg Yoshida, Pastor
> Fundamental

A small parking lot bordered the west side of the church, and on Sunday morning the prize of parking there was bestowed upon the early birds. Late arrivals were forced to park along both Church and Fifth streets. We, however, always walked to church, winter or summer, unless it was raining; then we would take the car, though probably not without some debate. This was no doubt just one of those quirks of having lived with an ex-marine. In fact we probably would have even walked to church for the funeral had not the funeral home picked us up.

On that day the July sun scorched the earth and blistered the world along with its poor inhabitants. The church was hot and stuffy, though all the windows and doors were open, and there were many flies, too, swarming and buzzing. Several large fans were droning on high but in vain. Sweat poured from everybody, and they were fanning themselves and swatting at flies, and it all looked quite silly except it really wasn't.

The pallbearers struggled carrying the casket down the six steps in front of the church, and when Harvey Wells tripped, for that brief instant, it looked like they would lose the coffin. Yet they recovered, making it down the steps and into the hearse, which then commanded the somber procession to Bethel Cemetery on the west edge of town. Everybody who lived in Bethel eventually ended up in Bethel Cemetery, whether rich or poor, lost or saved. Now Thomas Collins rested there too, near a tall oak tree.

But on this Sunday a cool breeze from the north continued to temper the oppressive August heat, making the day feel very pleasant. Puffy, white clouds floated in the sky, and the sun shone around the clouds. The breeze captured some trash and skipped it across Church Street into the tree row then, after a moment of incarceration, dislodged it free into the field beyond.

We walked up the front steps of the church and opened the large double doors. As we entered, we saw the Cornetts walking around the corner toward the front sidewalk and steps.

"Good morning, Mr. Collins," Pastor Greg said. Greg Yoshida, a short man around thirty, had been born in Los Angeles to Japanese parents. He had recently graduated from Bible college and seminary and just completed his second year at Bethel Baptist Church.

I quietly shook his hand.

Pastor Greg had been elected to the school board back in April, demonstrating his belief that Christians should be involved in politics. He often referenced the fact that he had spent time as a boy in a Japanese internment camp in America during the war, though he actually said little about the experience.

"Good morning, Miss Collins," he said.

"Good morning, Pastor," Debbie cheerfully replied. She enjoyed going to church.

Though likable, Pastor Greg was a green pastor, having spent most of his time in books. He was therefore unprepared for living in the real world—at least the world of paved streets, city blocks, and houses that comprised Bethel. Despite his great education, Greg Yoshida was unable to explain accidents or funerals or cemeteries.

"How are you, Angela?" he asked, grasping her hand.

"I'm fine," Mom said. She attempted a smile.

I knew she was lying, and I hoped that he would know it too.

The front doors of the church opened into a foyer, and here Pastor would stand every Sunday and greet his people. To the left were other doors that led from the foyer into the sanctuary. A full basement, which sometimes leaked when it rained, accommodated all of the Sunday school classes.

Debbie and I walked toward the stairs that led to the basement.

"Matt, you didn't even speak to him," she whispered.

"Yes, I did."

"You did not!"

"I shook his hand."

"He's nice, Matt. You need to be nice to him."

"Good morning, Wendell. Dorothy. Miss Cornett."

I looked back. Pastor welcomed the Cornetts. The three returned cheerful greetings.

The Cornetts had built a new home that bordered the north property line of the church. A decorative brick sidewalk led from their back porch to their back gate, so they had an easy stroll every Sunday, through their back gate onto the church grounds. They would usually walk to the front of the church and enter by the main door. I supposed that was more proper. Wendell Cornett owned Cornett Ford and was also one of the deacons of the church.

"Greg," Wendell said, "Jack's going to call today for a special business meeting."

"Special meeting? What for?"

"Whether to retain you."

"Oh no. Has it come to this?"

"Afraid so."

I remained on the top step and watched them.

Greg shook his head.

"Come on, Matt," Debbie said. "Let's go."

"Just a minute."

Mrs. Cornett quietly walked into the sanctuary.

Catherine Cornett walked toward the steps where we stood and smiled at me. "Hi, Matt."

"Hi, Cathy."

She spoke to Debbie, then walked down the stairs.

"Come on," Debbie repeated. She also headed downstairs.

"Be there in a minute."

Wendell and Greg were still in deep conversation.

"When will the special business meeting be?" Greg asked.

"Next Sunday night. Jack called me earlier this morning with the decision."

"Is there anything that can be done?"

"Not according to our bylaws," Wendell said. "Any two deacons can call for such a meeting if they think there is a problem in the church."

"And of course Jack and Forest called for the meeting."

"Of course."

"And they'll push this teacher-raise stink as the reason?"

"Well, in all fairness," Wendell said, "there are quite

a few in the community who are upset with the school board. And this is beginning to spill over into the church."

"That's simply because we have a superintendent who is keeping the pot stirred."

"And letters to the editor in the paper."

"Yes. And the paper."

I took one more step down, and my eyes were just above the level of the floor. They did not notice me.

"Will I get voted out?" Greg added after a moment.

"That is a very real possibility. Of course, you could do one thing that might save yourself."

Debbie reached the bottom of the steps, and Catherine was now out of sight.

"What could I do?" Greg asked.

"You can present your information about Forest to the church. That's what started everything. And it would show everybody what's behind it all."

"Wendell, you know I can't do that. I don't have any proof. And besides, that wouldn't be fair to Forest."

"Forest and Jack aren't worried about being fair to you," Wendell said.

"But a meeting? With the whole church? Over a school board issue?"

"It's a church issue now."

"I guess it is."

"My bet is that Jack simply wants to be the one in charge. The one who runs things. Now that we no longer have . . . well, now that Tommy is . . ."

"And of course Forest is embarrassed by everything."

"I'm sure he is."

"But before the whole church?" Greg shook his head. "This should be kept in a deacons' meeting."

"It should. We know it should. But as you know, we've tried lots of meetings and failed. Now Jack and Forest want to bring this other issue before the whole church. To get rid of you."

"Come on!" Debbie called from the bottom of the stairs.

"You could resign," Wendell continued. "From the school board."

Pastor shook his head. "How would that look in the community?"

I turned and walked down the steps to class.

The entire church smelled old and musty but especially the basement because of the occasional water seepage and mold. I arrived at the bottom, where Debbie was still waiting for me.

"Please be nice to Mrs. Yoshida," she said.

We headed toward Debbie's classroom, where Paula Yoshida taught.

"I will."

"I mean speak to her."

"I will."

Debbie believed it was necessary to keep me in line. I usually didn't mind; in fact I thought it was funny with her being my kid sister and all. However, sometimes she was a royal pain.

We reached her room and she started to enter. "Where's your Bible?" she gasped.

"I forgot it," I lied.

She scowled at me. I walked down the hall to my class, her eyes burning in my back.

I entered my classroom and braced myself for a boring lesson taught by Harvey Wells, the church's song leader. Harvey was an older, graying man who always wore gray suits and projected . . . well, he projected a gray personality that matched his appearance. His Sunday school classes were simply awful. He also served on the deacon board, along with Wendell, Forest Parker, and Jack Metzge.

"Good morning, Mr. Collins."

"Good morning."

"Where's your Bible?" Mr. Wells asked.

"I forgot."

"You've forgotten several weeks in a row, haven't you?"

"Have I?" The truth was I had not brought my Bible since the accident in July. God didn't need it and neither did I.

"Is there a problem?" he asked.

"No, sir."

Harvey Wells seemed to consider.

I sat down in the back of the small room behind Catherine, wishing the time would fly by and dreading the appearance of Wade at any moment.

In the next several minutes, a few other students entered.

After an opening prayer, Mr. Wells passed out the Sunday school work sheet while I stifled a yawn.

We heard a light rap on the open door.

"Excuse me, Harvey." Pastor Yoshida stood in the doorway along with Wade. My heart sank.

"Come in," Harvey said.

"You have a visitor. This is Wade Scott. He has just moved to Bethel."

"W-Wade Hampton S-Scott."

"Excuse me. Wade Hampton Scott."

"Welcome to class, Wade. My name is Harvey Wells. I'll be your teacher."

"P-pleased to m-meet you."

"We're glad to have you."

Speak for yourself.

"Th-thank y-you." A trickle of drool appeared from the corner of Wade's mouth.

"Here is a lesson sheet," Harvey said, handing Wade the lesson.

"I'll be going," Pastor Greg said. "I'm sure all of you will make Wade feel welcome."

"H-hi, M-Matt."

I nodded.

"M-Matt and me are n-neighbors."

"Is that so, Matt?" Harvey asked.

I nodded again.

"M-me and Matt are b-best friends."

You have no idea how to be a friend.

"I'm happy to hear that," Harvey said.

This friendship claim was an exaggeration at best, considering he did not know me and I really didn't want to have him around.

"I-I been called to p-preach."

Just don't preach at me ever again.

"You have?" Harvey Wells did not appear to know how to handle this profound revelation. "Well, that's nice," he finally said.

You just preach to God and leave the rest of us alone.

We watched him shuffle to a chair and struggle to sit down.

Look on the bright side. At least he didn't bring his sword.

Harvey Wells then began the class, and within moments I began to lapse into a deep coma. Paint on the cinder-block walls had yellowed and was peeling, and several floor tiles at the base of the wall had popped up. A spider crawled on a low ceiling tile behind Harvey, and I watched it intently. There was nothing else to watch, for there were no windows in the basement room. Seconds became hours and minutes became eternities as Harvey Wells droned on.

"We are gathered here . . . gathered here today . . . to say . . . to say good-bye . . . good-bye to our dear friend . . ."

I shook my head and attempted to snap out of it. If only God would be merciful and actually allow missiles in Cuba, and if they could launch one of them right now, it could be aimed at Bethel or at least hit it accidentally. Of course, God was not capable of such mercy. *All good things must end, so if it never ends, then it must not be good; therefore, the class is not good.* I was surprised that Harvey Wells did not put himself to sleep. I fought to keep awake.

"... *good-bye to our dear friend* ..."

Just don't cry.

"... *our good friend* ..."

Please don't cry.

"... *Thomas Collins.*"

"Would you please?"

Please don't—what?

"Y-yes, s-sir." Wade stood with great effort. "Th-thank You, Jesus, f-for this class. I so th-thankful to be here. A-amen."

Everyone knew class was over. With my superior speed, I managed to be the first one who bolted out the door.

People gathered around the top of the stairs and in the foyer, too. They hovered there before slowly drifting into the sanctuary.

I entered the sanctuary and sat down in the very back pew by myself, as was my recent custom.

"Sit down—now!" Mrs. Metzge ordered.

Her twin boys just looked at her before running back out into the foyer. They were only eight years old and were the wildest kids around.

"Jerry! Jimmy! I'll tell your father!"

I heard them race down the stairs to the basement. She followed.

The church was constructed of wood floors and oak pews and had a sound system that guaranteed the speaker could be easily heard though not always understood. The sound echoed around the sanctuary if the system was turned up too high. The church typically drew well over a hundred people for Sunday morning worship, an amount above average for the churches of Bethel.

"Hello, Mr. Collins."

I stood up for Paula Yoshida, the pastor's wife. "Good morning," I said, taking her hand.

Paula had met Greg in Bible college, and they had been married for five years. Paula was not of Asian descent. She had a pleasant smile and was short and round, and she glowed with child, for she was five months pregnant. Her due date was December 25.

"How are you today?" she asked.

"Fine."

"Debbie was sure cheerful."

I shrugged. "How are you?"

She patted her belly. "I have good days and bad days. This is a good day."

I looked beyond Mrs. Yoshida and watched Catherine walk down the aisle to sit with her father. Dorothy Cornett was already at the piano on the platform at the front of the church, and she talked with Harvey Wells and also with Pastor Greg.

"Matt?"

"Yes?"

"Didn't you hear me?"

"I'm sorry."

"I asked, how's your mother?"

"She's doing fine," I lied.

"That's good." Paula walked down the aisle and sat behind Catherine and Wendell.

I sat back down in my spot.

Grandma Pine entered the sanctuary with Mom, and they sat down near the front. Debbie finally entered too, and she joined them. We used to sit as a family back when it was fun to go to church. However, that all changed after I saw things nobody should have to see. Mom still sat up front because she believed Dad would have wanted that, and she wanted me to continue to sit with them. I had no desire to be near the front—or anywhere else in the church for that matter—and thankfully Mom did not push the issue. I did not know what Mom now thought about God, but I certainly knew what I thought.

Windows on both sides of the church were open, allowing a cool breeze to blow through, and this made everything quite pleasant. The Scotts entered the sanctuary and walked down the main aisle, Wade lagging behind.

Why is he here?

We must thank Debbie. Her big mouth. Of course, he probably would have come here anyway. To spit for God.

They sat down in the middle of the church on the other side of the aisle. Wade sat on the end of the pew. It probably was easier that way.

So he moved in next door just to . . . just to torture me. And why? Because there's no mercy. That's a fact.

The church began to settle down, and the clamor that accompanied the saints' assembly started to settle down too. We all knew that the service was about to begin.

And not only to torture but to preach at me. Well, he just better keep God to himself.

Bethel proudly boasted twelve houses of God, and

this multitude meant the Scotts had twelve choices from which to make their decision. Bethel had churches of every size, shape, and flavor—churches that babbled every imaginable message and would cater to any theological whim or desire.

But no, they just had to come to Bethel Baptist Church.

Pastor Greg walked to the pulpit and spoke into the microphone, giving the usual announcements. I suspect they were the same ones that he gave last Sunday. That was the nice thing about announcements. You could say anything you wanted because nobody ever seemed to listen. Greg then turned to sit back down on the platform, leaving the beginning of worship in the hands of Harvey Wells.

"Pastor?" It was Jack Metzge. He stood up three pews ahead of me.

The entire church turned and looked at him.

"I need to announce to the entire church that according to our bylaws the deacons are calling for a special business meeting for next Sunday night after the evening service."

A murmur circulated around the church.

"For what purpose?" asked Harvey Wells. He seemed surprised. There apparently had not been time to fill him in on what was going on.

"We will have a confidence vote on Pastor Yoshida—whether to retain him or not," Jack said.

The murmur grew louder. Harvey looked astonished. Pastor Greg remained seated, his face tense and grim.

"Why?" somebody dumbly asked.

"We all know about the school board's decision denying the teachers' raise. And we know how this has raised a stir in the community. Especially with all the stuff in the paper and all. Unfortunately for us, it has also directed some hostility toward our church. The church has now been linked to the actions of the school board. We believe a pastor should not be in politics, and this incident just proves it. So for the good of the church . . ." Jack's voice tapered off, and the murmurs continued.

Jack sat back down next to his wife and their twin boys. Jerry and Jimmy poked each other and squirmed, unaware of all the people looking in their direction. The announcement had fallen upon the church like a bomb-shell.

Harvey Wells clenched his teeth. "Let's stand and turn to hymn forty-five," he finally said.

The congregation dutifully obeyed. Harvey Wells began the singing, Dorothy Cornett played the piano, and church began. Hymns were sung and money was collected and Greg Yoshida preached, much the same as the Sunday before and the Sunday before that, and it would probably be the same the next Sunday. The future appeared a little uncertain beyond that.

I sat in the back and did not pay any attention to the activity. If God was so powerful, He did not need anything from me. Pastor Greg preached and rambled; I looked outside.

"*. . . good-bye to our dear friend . . .*"

Just don't cry.

"*. . . our good friend . . .*"

Please don't cry.

"*. . . Thomas Collins.*"

But on that July day, Greg Yoshida did cry. He began bawling like a baby in front of everybody. Then Mom, who sat next to me, exploded into uncontrollable tears. The July day was oppressive, and sweat drenched our best clothes, and there were flowers, too, tons of them around the church and on the casket, and you could not help but gag on their pungent fragrance in the stifling heat. So Pastor Greg started his crying, then Mom, and this began an instantaneous chain reaction throughout the church and probably beyond until the entire world was wailing, offering a lament for the dead.

Everybody, that is, except me. I did not cry.

I stifled a yawn and looked back around the church while Pastor Greg continued to ramble on about who knows what. I noticed that even God's buddy Wade yielded to a big yawn, though I could not see how much saliva he lost.

Yep, there's no mercy. That's why the Scotts showed up. And I'll have to see Wade every Sunday, too. After the service, Greg talked to the Scotts, and Paula joined them.

I ducked outside and sat down on the bench behind the church sign and waited for Mom and Debbie to finish visiting with friends. After they were through, we would walk home, probably with Grandma Pine, and have dinner.

Catherine Cornett left the church, walked over to

the bench, and sat down beside me without comment.
Though several months younger than me, she had been
in my class all of these years. We had grown up together.

Cathy wore a blue dress and hose and black shoes,
and her light brown hair was in a ponytail and tied back
with a light blue ribbon. She wore glasses, and several
freckles graced her cheeks and nose.

"Ready for school tomorrow?" she asked.

"I suppose."

"What homeroom did you get?"

"I'm in 209."

"So did I. That's Miss Edmonds. English."

"I was afraid it might be."

"Matt, you are good at reading and handling words.
Don't you like English?"

"I suppose it's okay. It's Nancy Edmonds I don't care
for."

"She's not that bad. We had her last year. You
survived that. You will survive this year too."

"I guess I will."

People streamed out of the church, and everybody
was talking about the announcement from Jack Metzge.

"Are you going out for cross-country?" she asked.

"No."

"You're not going to run with Colby?"

"No," I said.

"Why not?"

"Oh, I don't know. Dad was proud of me running on
a team. Now it doesn't seem to matter. You understand,
don't you?"

"Actually I do," she said.

We watched the Metzge twins race out the doors and run behind the church.

"Though I bet Coach Garrett won't understand," Cathy added.

"I really don't care. He can rant and rave and stomp around all he wants with that cane of his."

"That makes him sound awful."

"He is awful. He stomps around like Captain Ahab and his wooden leg."

"Captain Ahab had an ivory leg," she said.

"Well, Garrett stomps around with his cane like Ahab stomped around with his ivory leg. Garrett is just as nasty. He's impossible to get along with."

"Matt, you're being harsh."

"I'm being truthful. You never had him for gym."

"You're right. I never had him for a teacher."

"Or for a track coach."

"Or cross-country."

"Or cross-country. It seems stupid anyway for a cripple on a cane to teach anybody running."

We sat silently for a moment. I stared straight ahead while Cathy sat holding her Bible in her lap.

"His wife just left him," she said.

"Garrett's?"

"Yes. She left a couple of weeks ago."

"Why?"

"She may have been having an affair. She went to California with their boy."

"How do you know?"

"Pastor was over at the house last week, and I overheard him and Daddy talking about it. They made the whole thing sound very serious."

"I don't know about an affair, but I sure can understand why she'd leave him. I imagine he's awful to live with. I'm surprised he hasn't gotten fired by now."

"I have heard that if he says another foul word or loses his temper again or turns up drunk or steps out of line just one more time, they will fire him."

"I hope he does. That would be nice."

"Oh, I don't know. I feel sorry for him."

"Sorry for Garrett?"

"Yes."

"That's like feeling sorry for a snake."

"He must have had a sad life, Matt. Now his wife might have done something awful and left him. He is all alone."

"He had it coming."

"I don't know. I just feel sorry for him. I wish there was something I could do."

"Like what?"

"I don't know. Take away the hurt, I guess."

I turned and looked at her. Cathy was like that. Colby couldn't stand her, and she didn't like Colby. Colby claimed she was ugly, but this was not the case. Cathy might not have been the most beautiful girl in the class, but she was a lot better than average, and I always thought her attractive, though I never argued the point with Colby. Some things in life you just have to see for yourself.

Mr. and Mrs. Cornett walked out of the church, and Cathy got up to leave. "Bye," she said.

"See you tonight."

The Cornetts walked around to the back of the church and out of view. They had the quickest walk home of anybody in the church.

In time Mom, Debbie, and Grandma came out the large front doors, and we began our walk home.

"I was going to invite the Scotts over for dinner," Mom said.

I took a deep breath.

"They're going over to Greg and Paula's instead."

I slowly let my breath out.

"We'll have them over soon. Help them get settled in."

"Angela," Grandma asked, "what's all this about a vote of confidence?"

"I have no idea."

"Why would a school board decision affect the church?"

"Mom, I don't understand."

"Neither do I. I was just hoping you knew."

"I'm afraid I've fallen behind on church business." She then let out a deep, soul-shaking sigh, the kind that vibrates the entire body.

"I know, dear," Grandma said. "I was just hoping you might know something about all of this."

"Are they going to join the church?" I asked.

"Who?" Mom asked.

"The Scotts."

"Probably. They went to a Baptist church in San Antonio."

Figures.

We walked by the Scotts' white house, then into our own yard.

"Why did they move here?" I asked.

"Mr. Scott drives a truck for a grocery chain, and they had some openings over in the city, so they moved. Wade suffered with the Texas heat."

Bethel has heat but not as bad as Texas. After all, Bethel is way north of San Antonio.

"He's gone a lot, on the road and all," Mom said.

"What's wrong with Wade?" Debbie asked. "Mrs. Scott didn't say much."

"He has cerebral palsy."

"What's that?"

"He has suffered some brain damage, honey, from when he was tiny."

Brain damage? Try brain death.

"Is it real bad?" Debbie asked.

"Not too bad. Elaine says he gets along pretty good. He's seventeen now."

Seventeen? Two years older than I am.

"He's kind of strange."

"I suppose we all are in our own way," Mom said.

I could understand strange; however, Wade was beyond strange.

"We all have our problems that slow us down," added Grandma.

"He's more than strange," I chimed in. "He jabbed a

sword at us, and that's not right. And I won't stand for it
again."

"Matt!" Mom exclaimed. "What's this about?"

"He attacked us with a sword."

"Attacked you?"

Debbie explained to Mom what had happened when
we first met Wade.

"I think you're exaggerating a little," Mom said. "I'm
sure he didn't mean anything by it."

I'm not so sure.

"He seems to be a very nice boy," she went on.

"D-did your dad just d-die?"

"I think he'll make a very nice friend," she concluded.

"Mom, you don't understand."

"Matt, I do understand."

*No, you don't. He's such a . . . a retard. I can't stand
him.*

"Don't you remember the pastor's sermon last week?"
she continued. "He mentioned how we are all created in
the image of God? This is just the kind of thing he was
talking about."

Looks like both God and His image need to be slapped.

At home we had dinner, and later that afternoon I
went running. I felt good and ran well. The gentle afternoon breeze had changed direction and now came from
the south. The breeze felt warm but not hot, and even
though it stirred little dust swirls, breathing was easy.
I ran a good time—5:39—but nowhere near the five
minutes Garrett wanted us to be to compete at the state
level.

Yet I cared little about competing at state and absolutely nothing for Garrett.

That evening we returned to Bethel Baptist Church for the seven o'clock service. At church we discovered that the Scott family had been at the Yoshidas' house all day. Both families appeared to have had a grand time because everybody was smiling and laughing. I knew what this meant.

So on the Sunday evening before the first day of school, I sat in the back pew and watched the people play church to a God they probably did not understand. Dorothy Cornett played the piano, Harvey Wells led the singing, and Greg Yoshida preached. During invitation time at the end of the service, the Scotts went to the front of the church.

"These are the Scotts," Pastor Greg said. "Arthur, Elaine, and Wade."

"W-Wade Hampton S-Scott," he said.

Pastor Yoshida smiled. "Excuse me. Wade Hampton Scott."

Wade gave a poorly executed bow. "I-I so th-thankful to be h-here. Yes-sir-ee."

Of course they joined the church.

FOUR

"Hey, Matt!"

I was standing in the noisy, crowded hall near the front office of the high school. I looked up and watched Colby make his way through the sea of students toward me.

"What's your homeroom?" he asked.

"I'm in 209."

"That's Edmonds and English?"

"I think so."

"Have your schedule yet?"

"No, I haven't made it up there," I said. "How about you?"

"I'm a gym aide for Garrett first. Here's mine."

I dropped to one knee and opened my notebook to the front page. We were in the middle of the hall, and students rushed all around us as if we were boulders in a fast-moving stream. I wrote down the room numbers from Colby's schedule for later comparison.

"Garrett asked about you," he said.

"Did you tell him?"

"No. I'll leave that pleasure to you."

"Thanks a lot, Colby."

"No problem. By the way, his wife left him."

"She did?" I acted surprised.

"Yep. That's the big rumor flying around."

"That's too bad, I guess."

"Well, I need to get back down there. See you around."

"Sure."

We had taken our high school gym requirement as freshmen, but Colby had signed up for another year of gym, which meant he would be a gym aide. Gym aides ran the gym classes. Garrett did very little as a teacher. I had no desire to be a gym aide, and by not signing up, I had probably created such a different schedule from Colby's that we might not have any classes together. That would be hard to take.

Stanley Colby disappeared into the crowd. Boys wore dress shirts and slacks while girls wore skirts or dresses. Girls with money wore makeup, and those with less money wore little or no makeup.

I worked my way toward the stairway at the end of the hall. From there I noticed Wade coming through the front doors with Elaine Scott. They entered the front office.

Bethel High School—a massive, sprawling, brick structure on Church Street—bore a striking resemblance to the state penitentiary located thirty miles northwest in another city. Both structures had been built of dark red bricks in the 1920s and were square. The prison was larger and surrounded by barbed wire with many outside lights mounted on very tall poles. This might be the only difference between the two. The prison held captive physical bodies, and the high school held captive minds and souls.

Children who lived out in the country received bus service, but those who lived in town walked to school. The high school was five blocks east of Bethel Baptist Church and ten blocks east of the little gray house where we lived.

Inside the penitentiary, I walked up the stairs to the second floor and from there to room 209.

Sure enough, Miss Nancy Edmonds sat at the desk awaiting the arrival of her homeroom class. "Here is your schedule, Mr. Collins," she announced as I entered.

Nancy Edmonds, a round, barrel-shaped, homely woman of at least thirty years, sat at her desk acting like the Queen of Sheba or something. Many students liked her. Many did not. Catherine liked her. I did not.

"Thank you." I took the schedule and sat down at the second desk in the row closest to the door and opposite the windows. Several windows were open, and a gentle morning breeze filtered in. A large fan on a pedestal stood in the corner of the room ahead of my row; however, the room was pleasant enough, so it was not on. I immediately compared my schedule to Colby's.

Not a one. Not a single one.

For the first time since the first grade, we would not have any classes together. Of all the rotten luck. I struck my notebook with a fist.

Cathy walked in wearing a pink dress and no makeup. She could afford to wear anything but always chose to dress simply. She didn't even wear makeup to church. Other girls struggled to look grown-up; Cathy remained content the way she was.

She picked up her schedule and sat behind me and immediately began talking to several girls behind her.

Squareface Kindle was already seated next to the windows, where he would be able to gaze out and find entertainment for his dull mind.

The beginning bell rang, and Miss Edmonds took charge.

We stood and faced the flag in the front corner of the room by the windows and recited the Pledge of Allegiance. After that, before Miss Edmonds could really get started, Wade shuffled into the room.

Oh no. There he is. This proves there's no mercy.

"I-I'm Wade Hampton S-Scott," he said.

Miss Edmonds took the papers he handed her, and after a brief scanning, she nodded to him with a smile. "Welcome to Bethel High School, Mr. Scott."

"I-I'm so thankful to b-be here."

"Well, we're glad to have you."

Speak for yourself.

"I-I'm a famous g-general."

I busied myself with rechecking the two class schedules in my notebook.

"You're a famous general?" Miss Edmonds asked.

"Y-yes. General W-Wade Hampton was one of Robert E. Lee's b-best lieutenants." The sentence concluded with of shower of spit.

"I'm very happy for you." Clearly Miss Edmonds did not know what to say.

Even the class did not know how to react. I heard a few snickers. I could have died.

"Yes-sir-ee. F-famous general." Wade waddled in my direction and sat down in the chair ahead of me.

Is there no getting rid of the retard?

I did not have a single class with Colby but certainly had one with Wade. And maybe more.

There is no mercy.

"The first order of business is to get lockers assigned," Miss Edmonds pontificated. "I'll give you a few minutes to choose locker partners, and when you have decided, come to me for your number and lock."

"I'll take M-Matt," Wade announced.

The entire class looked at him, then me.

I was caught off guard.

He continued before I could respond. "W-we're b-best friends. We're n-neighbors."

"That's great," Miss Edmonds said. "Your locker number is 251. Both of you come up to get your padlock and combination."

My mouth dropped open and I pinched my arm, hoping to awake from the nightmare. Wade shuffled to the front desk, and I followed, all the while preparing to address this great miscarriage of justice. "Miss Edmonds, I—"

"This is just wonderful, Matt," she said, "taking the newcomer under your wing."

I had no intention of taking this newcomer anywhere, unless outside to maybe slap him or something.

"So you two are neighbors. That's great."

I was trapped. Suffocating. He clung to me like a leech.

Wade beamed.

I took the lock with the combination and went out to the hallway to find locker number 251 while Wade ambled behind. My teeth began to grind. "You might have asked me first," I said.

He looked at me questioningly, like a puppy might when it knows you are talking to it but it cannot understand a word you are saying. The thought that I had no desire to be a locker partner with him never crossed his inconsiderate mind. I could see speaking to him was useless.

We found the locker and I inserted the lock. I gave the combination to him and watched him fumble with the lock. It took him three tries before he got the lock opened. By this time, other pairs were finding their lockers beside us.

"So this is your new best friend," said Squareface. He wore a big grin.

I glared at him. Wade grinned.

"I'm sure Colby will be interested to hear about this."

I said nothing. I had never cared for Squareface because he was a coward and everybody knew it. I closed the locker, inserted the lock, then secured it. While my back was turned, Squareface gave Wade a shove. Wade crashed into the lockers, knocking his glasses askew.

I whirled around and faced Squareface.

"I think your new friend here is a nerd," he said.

Wade had a silly look on his face. He awkwardly straightened his glasses and rubbed his left shoulder. I said nothing. Squareface went down the row of lockers to find his. I returned to the room with Wade behind me. I watched him sit down.

Nerd. It does fit.

After the class had reassembled and completed home-room duties, Miss Edmonds immediately began her brand of torture. "We will be doing a lot of reading this year," she stated.

I enjoyed reading so did not have a problem with this announcement.

"Our first book will be *Silas Marner*, and you can pick up copies in the back corner of the room."

As one person we all looked behind us and discovered the stack of books in the back corner that had gone unnoticed until now. I had never heard of *Silas Marner* or George Eliot, so I had no immediate reaction.

Later, at the end of class, Wade and I gathered the books and went to our locker to leave them. I gave Wade the lower shelf while I took the upper.

"C-can you help me, M-Matt?"

No. Leave me alone. Go fly a kite.

He was showing me his schedule. I stared at him.

"W-where's my n-next class?" he said.

I looked at his sheet, and thankfully we had no other classes in common. I pointed him in the direction of his next class and watched him scuffle off into the noisy crowd. I went my way.

The remainder of my first day of school—math, chemistry, lunch, and the rest—went without incident.

Without incident, that is, until after last hour. On my way back to the locker, I cut through the cafeteria for a shortcut to one of the east stairways. This course took me past the gym locker room, and I didn't even think of the possible consequences until it was too late.

"Hey, bud. Collins."

The gruffness of the voice startled me. I turned. Coach Garrett stood beside the locker room doors. He stomped down the hall toward me using his cane. His right leg was shorter than his left, and he used his cane to keep weight off his bad leg.

Oh, great.

Garrett always wore a Chicago Cubs baseball hat, even inside the school building in defiance of the rules. Gray stubble covered his face, and there was gray on his temples just under the hat. He always stomped his cane when he walked, and he would wobble from side to side. He sported a soft gut, and we always called it a beer belly, which was probably true. He came near me and leaned against the wall, all the while chewing on a toothpick and idly tapping his cane on the floor. He looked gruff and mean. He *was* gruff and mean.

I faced him directly. I always believed it went better if I faced him directly.

"Why haven't you been to practice?" he asked.

"Practice?" That was dumb. I instantly regretted it.

"Don't play stupid, Collins. Cross-country. Why haven't you showed up?" He spoke harshly through clenched teeth. The toothpick hung precariously on the side of his mouth.

"I'm not doing cross-country," I said. "Sir."

Garrett stood glaring at me while idly tapping his cane. His eyes looked a little red, and it was difficult to determine whether he had been drinking again. Most people were afraid of Garrett. Even the principal. And rightly so.

"Why?" he finally hissed. I could tell he was mad. He was always mad.

"I don't want to," I said.

He stared at me with his typical angry look and bit the toothpick with his front teeth. His cane tapped the floor. He looked like he wanted to say something—perhaps strike me with his cane—but instead he turned and stomped back to the locker room without another word.

That was close.

Garrett was deformed, mean, evil—someone to be avoided. I understood why his wife left him, affair or no affair. I did not understand how Colby could stand to be near him. Still, gym aides had little contact with him, as they did all the work while he hid in his office, probably drinking. If he ever got caught, he would be history, and that would be fine with me.

I reached my locker to find the lock missing. I jerked the locker open and found the lock hanging inside. Wade had neglected to secure the locker when he left.

My teeth began to grind again. *The nerd.*

I had a miserable year ahead of me if he couldn't even keep it locked. I threw my books in, grabbed the copy of *Silas Marner*, secured the locker, and made my way outside. I quickly overtook Wade as he shuffled off the school grounds on his way home. "Hey!" I yelled.

He stopped, turned, and smiled.

"What's the matter with you?" I was mad. "Can't you even lock a locker?"

He stood with a blank look.

"The locker," I said. "You left it unlocked."

"I sorry, M-Matt."

"Look. You're going to have to do better than that."

"I didn't m-mean to."

"Hey, Matt." Colby and Squareface rode up on their bicycles.

"Here he is." Squareface pointed proudly.

"So this is your new friend," stated Colby with a grin.

I just rolled my eyes and shrugged.

"And locker partner to boot," he added.

"He said he was a general," Squareface said. "I told you he's a nerd."

Colby hopped off his bicycle and walked around Wade, looking him over. "See what you mean," he said.

Wade just looked at both of them.

Colby put his hand on Wade's shoulder. "I officially name you Nerd," he pronounced.

Squareface laughed and clapped.

Wade remained silent.

"Matt, my boy," Colby continued, "you have your hands full here."

"You're telling me."

"I guess we don't have any classes together," he said.

"Not a one. This has been a real bad day."

"I can see why," he said, "with the nerd here."

"That's not all."

"Oh? See Garrett?"

"Yep."

"How did he take it?"

"Not too bad. He really didn't say much."

"Did he hit you?" he asked.

"No. He thought about it, though."

"Garrett can make any day bad."

"So can he." I jerked my thumb at Wade.

Colby laughed. "You sure have your hands full," he repeated. "Well, better get going. See you around, buddy. See you, Nerd."

Both Squareface and Colby laughed as Colby got back on his bike. They rode off.

I had no desire to walk home with Wade. "You go on," I said. "I have some things to do. By the way, the idea of the lock is to keep the locker secured. You think you can use it?"

"Yes, M-Matt."

I turned and doubled back beyond the school to Delaware Street, ran down Delaware several blocks, jogged south to Church Street, then ran the rest of the way home.

I ran so far ahead of Nerd that I did not even see him.

FIVE

The Sunday morning before Labor Day was cool and clear, and you could look into the rich blue sky and see into forever. A gentle breeze drifted across town from the southeast, and we were all hopeful that the awful heat of August was forever gone.

That Sunday we left a little early for church. Mom and Deb wore matching white sweaters, but it was not really that chilly. As we walked, we could see one of Bethel's police cars parked on the street in front of the church. We arrived in time to see Monty Brewer, Bethel's police chief, drive away in the car.

"What's going on?" I asked.

Pastor Greg and Wendell stood around the church's sign out in front. They had rather stupid looks on their faces. It was easy to tell that they both were tense. "Looks like we had visitors last night," Wendell said.

A red line had been painted on the sign through the name *Greg Yoshida, Pastor*. Obscenities decorated the rest of the sign, and these obscenities were essentially used as adjectives for the noun *Jap*. It looked like the red paint had been sprayed.

"Oh no," Mom whispered. She spun away from

the sign with her hand covering her mouth. I could see she was trembling, and I was afraid that she might start crying.

Debbie seemed to understand that something terrible had happened but did not fully comprehend what.

"Come on, Debbie." Mom grabbed Debbie's hand and hurried them both inside the church. She said nothing to me.

"Chief Brewer just made a report," Wendell said.

We just stood around, looking at the sign and each other, with that sick feeling in the stomach that vandalism brings. It is always distressing to witness the results of a crime, even if it is just a church. However, I'd noticed that bad things did not seem to bother God all that much, and from the looks of life it appeared He was rather lenient about it all. It seemed like it only bothered us.

"Who did this?" I asked, but I knew it was a stupid thing to say.

Wendell shrugged. "Have no idea," he eventually said. "We just suspect that it has something to do with Pastor being on the school board."

The school board controversy did not really appear to be that big a deal. In August, Wilcox, the superintendent, had proposed to the board a 1.5 percent salary increase for the district's teachers. But since the school district was already over twenty thousand dollars in the red, the board voted the proposal down by a vote of three to two. Pastor Greg was one of the three no votes.

We had known little of the matter until the *Bethel*

Sentinel, the town's weekly newspaper, ran an editorial in favor of the raise and decrying the school board's action. Moreover, they printed an interview with the superintendent, who, in spite of the risk to his job, was quite vocal in his criticism of the board. Apparently Superintendent Wilcox took the board's rejection of his proposal quite personally.

The next week the paper had published a letter that recommended pastors should stay with church business and leave the running of the school district to those who knew what they were doing. Though no names were mentioned, everyone knew that Greg Yoshida was the only pastor on the board. The week after, another letter to the editor appeared that labeled the board's salary denial un-Christian. Now, on the Sunday before Labor Day, we arrived at church to see the sign and the paint and the obscenities.

"So what are you going to do?" I asked.

"We don't have time to paint over it this morning," Wendell said. "I sent Dorothy home to find something to cover it with. Harvey went to get some rope or something."

After a minute, Dorothy Cornett emerged from her back gate carrying a large sheet. Greg and Wendell covered the sign with the sheet. A moment later, Harvey Wells appeared from the side parking lot with some twine. They secured the sheet with the twine, thus sparing the faithful from the full impact of the defacement.

"This really does not help matters," Wendell said to Greg.

"No, it doesn't," Greg said.

"It's the worst possible timing."

Tension pulsated throughout the entire church that morning, pounding and reverberating off the walls. All that was talked about was the sign. Speculation flew concerning who could have possibly done such a thing and why. I noted that both Jack and Forest were rather quiet and added nothing to the speculations.

Everybody was upset by it all, and this disruption made it difficult to play church. Yet Sunday routine finally took control, and church—at least on the surface—became pretty much the same as it usually was, the same as last week and the week before that. When church was over, our routine continued as the four of us went home for dinner.

Later that day, after Sunday dinner, Mom and Grandma Pine were doing the dishes and talking while I sat on the back porch next to the kitchen door and debated whether to run later on. The day was now warm, and there were clouds forming in the hazy sky. Still, I could not tell whether a storm might be brewing or not.

"I was just wondering . . . " Mom's voice trailed off.

"Yes, dear?"

"I was just wondering. You know. When you lost Dad. How long? I mean, did you ever get over it? Completely?"

There was a long blast of running water from the kitchen faucet.

"Not completely," Grandma said. "How long has it been now? Eleven years? I guess the day does come when you can mention his name without crying. But it takes time."

"It's just that . . ."

"I know."

"I can't stop crying. Won't it stop? Will I ever stop?"

There was a banging of some kind on the counter, and then I could hear Mom sobbing.

"Yes, it will get better."

"I thought those miscarriages were the worst thing. Until this."

"Oh, Angela."

"You know, at times I wish I wasn't even alive. Nearly every night I hope I don't wake up."

"Don't talk like that. It's not good for you."

"I can't help it. I know I have to keep going. For the kids."

There was another blast of water from the faucet.

"I haven't even been able to go through his clothes," Mom said.

"It takes time, dear."

"But how long?"

"Time."

There was the clinking of dishes and the opening and closing of cabinet doors. Dishes were being returned to their resting places. However, they, in time, would be retrieved.

"We had just celebrated our seventeenth anniversary," Mom said.

"Angela, it breaks my heart too. Tommy was such a good man."

Mom was sobbing, but I could tell she was trying to stop. There was no sound of any work being done.

"Have you heard back from the life-insurance company?" Grandma asked after a minute.

"Not yet. And we need the money, too."

"How much was the policy?"

"Fifteen thousand. It will pay off the house and all the debts plus give us some cash. It would really help."

"So why the delay?"

"I have no idea, Mom. Nothing is going right. I just feel so helpless about it. Helpless about everything."

"There are people to help you."

One of the counter drawers opened, and I heard utensils being dropped into their places.

"I know. And they are helping. Wendell is helping me with the insurance. After I get that, some people at the bank have promised to help me with the mortgage and the papers and all. It's just that . . . I just miss Tommy so."

"We all miss Tommy," Grandma said. "Even the church."

"I don't know what is going on there. Seems like everything is just . . . well, out of control too."

There was a loud crash and the scattering of broken glass.

"Oh my. I'm sorry, dear. I guess these old fingers are covered with butter."

"That's okay, Mom. These are cheap glasses."

I heard the pantry door open, and after a moment there was the sound of sweeping glass.

"Yes," Grandma said, "the church is sure in an uproar."

"It just makes me sick. The sign and all."

"And then there's the special business meeting tonight."

"I can't believe it," Mom said.

"Neither do I. Greg is such a nice man. I don't understand why they want to get rid of him."

"This I do know: It is not *they*. It's just Jack and Forest. They're the ones behind this. They even gave Tommy some trouble when he was chairman of the deacons."

"I remember you telling me."

"He had to keep his thumb on them to keep things calm and running smoothly."

"So why are they causing trouble?" Grandma asked.

"Oh, I don't know. Tommy once said that Jack wanted to be in control of things. He also said that ultimately church problems arise when people are not following Christ."

I heard the broken glass being dumped into the trash.

"I'm sure sorry about the glass," Grandma said.

"Don't give it any thought."

"I do have a question about this school board thing."

"What's that?"

"Did Tommy have an opinion about Pastor running for the school board?"

"He didn't want him to do it."

"Why?"

"He thought an incident might arise between a

church member and the school district, and Greg could be forced into the unpleasant position of upholding some awful school policy against someone in the church. Tommy thought the potential was there for harming Greg's ministry, which must have first priority."

"Too bad Greg didn't follow that advice."

"Well, the way it's turning out . . ."

I heard the sound of pots and pans being put away.

Grandma soon began to hum a tune, but she hummed too softly for me to identify it.

"So, Angela, how are you going to vote?" Grandma asked.

"What do you mean? Tonight? Pastor Yoshida is a fine pastor. A very fine pastor. I like him very much. Don't you?"

"Yes. I think he is a fine pastor too."

"Then why did you ask?"

"I was just wondering about tonight."

"I will tell you one thing," Mom said. "There's something more behind this. More than . . ."

"You're right. I just don't know what it is."

"We'll probably find out tonight."

"We probably will," Grandma said. "In any event, I hope everything settles down."

I heard them move the chairs of the kitchen table to sit down. The dinner cleanup was complete.

"Do you think this might be a racial thing?" Grandma asked.

"Racial?"

"You know. Him being Japanese and all."

"Mom, he's an American. He was born in Los Angeles."

"I know," Grandma said. "I meant being of Japanese origin. After all, that appeared on the sign."

"I wouldn't think so. I think this is just a Jack and Forest thing."

I walked around to the front yard and sat under a pin oak, resting my back against the trunk. The sky was beginning to become overcast, and I watched a pickup drive into town with a cloud of dust following.

Later that afternoon I ran but did not run hard or keep time. The sky was graying and the wind had picked up, but the dirt road still stretched lazily before me. I decided to run hard on Monday because it was Labor Day. There would be no school, and I would not be rushed by evening church or anything else.

When evening arrived, we sat in church with great anticipation. Pastor Greg kept the sermon short, and after the service, the church quickly reassembled for the special meeting. Attendance was very high for a Sunday evening. Jack Metzge was the moderator, taking the place of Thomas Collins, who was no longer attending church. Jack was a middle-aged man who stood tall and wore a dark blue suit and looked quite official and distinguished.

I sat in my place in the back pew and eavesdropped.

I saw Wilmer and Ethel McLean, and this was unusual, for they rarely attended evening church and Wilmer often missed Sunday morning. Wilmer wore overalls and a flannel shirt while Ethel was dressed in a faded yellow dress with a white sweater. They looked like poor migrant workers, but everybody knew that Wilmer had bought a new combine that very spring and had paid cash. They sat in the back too, on the other side of the main aisle.

"You best leave now, Pastor," Jack said.

Greg and Paula gathered their Bibles and her purse and started down the main aisle.

"No," Wendell said, standing up in the aisle in front of them.

Jack glared at him.

"He needs to be here," Wendell continued. "To explain the school board situation."

"He should be gone," Jack said.

"No. He needs to be here. To be fair. If this is only about a pastor on the school board, then the church needs to know all about what happened. On the school board."

"No."

"Yes. To hear his side."

Greg had a blank look, glancing first at Wendell, then at Jack behind him.

"It won't hurt none to let the pastor stay," said somebody near the front.

Jack gritted his teeth.

"To be fair," Wendell repeated.

"Very well," Jack said.

Pastor Greg and Paula turned around and sat near the front, opposite my side of the church.

"Well, let's call this meeting to order." Jack rapped the lectern with his gavel in an official manner.

He was standing at the head of the main aisle directly in front of the pulpit behind a portable lectern used only for business meetings. The microphone and sound system were not used for business meetings. The church's secretary sat in the front pew to Jack's left to record the minutes.

"What's this all about?" somebody asked.

"You're out of order," Jack said.

The Scotts were two pews ahead of me on the other side. Wade sat between his parents with his usual moron look.

Greg immediately stood up. "Let's begin with a word of prayer."

The sanctuary fell silent, though Jack had an irritated look.

"Our Father and our God," Greg began, "we praise Your name and give You thanks for all things. Please be with us in a special way this night, so that we may do Your will. In Jesus' name we pray, amen." He sat down.

The windows were open, and a gentle breeze drifted through the sanctuary. Evening was beginning to settle, and we could hear cicadas from the large elm in the front. We could hear laughter, too, from some of the children playing outside in the churchyard.

"So what's this about?"

I looked back up front but still wasn't sure who had asked the question.

"There will be order," Jack said. He rapped the gavel again.

"Mr. Chairman?"

"The chair recognizes Forest Parker."

Forest stood up. He was a big, rotund man with dark hair that was beginning to thin. He wore a perpetual scowl that fit his reputation as a hard businessman. He was dressed in a white shirt with a blue-and-red-striped tie. He had been sitting next to Cindy, his wife.

"Mr. Chairman, we believe Pastor Yoshida should resign his position at this church. His political activity has hindered the gospel message. Also, as recent events have shown, the name of the church now stinks in the community. We've even become a target for vandals. Therefore, we believe he should resign. For the good of the church."

A murmur arose from the church.

Forest sat down beside his wife.

"Thank you, Mr. Parker," Jack said. "But do I have a motion?"

Forest stood back up. "Mr. Chairman, I move that we remove Pastor Greg from his position of pastor."

Aren't we supposed to read minutes from the previous meeting?

"Do I hear a second?"

"I second it." The voice came from the center left.

I could not tell who had spoken. I was still watching Forest as he sat back down next to Cindy.

"It has been moved and seconded that we remove Pastor Greg," Jack said. "Is there any discussion?"

"So why should we fire Pastor?" somebody asked.

"He has hurt the church by being on the school board," Forest said.

"Well then, why doesn't he just resign from the school board?"

"It's too late for that."

"Why is it too late?"

"How has he hurt the church?" someone else asked.

Several people began talking at once.

Jack pounded his gavel. "Order!"

The church quieted down.

"Mr. Chairman?" Gladys Summers stood up. She was a widow and the oldest member of the church. The trustees took turns bringing her to church.

"The chair recognizes Mrs. Summers."

"Mr. Chairman," she said. Her voice was shaky. "Pastor Greg preaches a long time. Some of us would like to get out at noon." Gladys sat down.

Jack looked puzzled.

"What does that have to do with the school board?" someone asked.

"Yes. The pastor on the school board seems to be the problem."

"Why?"

"Pastor should resign."

It was becoming quite animated, and I could not tell who was speaking. Jack was having trouble quieting it.

"The sign."

"Yes. Somebody has ruined our sign."

"And it's because he is on the school board."

Once again, a number of people talked at once.

"Order."

"Who ruined our sign?"

"Maybe someone here in the church!"

"Order!"

"That would make sense if they were trying to get rid of—"

"*Order!*"

The church quieted down.

This meeting is sure different.

"So what is this really about?" Wilmer McLean asked, standing. He stood slightly bent forward, his eyes shining brightly. His face was wrinkled and weathered, and his gray hair was unkempt.

"You are out of order," Jack said.

"I'm in plenty of order. Cut the nonsense. What's this really about?"

Several people voiced approval.

"We don't believe Pastor Greg is right for our church," said Forest while still sitting in his pew. "He has told us how he suffered in an internment camp here in America and that Christians need to improve the political system. But the truth is that he has served the school board to the neglect of the church."

"How has he neglected the church?"

Did Grandma say that?

"What's wrong with the pastor?" another woman asked.

"He has chosen Caesar over Christ," Forest said.

The church erupted into mass chatter again.

"Don't forget about all those downer sermons," someone added.

I sat up straight. This meeting was becoming far

more interesting than I had expected. I was trying to see who was saying what, but my position in the back was a hindrance.

"He only preaches the wrath of God."

A number of people were talking while others were calling for the chairman to recognize them.

"He just preaches judgment."

"Isn't God a God of love?"

"Pastor Greg has not neglected the church," Grandma said, standing, though her voice was lost in the din. "I think he is a very fine pastor." She sat back down, and I doubted if many had heard her. I barely had.

"Mr. Chairman? Mr. Chairman?"

"*Order!*" Jack pounded the gavel again. "For one thing, we haven't been growing. We haven't had one new member in the two years he has been here."

"You are now out of order," said Wilmer, "Mr. Chairman. Sir." He had remained standing and was now staring at Jack Metzge.

Jack bristled.

"What about the Scotts?" somebody said. "They've joined."

"So what's this really about?" Wilmer repeated.

"What this is about," Harvey Wells said as he stood, "is that Pastor Greg asked Forest to resign from the deacon board. Forest is just trying to beat Pastor to the punch. That's what this is all about."

"Mr. Wells! Order!"

"It's true and you know it," Harvey said, glaring at Jack.

"Not so," said Forest. "This is about a pastor on the school board."

"No, it's not," Harvey said. "This is about all of the rumors concerning Forest. Rumors in the community."

"We'll not circulate rumors around this church!" Jack said.

"You called this meeting," Harvey said, pointing his finger at Jack. "The church needs to know what this is all about!"

"What is spoken in deacon meetings is to be kept confidential!"

Several people began to speak at the same time again, and the volume had increased to the point where their voices echoed off the walls.

"Who says?" Harvey asked over the growing noise.

The congregation became a cacophony.

This was the most animation I had ever seen from the gray Harvey Wells. Perhaps there was more to him than I had realized.

"Order!"

"Mr. Chairman, may I have the floor?" Greg spoke the words softly.

"No!"

"Let the pastor speak!" somebody shouted from near the front of the church.

"Let him speak!"

Jack's ears began to turn a little red. "The chair recognizes Pastor Greg," he finally said.

All who were standing sat down. A hush settled over the church.

Greg stood and turned in his pew to face his people. "I did ask Forest Parker to resign," he began.

I noticed that Forest placed his hands on the pew as if he were preparing to launch himself straight into the air. In the hush, we heard one of the giant red balls that the children were playing with outside hit the side of the church.

"There were rumors floating around the community concerning Forest. These were only rumors and were not substantiated and can be very damaging and embarrassing to Mr. Parker. It is unnecessary and inappropriate to repeat any of these rumors. They are never to be discussed. But under the circumstances, I believed it would be best for the church and for the reputation of Christ if Forest would resign from the board until the rumors were proved false. That is all I asked and why I asked it."

"What were the rumors?" somebody asked.

"That is not important. The church will not engage in gossip. I asked Forest to resign. He did not think it was necessary. That closed the matter. Now as for my position on the school board, well, my heart is with you people. Since some of you believe that my service on the school board is a hindrance, I am willing to resign that position as soon as it can be graciously done. Especially in light of this morning's incident with our sign." Pastor Greg looked out over his people. "Hopefully this matter can now end." He sat down.

"But it's too late," somebody said. "The damage has been done."

"What about the name of our church?"

"Who painted our sign?"

The church then exploded into chatter.

"Pastor still needs to resign," Forest said. He had settled back some in his pew.

"Pastor hasn't done anything wrong," Wilmer said, standing back up and looking in Forest's direction. "Why should he resign?"

"Only Forest wants him out," someone said.

"Why?" This question came from the front.

"What were the rumors?"

"Yes. Why did they want Forest to resign?"

"What is circulating around the community?"

"What did Forest do?"

I instantly lost track of who was saying what. I half stood and peered over people and noticed that the church's secretary was no longer attempting to record anything.

"What rumors that harm the cause of Christ?"

"Yes," Ethel said. She had leaned forward and was touching her husband's sleeve. "What could he have done to harm the reputation of Christ?"

Wilmer turned toward her. "Do you suppose he—?"

Four people jumped up and demanded to be recognized by the chair.

"Order!"

"What rumors?" someone shouted.

The questions echoed around the entire church.

"Order!" Jack pounded the gavel.

"Pastor has agreed to resign from the school board," Wendell said. "This should end all discussion."

"Pastor Greg needs to resign from the church," Forest repeated.

"Mr. Chairman," Wilmer said, "in light of this morning's incident with the sign, the church—"

"What do you know about the sign?" interrupted Todd Streeter, turning around in his pew. He was one of the mail carriers who worked out of the Bethel post office.

Wilmer looked puzzled.

"You weren't even here," Todd said.

"The church needs to know what is going on," Wilmer concluded.

"You need to sit down," Todd said. "I don't think anybody who doesn't attend all the time should be allowed to speak at meetings."

"*Order!*"

The church ignored their chairman.

"What has Pastor done?"

"What rumors are circulating?"

The church door slammed, and it sounded like several children were running in the foyer on the other side of the sanctuary doors.

Everybody in the church, along with the person sitting next to them, all started talking. Jack was gritting his teeth and beating his gavel, but I couldn't even hear his pounding. I could barely hear the children.

"What rumors?"

"*Adultery!*" Harvey Wells stood up as he shouted this announcement. "Forest Parker is guilty of adultery!"

"That's a lie!" screamed Forest as he bolted into the center aisle. "A dirty lie!"

Jack pounded the lectern. *"Order!"*

"There're no rumors!" Forest shouted. "Pastor has made them all up so he can gain complete control of the church! Especially the money! That's the real issue!"

Pastor Greg turned around. His face looked pale and drained. He faced Forest. "Money?" he mouthed.

The church exploded in a verbal ruckus. Jack Metzge pounded his gavel but in vain. Forest was red faced. Cindy disintegrated into tears.

"Pastor has made nothing up," said Wendell Cornett as he stood, though I suspected that very few people heard him.

Grandma and Mom had both turned around to see who was speaking. Grandma was pale, and Mom bit her lower lip, looking ghostly. Several other ladies were trembling. Cindy Parker was crying hard now. Dorothy Cornett looked upset, and even Cathy looked very near to tears. Arthur and Elaine Scott appeared perplexed. They hadn't a clue what was going on, other than the fact that they'd somehow got mentioned in all of this. Wade looked so much like a moron that I suspected he didn't even know that he was sitting in a Bible-believing church.

From my position in back, the carnage seemed pretty serious.

"We need Tom Collins!" somebody shouted. "Tom would have stopped this!"

Jack slammed his gavel on the lectern.

Pastor Greg jumped up and waved his hands. "Please! Please!"

The church began to settle down.

"Please! Let's calm down," Greg said.

"*Order!*"

"We can't do this to one another," he continued.

"I'm innocent!" Forest shouted. "You've ruined my reputation!" He pointed at Greg. "So help me, I'll sue! You can't ruin a man's name and reputation and family and not pay! You'll pay for this!"

Greg took a deep breath.

Mom jumped up and ran down the main aisle toward the back of the church. Tears poured from her face. When she reached the back pew, she whirled around. "You need Tommy," she said, her voice trembling. "I need Tommy. We all need Tommy. But we don't have him." Her crying overcame her for a moment. "I can't stand any of this." She then erupted into a flood of tears.

Though quiet for an instant, the church looked poised for a major explosion.

"He always told me we needed revival in this church," she continued between sobs. "He was right. We need to act like Christians!" She turned and quickly walked to the door leading to the foyer.

The hush continued over the church.

When she reached the door, she turned once again. "I'm going home. Debbie, come here."

Debbie immediately got up and walked back toward her. Grandma also got up and followed. Mom did not speak to me, so I did not move. "I can't take any more of this." She left the sanctuary with Debbie and Grandma.

The sanctuary door closed.

The hush lingered.

Wilmer McLean stood. "Let's just keep the pastor till we have time to sort this all out."

There were several nods.

"We don't want to do anything rash," Wendell said.

The spell Mom had cast continued to hold.

"I've been ruined and I'm innocent!" Forest shouted. His shout was out of place with the calm that Mom had imposed.

"We have a motion on the floor," Jack said, pounding his gavel. That also was too loud. "We need to vote."

"Why?" somebody asked.

"Because we have a motion," Jack said.

"We can table it."

"Well, let's vote," somebody else said.

"We need a secret ballot," Jack said.

"Who says?" Harvey asked.

"It's better that way," Jack said. If looks could kill, Harvey Wells would be a dead man.

Harvey glared back.

"Can I have some ushers?" Jack asked.

Several men went forward. They found some paper and started ripping it into strips.

"Write *yes* if you want to get rid of the pastor," he said, "and *no* means—"

"Too confusing!" shouted Wendell, jumping to his feet. He was real mad, but I wasn't sure why.

Jack looked furious.

"Write *keep* to keep him and *rid* to get rid of him," Wendell said.

Jack regained control of himself. "Very well, write *keep* to keep Pastor Greg and *rid* to remove him."

The church quieted while the ushers passed out the paper. Greg and Paula stood up and walked down the main aisle toward the back. Greg's face looked drawn, and Paula's was red and puffy from crying. They left the sanctuary, and I heard them go downstairs. I could hear the children laughing and squealing outside again.

After a moment, I left the sanctuary too, for you had to be twenty-one to vote. Jerry and Jimmy Metzge ran wildly past me and down the stairs. Other kids were running in and out of the foyer and also outside in the dark evening. I crept down the stairs and found Greg and Paula in the pastor's office, kneeling on the tile floor, praying. I did not disturb them.

I walked back upstairs and entered the sanctuary.

The ushers had finished counting the vote and had handed the results to Jack Metzge. He announced the results through clenched teeth. "Keep, forty-two. Rid, eleven."

I retreated to the foyer, then stepped outside and sat on the front porch. Crickets dominated the outside sounds of late summer. Children were playing red rover in the growing darkness by the outside lights from the front of the church and under the cover of the large elm.

Pastor Greg had survived the vote.

It was crystal clear that God was unable to control His church. That was an indisputable fact. It was also an obvious fact that it was much safer to stay away from both God and His church.

But I had witnessed something else. Something surprising. Unsettling. Dad was dead and forever gone and buried in Bethel Cemetery. Yet at the mere mention of his name, troubled waters were calmed.

What sort of man was he?

SIX

We would leisurely jog from the little gray house along the county road, out of the world of Bethel into another world of rolling fields, gravel roads, and tree lines. Hills and gravel dominated the county road, and this combination made for poor running. We would jog west one mile down the road just to reach the dirt road and, of course, to warm up. Once we reached the dirt road, we would sprint our fastest. The hard-packed gumbo made excellent footing in all seasons and most conditions.

We would race down the dirt road between the fencerows and trees, and there would be fields at either hand and tiny dust clouds at our feet from our shoes slapping the dirt. Along the road we watched the seasons come and go, crops sown then reaped, cattle grazing then resting. We would race, and Colby would always win. I had never beaten him in my life, but this did not matter because we were best friends. We would jog, then race, and we had a fine time for we shared a deep joy for running.

But with the passing of summer and Labor Day, I rarely saw Colby. We shared no classes, and after school he trained for cross-country with the team; I ran by myself. Colby trained for meets; I had no desire to participate as I once had.

I remembered how Dad had enjoyed going to meets. He worked odd shifts at the plant, and he was often able to attend.

They once held a meet on a blustery spring day when the sky was gray and low and the wind was from the north, stiff and frigid. You could see people huddled in the stands and by the fences, wearing coats and hooded sweatshirts, and you could hear the loudspeakers crackle out the events. You could smell too the occasional whiff of cigarette smoke that always seemed to be present at sporting events—this in spite of the wind.

Well, we were lined up to run the finals for the mile, and we could feel the excitement of the meet pound in our temples, and we could feel the sting of the cold wind though we felt hot on the inside.

The gun exploded and we were off. As I rounded the first curve, I heard Dad yell, "Go, Matt!" I thought he had not been able to make it, but when I heard his voice, I ran as hard as I could, like I had rockets on my feet, and I finished third, my best time ever. I knew Dad was proud of me. He bought me a stopwatch and would always ask about my time.

But summer followed spring, and July had forever changed all of that. He would not be attending any more meets, and I would never again hear him cheer me on. There no longer seemed to be any reason to run cross-country or track. I had no desire to be on any team. Now I only wanted to run by myself and to be left alone. I did not want to be seen, because I did not want to answer any questions.

But Wade saw me. I found that out one morning on the way to school.

"Y-you run, M-Matt?" he asked.

I didn't answer.

Cathy looked at me, surprised.

"I-I saw you r-run, M-Matt."

Then why did you ask?

We were walking east along Church Street toward prison. Cathy would usually join us as we walked past the church. Had it not been for her, the walks to school would have been intolerable.

"Y-you run g-good."

Shut up.

"Matt, are you . . . ?" Cathy began.

I frowned at her.

"W-why don't you r-run on the school t-team?"

"Don't want to."

"W-why?"

"Why don't you just shut up?"

Cathy's face turned pink, and she looked first at me, then at Wade. "We lost our JV meet the other day," she said after a minute.

I didn't care.

"Th-that's too b-bad," Wade said.

"Colby finished third overall. First for Bethel."

I had heard that around school.

"C-Colby good r-runner. Like M-Matt."

Colby *was* a good runner, for he ran hard, much like a freight train pounding by. He was the better runner, and we all knew it.

"Did you go to the meet, Wade?" she asked.

"N-no."

"I didn't either."

"B-but I seen C-Colby r-run."

"I have too. He runs fast."

Like a freight train pounding by.

"Real f-fast."

We walked toward school on the brick sidewalk on the north side of the street. A yellow dairy truck drove up Fourth Street and parked in front of a house.

"M-Matt runs r-real fast t-too. I saw h-him."

Leave me alone.

"Y-you run as f-fast as C-Colby?"

"No."

"Y-you w-will."

Wade shuffled along, and we dawdled to keep pace. Mom had assured Mrs. Scott that I would be more than happy to walk to school with Wade and that I would also keep an eye out for him. But of course she didn't ask me first or find out whether I even liked the nerd, which I didn't, but Mom promised and I was trapped and there was nothing I could do and that was that. Wade clung to me like a disease. He stuck to me like Squareface stuck to Colby.

"P-pretty d-day."

Oh, please!

"Yes, it is," Cathy said. "We have had many pretty days."

That September, fall arrived early, and the days were unusually cool and usually cloudy. Changing colors appeared, especially red on the sumac and Virginia creeper.

"I-I so th-thankful."

"For what?" I asked.

"The d-day. F-for pretty days. E-everything."

The cool breeze drifted out of the north, and the day promised to be perfect.

"You're thankful for everything?" I asked.

"Y-yes."

"So you're thankful for birth defects, tornadoes, war, and disease, right?"

Don't forget head-on crashes.

He looked puzzled.

"You did say everything."

We continued to walk while the sun peeked through the clouds and shone on our faces.

"I-I th-thankful to God, M-Matt."

"What on earth for?"

"G-God's been good to m-me."

Don't start preaching at me.

"Very g-good."

I stopped walking, shaking my head. "You know," I said, "have you ever—?"

"Have you read your chapter of *Silas Marner* for today?" Cathy asked. She no longer looked embarrassed.

I glanced at Cathy, then started walking again. "I

didn't even try to read that stupid book," I finally said. "I think it's awful."

"Matthew Collins, you are being very difficult today. Quite difficult." Her face regained a tint of red, and this accented her blue eyes. Actually she looked pretty, and I enjoyed it when she turned color.

"I've tried to read it," I said. "I can't. *Silas Marner* belongs in the trash." It was more fun irritating Cathy than irritating Debbie.

"I don't think it's awful," she said. "In fact, I kind of like it."

"That's because you're a girl."

"What does that have to do with anything?"

"Just girls like things like that," I said.

"Matthew Collins!" She stared at me.

We stopped walking, and I stared right back at her. I wasn't sure about this stare down, so I looked cross-eyed. This made her laugh; then I laughed too. I won but just barely.

"Well, I do like it," she said. "Like it quite well."

"And I hate it."

"Don't let Miss Edmonds hear you say that."

"I don't care."

"She will skin you alive if she finds out."

"She won't find out," I said.

"You really should read it, Matt."

"I know about it from the class discussions."

"But, Matt, you should read it."

"I-I try to r-read it."

"That's great. See, Wade reads it."

"Look. You can spare me the agony. Just tell me what happens."

"You're a big boy. You can do your own work."

"I l-like it. Yes-sir-ee."

Why don't you just drop dead?

We reached school and walked to our lockers, then to class. Homeroom English was an awful hour because of the torturous studying of *Silas Marner* and because I had Wade in my class. The book was nearly impossible to read and the retard nearly impossible to tolerate.

I was not alone in my hatred of the book; other students hated *Silas Marner*. The book was boring. Worse than boring. It was the kind of book that, had you not known better, you would have sworn that Harvey Wells had written it.

Cathy liked the book and so did some of the other girls. I read well and could match any girl for vocabulary, word for word, so Cathy was quite surprised to learn I hated the book. My disgust for *Silas Marner* made reading agonizing, and I did not read all of each chapter and sometimes not even any of the assignment. I would skim the reading and figure out the rest through the class discussions, if I was able to pay attention to Miss Edmonds, which oftentimes I was not. The discussions were nearly as bad as the book, if that was possible.

After first hour, the day improved because I was free of Wade. Sometimes I saw him in the lunchroom but not always. Yet I could never leave school ahead of him on account of needing to check our locker. If left to himself, he would leave it unlocked. Therefore I walked home with him, as Mom promised I would, but Cathy usually joined us as far as the church.

When we went home, we would walk along the south side of Church Street, facing traffic. There were no sidewalks on that side, so we walked on the pavement. It posed no problem as there was very little traffic toward school along Church Street.

A ditch ran along the south side of Church Street, and a tree line grew on the other side of the ditch with fields beyond the trees. Several farmers planted wheat in those fields. We watched their tractors and drills stir up dust as we walked home. There were cool days and warm days, but the cool days were earlier in the season than they should have been. The farmers, including Wilmer McLean, planted their wheat in earnest, for they feared an early fall with early fall rains, so they were determined to redeem the time and work their fields while they had a chance.

After school I would run. I would change into shorts and running shoes, take my stopwatch, then jog west to the dirt road. Once there, stretched and warmed up, I would time myself running a mile. McLean might be out in one of his fields. The leaves were beginning to change, and the locust trees were starting to turn yellow. All that remained of the dead cat was a trace of fur, and the smell was long gone and forgotten.

It did not take long for the earth to reclaim the dead.

I always pushed myself hard down the dirt road. The ground felt solid, and the footing was sure. In earlier days, I would sometimes recite a psalm or pray during these runs. This fall I realized I was completely on my own; there was no use in praying.

I would leave God alone.

I loved to run. In running I escaped Wade, for he could not run, and I escaped life, too. In the world of running, I found peace, because at those times I was all alone except for the wind and the fresh air and the rolling fields and the changing colors of the season. Peace awaited me down my dirt road.

And I longed for peace.

SEVEN

"Matt!" Cathy said. "You're not listening!"

"I hear you."

We were standing in the hallway next to our gray lockers. Students filled the hall, and the ruckus and the occasional slamming of lockers echoed along the corridor.

"You cannot keep acting like this," she said.

I slammed my locker. You had to slam the stupid things for them to close properly. I inserted the lock then faced Cathy. She stood but a few feet away; her ponytail bounced in agitation.

"You're only making Miss Edmonds furious."

"I really don't care."

"You need to care."

"I don't."

"And you need to sit up straight," she said. "At least look like you're paying attention."

I don't need a keeper either.

The hall had a life of its own—swirling, laughing, moving, slamming, talking. Some of this life spilled into room 209. Nobody paid us any mind.

"Colby doesn't have Miss Edmonds for English,"
I said.

"Well, you're not Colby. And you do have Miss
Edmonds. And you must make the best of it."

"She's boring, the book's boring, and the class is
boring."

"She is about to chew you up and spit you out."

"I'm really scared."

Cathy stomped her foot in fury. "She can make life
miserable for you!"

"She already has." I turned to head for the room.

"Matt!"

I glanced back at her.

"Look," she said. "If she asks you a question, just say
you had trouble understanding that part. Then nicely
ask her to explain it to you. That way, she will be able
to talk about the book because she loves it so much, and
you will be out of harm's way. But sit up."

"I will."

"You must look interested."

"Okay. You win." I half smiled at Cathy before enter-
ing the classroom.

Class began, the discussion of *Silas Marner* began,
and I slouched at my desk and stared at the clock. Each
minute seemed like an hour. Perhaps Nancy Edmonds
took lessons from Harvey Wells. Twice during the class,
when Miss Edmonds wasn't looking, Cathy kicked the
back of my seat.

Why doesn't the bell ring? Come on, bell. Ring.

"Mr. Collins!"

I looked up. Every eye was on me. I had no idea how long Miss Edmonds had been talking to me.

"Now that we have your attention . . ."

Uh-oh.

". . . maybe you can share your opinion."

"My opinion?"

"Yes. It's about time you joined the class. Share your profound cogitations concerning the book."

My mind went completely blank.

"Perhaps you can share with the class the deep thoughts you are having," Miss Edmonds badgered. She moved her barrel-shaped frame to the head of the row and studied me.

"My thoughts?"

"Yes. Share them. Now."

"The truth?"

"Absolutely."

"You want the truth?"

"Of course."

"I was thinking how much better it would be if I walked over to the windows and jumped out."

The class took a collective gasp.

"Jumping from this second floor," I said, "would be better than this book. Much better."

Nancy Edmonds began to turn red; her legendary rage was about to explode.

"The only question left in my mind," I said, "was whether to take the time and open the window or to just jump through the glass."

She did say she wanted the truth.

"This book is awful," I concluded.

There. That should cover everything.

"Mr. Collins!" She began to unleash her fury. "Mr. Collins, you have gone too far!"

I knew I was in serious trouble, but she'd wanted the truth and truth is important at any cost, regardless of how one might feel. This was something that surely Nancy Edmonds would know and appreciate.

She took a deep breath as she prepared to chew me into bits.

Why doesn't the stupid bell ring?

"Miss Edmonds," Cathy said, "I would like to say something." She stood up and faced the furious teacher.

"Please do."

Catherine was her top student—a favorite. Cathy could say anything she wanted whenever she wanted.

"I would like to say how appalled I am by Mr. Collins's remark."

Great. Now Cathy was stabbing me in the back. I twisted around to face her, but she refused to look at me, so I turned back. Miss Edmonds had an evil gleam in her eye as her ace student joined the attack.

"Appalled I am."

'Appalled I am'? Where did that come from? I looked at Catherine.

"His statement is inexcusable." She stood with her feet together, hands straight down by her sides, her head held up, and her gaze directly at Miss Edmonds. "I have never been so horrified in all my life."

I turned back around. I knew I was a goner for sure. I

would flunk English. Mom would have to come for a conference. I might even get thrown into the penitentiary.

"For Mr. Collins to even think of jumping through a window," Cathy said, "well, that's just awful!"

An evil grin spread on Miss Edmonds's face. Of course, any grin of hers was evil.

"He is so selfish! For one thing, just think of the damage to school property!"

My death was slow and painful, and Catherine was adding to my misery.

"Mr. Collins should know in his heart the proper course of action!"

And I had thought Cathy was my friend. There was just no telling about girls.

"He should know the proper thing!"

You could hear a pin drop. Cathy took a deep breath. "The proper course of action would be for *all of us* to calmly walk to the windows, *open them*, then jump. No book—especially this silly *Silas Marner*—is worth glass cuts by jumping through windows. Thank you." She hastily sat down.

The class instantly erupted into laughter and then applause. Several boys by the windows stood and gave an ovation. One boy even opened a window.

Nancy Edmonds turned bright red, then purple. She stupidly opened and closed her mouth like a fat fish. She was stunned and speechless. "Class!" she screeched.

Yet the applause turned to more cheering and laughter.

I glanced back toward Cathy. She sat calm and expressionless, her hands folded on top of her desk. Yet her blue eyes sparkled and her cheeks flushed red. She still refused to look at me.

The bell rang.

As one person, the class leaped for the door.

"Class!" Miss Edmonds continued to screech. It was no use. She had lost control. "Read the next chapter for tomorrow! *We will continue* Silas Marner *until it is done!*"

I ducked by the raging teacher and managed to be the first one outside in the hallway. The noise and chaos poured from the classroom into the hall; everybody was laughing and cheering. I waited a safe distance from the doorway of room 209. Cathy walked out of the classroom surrounded by several of the other girls. When the girls saw me, they giggled.

"Miss Cornett," I said.

The procession stopped. Cathy looked directly at me. Her face still showed color.

I knew I had better choose my words carefully or her giggling friends would really have a time. "Thanks."

That was the simplest. She had saved my hide, and I knew it. Now Miss Edmonds could do nothing to me without also dealing with Catherine. And she would do nothing to her. Catherine was her pet.

Cathy said nothing but turned with the girls who still giggled and continued on her way. When she had passed, she looked back and smiled, still saying nothing, but the red tinge remained in her cheeks.

We went to our classes, and the day settled down to normal. The relief of my narrow escape remained with me all morning until another ruckus destroyed it. We were sitting in the cafeteria during lunch when we heard a crash followed by a roar of laughter. Several tables over, Wade had dropped his lunch tray. A nearby janitor walked over to help clean up the mess. Everybody was laughing because Wade had spilled food on himself also. He was a mess.

What a nerd. A good detective could tell what he had for lunch by just looking at his shirt.

The janitor cleaned up the mess with the help of a lady from the cafeteria. Wade stood by and watched.

In fact, even a poor detective could tell.

I stood up and walked over to the exit and dropped my half-eaten lunch in one of the barrels stationed for that purpose.

What a loser and a nerd. And he's my neighbor and locker partner. I guess that makes me a loser and a . . .

I shook the thought out of my head. *He's certainly no friend of mine.*

"Hey, Collins." Squareface sat nearby, laughing. "Just look at your friend."

I tell you he's not my friend.

"He's struck again." Squareface cackled.

I said nothing and escaped down the hall to my next class. I was early, so I sat by myself in silence.

That afternoon after school, Cathy stayed in the library, so I was forced to walk home alone with Wade. I locked the locker after him; then we dawdled down Church Street.

Maybe I'll leave him. Just run on home.

"Hey, Matt."

I turned.

Colby and Squareface came running up. "Heard you gave Miss Edmonds a time." Colby wore a big grin.

I grinned back. "Sure did."

"She had it coming."

"That's what I thought."

"Are you going to the tri-school meet next Thursday?" Colby asked.

"I don't know." I didn't know what to say.

"It's the big meet of the year. Garrett's sure antsy."

"Why aren't you in practice?" I asked.

"I skipped out. I told him my foot hurt."

"You injured?"

"Not really," he said. "Just wanted a day off. I get tired of running."

Tired?

"It's boring," he said. "Same old thing every day."

I figured he was joking, but I couldn't be sure. I looked at Squareface. "It's unusual to see you guys without your bikes," I said.

"We're walking today," said Squareface. "We wanted to be with you. And your friend." He pointed at Wade.

Wade wore a dumb expression.

"How's your time?" I asked Colby. Wade was not a good topic for conversation.

"Not bad. I feel great. Garrett's piling on the pressure for this meet. He's been working us hard."

"He always does."

"He struggles with the JV team. I suppose I'm the best runner on the team."

"No question about it," I said.

"Well, Nerd—" Squareface focused on Wade—"what did you spill today?"

Wade stared at the ground, saying nothing.

"Doesn't he become a bore to you, Matt?" Colby asked.

"Sure does."

"Why don't you just dump him?"

"Not a bad idea."

"I'll help," Squareface said. He took two steps toward Wade and gave him a hard shove.

Wade went sprawling backward and fell into the ditch beside the road. His glasses went flying in one direction, the book he carried in another.

Squareface and Colby laughed, Squareface the loudest. "Nerd!" he said.

Wade began to spasmodically thrash about, searching for his glasses. He awkwardly put them on and stared stupidly at us, saying nothing.

"Come on, Matt," Colby said. "Let's go to the store and get some pop."

We left Wade in the ditch and walked to the Bethel Superette. Colby bought us all root beers, and we had a fine time drinking them outside the store. After a while, Squareface went back inside the store to buy some gum.

"There's somethin' you should know," Colby said.

"What?"

"Garrett's sure mad at you."

"What did I do this time?" I asked.

"Not what you did; rather what you didn't."

"You mean not running cross-country?"

"That's part of it."

"I don't want to run. Shouldn't bother him none."

"It does," Colby said.

"Well, Garrett doesn't bother me."

"He can be awful mean, Matt."

"So can I. Watch this." I searched around for a stick that I could use as a cane, but finding none I improvised without it. I limped around Colby and pretended to be stomping a cane, and I barked out orders. "Colby! Get the lead out! Speed up! Where's Collins?" I then swore.

Colby laughed. "You look just like him," he said, grinning.

"All I need is a Cubs hat," I said.

"That's funny, Matt. You make a great Garrett."

"It's real easy to be Garrett."

We watched a Buick angle park in front of the bank. Buicks were easy to identify because they always had holes in their front fenders.

"Well, anyway, be careful," Colby said. "Garrett's mad at you."

"I'm scared."

"And also your church."

"Church?"

"He blames your church for his wife leaving him."

"Why? She never attended."

We watched Chief Brewer creep west on Main Street in his police car. He drove a black-and-white Dodge that had a high-performance engine, and there was a single red rotating light on top of the car.

"He hates your church," Colby said. "You should hear how he carries on. About your pastor and all."

"Greg? He's harmless."

"Sounds like Garrett wants to kill him."

"What on earth for? His vote on the school board?"

"I have no idea," he said. "He just hates him. You should hear what he calls him. And the rest of your church as well."

"Well, he can hate the church for all I care. It's not my church."

"You go there."

"Not by choice."

Colby studied me for a moment. Squareface came out of the store with his gum. It cost five cents a pack or three packs for a dime. Squareface had bought three packs. He gave us each a stick.

Later I walked home. Debbie was home by then. I changed and went running, for the afternoon was cool and beautiful. When Mom came home, we had dinner, then helped clean up the dishes.

"I talked to Elaine," Mom said to me.

Elaine?

"I guess Wade has had a time of it."

Did she say anything about today?

"He has had cerebral palsy ever since he was an infant."

"You already told us that, Mom," Debbie said.

"He has a lot of other health problems as well," Mom said.

"Like what?"

"Elaine said he has a heart condition. His heart beats

irregularly and often fast. Elaine says it beats pretty wild sometimes."

"Is it serious?" Debbie asked.

"Yes. If he becomes excited or startled or scared, he could die."

"Oh my," she said.

"Elaine says it's a rare condition. That's why he has been excused from physical education."

"So that's why he escaped Garrett," I said.

"What did you say?" Mom asked.

"Oh, nothing. He just escaped Garrett; that's all. Usually transferees get stuck in gym, regardless of what they already have had."

"Oh."

"He just escaped gym."

"Anyway, his condition is serious," Mom said.

I picked up the plates Debbie had dried and put them away in the cabinet.

"He's taking medication for his heart," she added.

"And he might die?" Debbie asked.

"Elaine said there is always that chance," Mom said, "though unlikely."

Debbie remained silent. We got everything washed, dried, and put away.

"Elaine said something else," Mom said.

Oh no.

"She said Wade sure likes you, Matt."

"He does?"

"She said he is very thankful to have such a good friend like you."

EIGHT

Darkness descended on Bethel Baptist Church. I stood at the main doors and watched large drops of rain begin to fall from the low sky; the water fell hard, spotted the porch and sidewalk, then stopped. The low rumble of thunder rattled the windows. A car with its headlights on drove east on Church Street.

"You were right, Matt," Mom said. Sunday school had ended, and she had been standing in the foyer visiting. The rumble had brought her over to the doors and beside me. She too looked outside. "We should have taken the car this morning."

Bethel Baptist Church was one of the older churches in town—in some ways a town landmark. The old church smelled musty in a nice museum sort of way, not enough to gag or be objectionable, but more along the lines of a stately institution that was locked into rigid tradition. Yet behind us the dark day had created deep shadows within the church, and this darkness dominated the interior. Lights glared in stark contrast to the darkness but failed to dispel the gloom.

"I'll try to get us a ride home from someone after the service," she said.

"Unless you want to swim home," I said.

She looked up at me with her sad eyes and half smiled, then turned back toward the sanctuary.

Yet inside the museum, the people who were to be lights to a dark world appeared to be ignorant of that calling. They rushed about the church, restless and animated, as if they did not comprehend that darkness surrounded them.

During the week they had circulated rumors, wild and unabated. Telephones carried those rumors, and they had also been spoken in small groups. The saints talked about the school board and the church sign. They talked, too, about Greg Yoshida's recall vote. Then when sufficiently warmed up, they took a deep breath and talked about how Forest Parker might have had an affair and poor Cindy, but of course nobody knew who the mysterious woman might be, but she probably had already left town, and can you imagine such a thing happening in our church, and by the way did you know that Forest's hardware store here in Bethel is nearly bankrupt . . . and on they talked. The gossip continued hot and frenzied. The gossip masked the embarrassment that they no doubt felt for having been a part of the blowup meeting.

"Hi, Matt." Cathy walked up beside me, her light brown hair loosely brushing her shoulders.

"Hi, Cathy."

"Looks angry out there."

"The wrath of God," I said.

"No, it's not," Cathy said. "We have to have rain.

Rain is a blessing from God. You know, it rains on the just and the unjust."

"I suppose."

Yet inside the church, among the assembly of the saints, the rumors ceased and were replaced with other topics. It was not proper to discuss such things within the house of God—or at least within the hearing of those they were talking about. People talked with great energy, and they talked about everything—everything except Forest Parker's affair or nonaffair and Pastor Greg's recall vote. These topics were reserved for conversations outside the church.

"By the way," I said, "thanks again."

"What for?" She wrinkled her nose, lifting her glasses slightly higher on her face.

"You know what for," I said.

"Tell me anyway."

"For saving my hide in English class."

Even from the outside doorway, we could hear the animated chatter from the sanctuary and see the frenzied activity in the foyer. They were people driven by unseen forces, not unlike mice in a maze, driven by the memory of a meeting they apparently wished had never happened. Yet the awful church meeting *had* happened, the carnage *had* occurred, and in its aftermath, gossip flew. Now there was an irreverent din in the house of God.

"Oh," she said. "You mean from Miss Edmonds."

"Yes."

"I tried to warn you."

"Yes, you did."

"She was sure mad at you."

"You took an awful risk." I was unclear why Cathy had taken the risk but reluctant to ask why. "I hope you didn't get in trouble."

"No," Cathy said. "She hasn't said a word."

The church sign had been whitewashed, but the lettering had not yet been painted back. As it currently stood, the sign gave the community no indication as to what the church might be or what might be going on inside. It was like the people were now without name or direction, whitewashed of their identity.

The *Sentinel* reported the vandalism, but ironically the tone in the paper dramatically changed. Regardless of a school board vote or a teacher raise or no raise, small towns do not like vandalism of any flavor, and the community opinion rallied around the church.

"Well . . . like I said, thanks."

Cathy headed toward the sanctuary. "You're welcome," she said softly over her shoulder.

I watched her enter the sanctuary.

Catherine had linked her good position in class with my poor one, gambling, and correctly so, that my hide would be spared from the wrath of Miss Edmonds without consequence to herself. Politically speaking, Cathy had nothing to gain in this gamble, everything to lose.

I then watched Wade make it to the top of the stairs and shuffle into church, his hair plastered, his tie askew, his feet pigeon-toed, his Bible held close to his body. At least he had a clean face and shirt, free from mess or food. For Wade, that was saying something.

Wade had smiled and spoken in Sunday school class, but I had said nothing to him, for I had nothing to say. I did not want him to get hurt, and he was not hurt by Squareface, not really. I just wanted him out of my life. I wanted to live free of him, but instead he butted into my life at every turn. Uninvited.

I couldn't tell Mom about it. She wouldn't understand.

Thunder rumbled again. I looked back outside at the gathering storm.

"Coming to church, Matt?"

I glanced over my shoulder. Wendell was standing by the doors to the sanctuary. The foyer crowd was beginning to thin.

"Yes, sir," I said. I closed the outside doors, walked back and picked up a bulletin from the foyer table, and followed Wendell inside. I sat down in the back pew on the right.

God's number one representative, Wade, was sitting with Mrs. Scott, who sat without Mr. Scott, for he was on the road and out of town. Wendell sat down by Catherine, who was sitting by Homer Oppenheimer, the president of the First State Bank of Bethel, and his wife. Homer went to another church in town but often joined the Cornetts. Wendell and Homer were close friends and business associates, and a mere word from Wendell had secured a job for Mom at the bank.

Inside the bulletin, Pastor Greg had written an article. He publicly announced his resignation from the school board, effective at the end of the year. He also reemphasized his heart's desire to serve the people of God.

And though he had survived the recall vote by his people, the atmosphere within the church remained heavy. No doubt everybody felt it.

So in a little Baptist church in a little town on a Sunday morning in the late summer of that year, announcements were read, Dorothy Cornett played the piano, hymns were led by Harvey Wells and sung by the church, money was dutifully collected, and Pastor Yoshida began to preach to a congregation, who finally calmed down and prepared themselves to drift into a deep sleep.

"A few years ago," Pastor Greg began, "I worked in a TG&Y store while attending Bible college. I worked with a high school girl who said something that has always stuck with me. I had witnessed to her about Christ, but she rejected the gospel. She told me she wanted nothing to do with a God who would allow little babies to starve and die."

Rain began to fall, lightly at first, then hard, the same big heavy drops that we had seen earlier. The rain fell in sheets, washing the windows. The gloom was so dark I could see inside reflections off the glass. The fall rains had begun early and in earnest, and we would definitely need a ride home from somebody.

"Her words always bothered me." Pastor Greg's amplified voice echoed around the church.

The rain became quite noisy, and we all knew that the basement would probably flood as it always did when it poured.

"I didn't know how to answer her. How do you

explain that God gives people the freedom to sin and that suffering is the result? I honestly didn't know what to say."

That was the problem with Greg. He didn't know. His great education had not properly prepared him for life's realities.

"I'm sorry, Mrs. Collins, but your husband is . . ."

At least Pastor Greg had heard the murmuring of his church, for he did not preach a doom-and-gloom sermon nor did he say anything about the wrath of God. Instead he preached on God's love, a new topic to torture us with.

I sketched with the pencil kept in the pew and drew geometric designs on the church bulletin while daydreaming about nothing in particular except I wished I wasn't in church. I watched the water splash the windows and fall from gutters probably stopped up with dirt and leaves. The roar from the storm threatened to drown out the boring preacher, and tuning him out proved easy. Though sincere, Greg lacked answers to life.

Cindy Parker sat with her head down as though she wasn't paying attention either. She had been keeping to herself and not visiting with the other ladies at all. She had not been the same after her husband had been accused of adultery. Forest sat with his arms folded.

Greg continued to preach on God's love.

The conversation within the church had been a bit shriller that day, and the people were a bit more abrupt with one another. Even Harvey Wells, who was usually gray and boring but friendly, had been terse and unfriendly. God's love, though spoken from the pulpit, was a bit hard to see in the pew.

I began to shade the designs I had drawn on the bulletin while the storm continued to rage. Grandma sat with Mom and Debbie near the front, and they sat straight and alert and learned all about God's love.

Mom's cheeks had once been decorated with natural color but now were colorless and pale. A few gray hairs appeared near her temples in her once-dark hair. She walked stooped with her shoulders sagging. By her own words, she spent her days crying and her nights wishing she would not wake up. I did not see God's love in any of these things.

God's love certainly did not exist in His church. The blowup meeting proved that.

And God's love did not exist in the little gray house on Church Street.

Dad had loved God, yet God let him die a horrible death. That July night I saw things that nobody should have to see and heard things nobody should have to hear. And now the crying goes on night after night and week after week, and I hear the crying. But God does not hear or care.

As for me, I don't cry. Nothing is worth such pain.

We would be sitting at dinner, and somebody would call on the phone selling siding or something, and they would naturally ask for Mr. Collins. But of course Mr. Collins is not around at the moment, and in fact we haven't seen him for quite a while, but we heard he might be over at the cemetery—or under—and perhaps you might check there, and although we would really want him to be able to come and talk to you, he can't make it to the phone just this minute, and could we take a message or maybe you should call back, for we could all hope that you would have better luck next time, or maybe you should dial heaven, but I'm sorry I don't have that number handy.

But no matter what you thought or wanted to say or actually did say on the phone, the call would trigger the memory of that horrid night, and that would be sufficient for Mom to disintegrate in a pool of tears, forcing her to run to her room and close the door.

Then there was that time when an old marine friend had been passing through a nearby city and had called, hoping to be able to see Dad. They had been war buddies and had been through a lot together. We had to tell this marine that Tommy Collins was now dead and then explain all over again for the millionth time about the drunk and the head-on collision and what had happened outside a small town on a July night.

If there was a hell on earth, it resided in a little gray house on Church Street, and I lived smack in the middle of it. If Christ had come to deliver us from hell, well, He certainly did not deliver us from this one. Let the great erudite Greg Yoshida with his wonderful degrees explain that.

So Pastor preached on the love of God inside a dark church, and he even got us out a few minutes before noon. Perhaps the sermon was called on account of rain, rain that was heavy and black. But I alone understood life, and I knew that there was no such thing as the love of God.

And it was very dark.

NINE

"Pick one." Colby leaned back against the lockers, his hands behind his head.

"I'll pick the Yankees," I said.

"You sure?"

"Yep."

"I figured you'd pick them," he said. "I wanted the Dodgers anyway."

Every year we backed teams to win the World Series. Baptist children could not wager, so no money was ever involved, and even if we could wager, I would never place money on teams I really cared little for. So we didn't bet money, but we always picked some team to win the World Series.

"Dodgers will get creamed," I said.

He shook his head. "You're wrong. The Dodgers'll win easy."

"No way."

"You'll see."

"No way."

"Koufax has won twenty-five games this year. He's hot."

"Mantle will hit him; you'll see. He'll bat right-handed against him."

We were standing by the lockers outside the cafeteria near the gym locker room. We had divergent schedules, and we rarely saw one another. Still, we got together to pick the World Series winner, and I knew the Yankees were the team to back.

Colby glanced at the gym locker room. "Garrett's been awful," he said.

"Why talk about him?"

"He's been just awful," he said.

"So what's new?"

"Matt, this is different."

"How so?"

"This coming meet has him on edge. You'd think *he* was playing the World Series."

Students walked along on the tiled hallway, and we were surrounded by a great din. Garrett sure had Colby on edge, and I was glad I did not have to face the old crank.

"He wants the JV team to win," Colby said. "He wants to win no matter what. And he's driving us all nuts."

"So win."

Colby shook his head with a grin. "You know how poor the JV team is."

"You'll just have to carry them. You can do it."

"I'll do my best."

The bell rang. At that instant we were both late. He turned to go down the hall, and I turned to go back through the cafeteria.

"Hey, Colby," I called.

He glanced back.

"Don't let Garrett bother you," I shouted. "He's nothing but a cranky old cripple. Cripples don't know anything about running. You carry the team."

Coach Garrett suddenly appeared in the doorway of the locker room. He stood and tapped his cane. He was scowling, even though his baseball cap almost covered his eyes. I knew he had heard me.

I hurried through the cafeteria to my next class, never looking back. I did not care. I would tell it again to Garrett's face.

• ◆ •

Bethel High School took little notice of cross-country meets, saving most of its energy for football. Yet in that very unusual year, and even with homecoming just a week away, the school devoted rare attention to the cross-country team. Bethel played host to two other schools in a big tri-school meet.

On the day of the meet, the school canceled last hour to hold an all-school rally in the football stadium. The day was cool and overcast, and there were many clouds—low and gray but not really angry—and the sun had taken some time off, so the afternoon lighting was drab. The stadium filled with students and teachers, and soon the pep band played some awful noise. Then the principal and vice principal spoke while Garrett stood nearby and glowered. The principal was probably unable to get Garrett to speak and relieved that he didn't all at the same time.

I had no idea where Wade was. After the rally,

I headed on home and caught up with Cathy. "Aren't you going to the meet?" I asked.

"No. Aren't you?"

"No."

We walked along Church Street on the left side, as was our custom.

"You surprise me, Miss Cornett," I said.

"Why?"

"I don't know. School spirit and all that."

"I don't feel like going; that is all."

The trees along the street displayed great colors, and these colors contrasted with the grayness of the October overcast. The air was damp from recent rains and a little chilly, too.

"You don't want to see Colby," I said. "That's why."

"No. That's not why. I just don't feel like going. But it is true. I don't like Colby."

"Why?"

"He is rude. Stuck-up."

"He's a good runner."

"I suppose," she said. "But you're a good runner."

"Not as good as Colby."

"I think you are."

"I'm not."

"Anyway," she said, "there is more to life than running."

"Like what?"

"Colby is not a Christian." The wind carried her words through the trees and over the fields to the very edge of the world, then beyond and into the overcast.

"So? What's that have to do with anything?"

"Everything," she said. "Being a Christian is important. Very important."

"It doesn't make much difference."

She looked at me. "Yes, it does. You know it does. It changes the way you look at things."

"Colby sees things the same way as I do."

"Not really."

"We're best friends."

"You only think you are," she said. "Colby is selfish. Insincere. He would turn on you in a minute."

She stopped walking while I continued several steps ahead of her. I collected my thoughts and was about to explain a few things to her.

"What's that?" she asked.

"What's what?"

"Didn't you hear it? There it is again."

I had heard nothing.

She stepped over the ditch to the tree line. "Oh no. Come quick, Matt."

I walked back and squatted beside her. Cathy had found a little white kitten—cold, skinny, starving, half dead.

"The poor thing," she said.

"Come on, Cathy. Let's go."

"We can't just leave it."

"Why not?"

"Matthew Collins! Sometimes . . . !"

I just stared at her.

She started to pick it up with one hand, and the

kitten attempted to arch its back and hiss but was so weak it could not. "Here," she said. "Take my book."

I looked at her, then the cat.

She turned to me. "Matt! Please!"

I took her copy of *Silas Marner* and held it.

She picked up the kitten despite its feeble protest, cuddled it against her, then began petting and stroking the animal. Soon the kitten tried to purr as it snuggled against her jacket. "If we leave it, it will die," she said.

"If you take it home, it'll die."

Cathy looked at me, her blue eyes moist with tears.

"Cathy, cats die all the time."

"Don't you have any mercy?" She spoke softly, not at all angry or accusing.

I said nothing.

"I'm going to take it home," she announced. "Come on."

We cut through the church lot, across her backyard, and into the house. The kitchen was tiled, and there were oak cabinets and a long counter. Light paneling graced the lower half of the wall, and the eating area had light wallpaper and open shutters. The house smelled new and clean. The Cornetts had lived in their home for nearly a year, but this was the first time I had ever been inside.

Cornett Ford was the only car dealership in Bethel or for miles around for that matter. Wendell Cornett had a fine business, and he sold many cars and made tons of money. Nearly everybody in town bought their cars there, whether new or used. Our car was a light green 1960 Chrysler Imperial. It had been a low-mileage trade-in to the Ford dealership, and Wendell had let us have it for a song earlier that year. Though the Cornetts were fine people, Catherine's simple dress and lifestyle reflected more her personality than her upbringing, for her parents did not share her simple, inexpensive tastes.

Cathy held the kitten in one hand while she poured a little milk in a pan, then heated it on the stove. She poured the warm milk in a little bowl and set the kitten on the floor in front of it. She found a box in the broom closet and put it in the corner near the refrigerator.

Dorothy Cornett stood silently in the archway from the living room and watched her daughter. The kitten had difficulty standing but somehow managed to lick up some of the milk. The warm milk gave the animal strength, and before long the kitten consumed the entire contents. By this time Cathy had found a towel, and she placed it and the kitten in the box. The animal licked itself, purred, then snuggled into the towel.

"Another stray?" Mrs. Cornett asked.

Cathy blushed slightly and did not look directly at her mother. "It was half-dead. I had to bring it home."

The kitten had no curiosity of its new surroundings and quickly went to sleep.

"Must you bring home every stray?" Mrs. Cornett asked.

Cathy looked pleadingly at her mother. "I couldn't just leave it," she said. "We can keep it. It will be no bother to you or Dad."

Mrs. Cornett shook her head but smiled at the same time. "I guess you just can't help yourself," she said at last.

Cathy looked quizzically at her mother. "It was half dead," she repeated.

"Have you asked Matt about working?" Mrs. Cornett asked.

Working?

Cathy blushed again. "No, I'm sorry. I haven't had a chance."

"Matt," Mrs. Cornett began, "Wendell's porter at the shop broke his leg and will be off work for a while. Wendell thought you might want to earn some money part-time."

I reacted without giving the situation any thought. "Yes, ma'am. I would like that very much."

"You would clean cars," she continued, "washing them, that sort of thing."

"That would be fine."

"He would use you on Saturdays and maybe several afternoons after school."

"I would like that."

"You probably will need to talk to your mother about this."

"Yes, I will. Thank you very much." I placed Cathy's copy of *Silas Marner* on the kitchen table. "When would I start?"

"Talk it over with your mother, then go see Wendell."

"I will. Thank you very much."

Cathy was still slightly red.

"See you tomorrow, Cathy," I said.

"Bye, Matt. Thanks."

I walked toward the back door. "For what?"

"For helping with the kitten."

I had not done anything, and had I been alone, I would have done less. "You're welcome."

I walked out the back door into the cool afternoon and headed home. I changed, then jogged down the gravel road to the dirt road. The damp air felt good and smelled good, and color was everywhere, and in fact, the gray day made the fall colors softer somehow. I could see McLean's wheat from the gravel road, for it had sprouted neat rows of green that looked like grass. I carried my stopwatch, and I just knew this would be a good time because I felt strong. I reached the dirt road and found it damp. I started my watch and began the sprint.

Immediately mud began to cling to my shoes; then mud began to stick to mud, and this added great weight to the shoes. Mud flung off as I ran. By the time I reached the willow trees, the road had become too soft. I had to stop. It was no use. Too muddy. I leisurely jogged back to the gravel road, then back home.

That night I asked Mom about working at Cornett Ford. She preferred that I be at home if Debbie came home, but Debbie rarely came straight home anymore. Debbie would usually go to the bank or to Grandma's or to a friend's house, usually Julie's. Therefore, Mom ultimately did not mind, and I looked forward to earning some extra money.

The next day I arrived at school to learn that Bethel had won the cross-country meet. Colby had carried the JV team.

I also discovered my locker open with the lock hanging inside. I had not checked the locker after the school rally, and Wade had messed up again.

Only this time there was another problem. Somebody had thrown mud into the locker, and the mud had splattered all of our books and papers, both Wade's and mine. There was mud on both shelves and everywhere inside the locker.

I wanted to kill Wade.

TEN

Cornett Ford covered an entire city block on the north side of Main Street. New cars filled the front of the lot, and there were many used cars too, parked on the north and east sides. An older brick building with large windows served as a showroom, and the service area was located in a large metal building adjoining the back. These buildings stood as islands in the huge sea of cars. Wendell Cornett provided automobile sales and service for the entire county, and his dealership was a very busy place.

The showroom inside was clean and well lit with plate-glass windows across the south end. The new model year had begun, and a white, two-door Falcon with a six-cylinder engine was parked on the east end of the room with a maroon Galaxie 500 convertible on the west. The Falcon catered to the economy minded, while the Galaxie was a deluxe model equipped with the high-performance package.

Parked between the two new cars was a 1930 Model A Ford town sedan. The car was black with gray mohair interior and had belonged to Wendell's father. We would often walk the two blocks from the Bethel Superette to Cornett Ford just to look at the old car. We would place a foot on the running board and look inside through the open window, and we could smell the gas along with the old smell from the interior. We thought cars with running boards were wonderful, and it was a shame that new cars no longer had them.

Wendell would often start the car and run it a little, just to keep the oil circulated and everything running properly. Because of this activity, a piece of cardboard had to always remain under the engine on the tile floor because the car leaked oil after it had been running.

Big Joe, Wendell's service manager who remembered Model A days, once told me all Model As leaked oil. The oil leaked backward from the rear main bearing and dripped out the flywheel housing. He said you never had to change oil in those cars, just add a quart from time to time. Of course he was joking, because the car did not leak that much oil. We all knew he was joking, but it was a funny thing to say anyway, and these stories just made us like the old car even more.

The car was a reminder of days long ago, simpler days. Yet past days are only simple when you look back. No day is simple as it happens.

A wall separated the showroom floor from the main offices, and on this showroom wall hung many pictures. There were pictures of old Fords and also pictures of Wendell and his dad, Frank, who had started the dealership forty years ago during the Model T days.

Inside Mr. Cornett's office there were pictures too, including pictures of Mrs. Cornett and Cathy.

"It's quite simple," Mr. Cornett said while leaning back in his chair with his hands behind his head. "Clean cars sell. Dirty ones do not."

I paid strict attention and only occasionally glanced at one of the pictures. This was the first time I had ever been in his office.

"I'm a little shorthanded at the moment," he continued, "with Jimmy being out. But I want to keep his job open for him to come back to."

I was beginning to understand jobs and the privilege to have one and keep it. We were very grateful Mom had landed a job. I respected Mr. Cornett for keeping the job available for Jimmy.

"Scotty will show you what needs to be cleaned."

Scotty was the sales manager, a gray-headed veteran of countless car sales.

"The other guys will show you where things are and how they should be done. Any questions?"

"When do I begin?"

"Tomorrow morning, eight o'clock."

"I'll be here. Thank you very much."

"Quite all right, Matt. I know you'll be a good worker."

I left Mr. Cornett's office and bumped into Mrs. Cornett and Cathy.

"Hello, Matt," Mrs. Cornett said.

"Hi."

She then entered the office.

Cathy stayed with me. "When do you start working?" she asked.

"Tomorrow."

The office door closed.

"So did you get your locker cleaned up?" she asked.

"Yes, a janitor helped."

"Was it bad?"

"It was awful. Everything got covered. We went to the office to report the textbooks. They all got ruined. Everything got ruined."

"Will you have to pay for them?"

"No, the school will replace them."

We were standing in the hallway outside Mr. Cornett's office. I could see the showroom and the Model A behind Cathy.

"But some things can't be replaced," I added.

"What do you mean?"

"Well, my notebook for one thing. And I have to redo a math assignment that I already had done."

"Oh my."

"And I lost my running log."

"What?"

"I had kept track of my running times for the last six months. By chance I had left that in the locker, and now it's ruined. I've lost all of those times."

"I'm sorry, Matt."

"That was kind of important." I started walking toward the showroom.

She turned and followed me. "Who do you suppose did it?" she asked.

"I don't know. I suspect Squareface knows."

"If Squareface knows, Colby knows."

"Colby didn't do it," I said.

"Don't be so sure."

"He couldn't have. He was at the meet."

We stopped at the end of the hall at the edge of the showroom floor. Scotty was talking to a lady who was standing by the Falcon. I just shook my head.

"What is the matter?" she asked.

"Oh, mud I guess. I can't seem to forget it. After all, it was meant for Wade."

"Wade?"

"Sure. He has a way of attracting these acts of affection. I'm the innocent one in this. Because of him I lose my stuff. And I couldn't believe it. He just stood around and watched us clean it up. He never helps. He's just worthless."

"Oh, Matt."

"He is. And he's the cause of this."

"No, he's not."

"Oh yes, he is. If he'd locked the locker, this wouldn't have happened."

We could see Main Street from the windows, and we watched a pickup from the parts store pull into the lot and drive toward the back.

"Well, I had better be going," she said after a moment. "We have plans for tonight. We will be eating out." She turned and headed back toward the office.

Must be nice to eat out.

"You really shouldn't blame him," she said as she opened the office door.

I walked through the showroom, then outside.

Of course I can blame him. I lost all my times, and it's his fault. I ought to teach him a lesson. Something to get even.

As I headed home, I tried not to think of Wade but rather looked forward to tomorrow and my new job and the money I would earn.

Saturday morning arrived, cold and windy, and Scotty started me washing some of the used cars on the north side of the lot. Trade-ins were first parked on the north side, where they were cleaned. The detail area for washing and cleaning cars was being remodeled, and none of the power equipment was even hooked up, so cars had to be cleaned on the lot. The hose and nozzle for washing were coiled against the north side of the service building, with the soap, rags, and bucket resting just inside the building.

The first car I washed was a '57 Chevy that had been traded in two days earlier. I got wet from washing the cars, and the wind froze my hands and chilled me. But I did not mind. I finished the car, then started on the next.

By early afternoon, I had washed all the cars that needed washing. I was quite wet and cold when I stopped for lunch. Mom had made several sandwiches and packed them along with some chips in a paper sack. Two of the mechanics worked that Saturday and also Big Joe, so I ate lunch with Big Joe out in the service area.

Big Joe, a tall man in his early fifties, had high cheekbones, sharp features, and jet-black hair. He was of American Indian descent, though I never asked him from what tribe. Big Joe really knew cars, and he had first started to work for Wendell's father. He was a friendly guy, and everybody called him Big Joe, from Mr. Cornett down to the greenest mechanic. I got to call him Big Joe too.

Big Joe told me more about Model As and then talked about the early V-8 Fords and how they'd had water pump problems and would overheat. The later V-8s were designed better, and he told me why. He also told me he remembered how the V-8 Fords would beat anything up Suicide Hill, located about two miles northwest of town.

"How do you know so much?" one of the mechanics ribbed him.

"Spent many a night racing up that hill."

"So you raced V-8 Fords up those hills?" the mechanic asked.

"Yep. All the way to the top."

"Would you race them up mountains?"

"I'll race 'em anywhere," Big Joe said. "I'll even race 'em in hell."

"You intend to go there?"

"You bet," Big Joe said.

"Don't let Mr. Cornett hear you say that. He's a Christian. And an important one, so I hear."

Both mechanics laughed, and I laughed too. Big Joe thought it all a good joke.

I thought the conversation grand and told them if Big Joe was going to hell, I might race V-8 Fords with him. They all laughed again, and they called me the kid. They accepted me and even offered me a cigarette, but I declined; that was going a bit too far. I told them I was trying to run super fast, and cigarettes slowed you down by taking your wind away.

After lunch, my next job was to vacuum out cars, which was much better. The dealership had a large portable vacuum that could be wheeled to each car, and this job was warmer than washing. The vacuum made a lot of noise, and I could not hear anything while it was running. I vacuumed the cars I had washed earlier and other cars as well. I did this for the rest of the day.

Everything closed early on Saturday, and they closed up the dealership around four o'clock. Scotty paid me in cash, and on my way home I couldn't help but think how great it all was.

"How was your first day?" Mom asked when I arrived.

"Just fine."

"You tired?"

"Yes."

"You look cold."

"I am. Had to wash cars. I got wet. Never warmed up."

She looked at me with that concerned, motherly look.

"I'm all right, Mom."

"We'll get some hot food in you. You go clean up first and get dry clothes on."

I took a hot shower and had some hot tea and felt

much better. Supper was ready by then, so we sat down and ate.

"By the way," Mom said.

Debbie looked at her in anticipation.

Mom hesitated, then started to cry but caught herself. Debbie looked at me, and we wondered what this was all about but suspected that it was nothing good. When Mom regained control of herself, she continued. "The stone is now in place."

"What stone?" Debbie whispered.

Mom took a deep breath. "Your father's tombstone. It's all done and now in place."

Debbie and I continued to look at each other, not knowing what to say but afraid to say anything for fear Mom would start crying again.

"I didn't know what to do or what to order. It took me a while. And it took them a while to make it. But it is made and in place."

We sat silently and picked at our food, not eating but looking like we were.

"There is just so much that I don't know what to do about. . . ."

"Thanks for telling us, Mom," I finally said.

• ◆ •

Sunday morning was cold and overcast for it had rained a little, but it was not raining by the time we walked to church. Dad always believed in walking. We did not mind.

The Scotts had driven, and they were there by the time we arrived.

Wade immediately cornered me. "I s-sorry, M-Matt."

"You're sorry?"

"'B-bout the l-locker."

I gritted my teeth. *Punch him. Punch him in the face. That would get even.*

"I-I feel real b-bad."

"How hard is it to lock a locker, Wade?"

Pastor Greg overheard me and looked my way.

"I s-sorry. I do better, M-Matt."

"The only reason I don't punch you," I said, trying to keep my voice low, "is because I don't think it will do any good. You're too stupid to learn. You're beyond help. But because of you, my stuff gets ruined."

One of the older ladies had stopped to talk to Pastor Greg, so his attention was diverted and nobody heard me.

"I real s-sorry."

"You sure are. You're a sorry sight."

"I don't b-blame you for being m-mad. P-please forgive. M-me."

"I'm not going to forgive you until you shape up," I said. I poked him in his shoulder with my finger.

He staggered back under my jab.

"I guess that means I'll never forgive you," I said, "because you'll never change."

Wade looked at me with his characteristic blank look. His eyes, distorted by the thickness of his glasses, contributed to his comical appearance.

I walked away from him and headed downstairs to the horrid Sunday school class. I tried to take a deep breath.

"I unders-stand," he called after me. He spoke with the accompaniment of a large amount of saliva.

I stopped halfway down the stairs and looked back at him.

"I-I thankful for you, M-Matt. You're good to m-me."

"What?"

"I give th-thanks for you, M-Matt. You m-my friend."

I stared at him.

"God is g-good—"

"Don't preach to me about God!"

"B-but God is—"

"God is not good!" I bounded back up the stairs toward him, not fully sure what I was going to do. At the very least clear the air about God and friends—and a forceful air clearing at that.

Harvey Wells appeared behind him and began to descend the stairs. "Good morning, boys," he said. "Ready for class?"

"Y-yes." Wade mustered a smile.

I said nothing. Wade had no idea what a close call he had just experienced.

They headed down the stairs, and several kids from the foyer followed. After a minute my breathing was normal, and I then went downstairs.

I put my mind into neutral and coasted through Sunday school, morning church, and later evening church. The lettering on the church sign had been repainted as before, though the incident had not yet been forgotten. The Parkers were not in attendance that Sunday, nor were several others, and you could tell that the congregation was a little smaller. The church remained anxious, unsettled.

I felt tense too whenever I thought of Wade. But when I did, I tried to think of something pleasant. For one thing, I now had some money, and that was truly a pleasant thought, and whenever I thought of Wade, I would simply think of the money to help forget him.

But thoughts about mud kept nagging me.

By Monday morning, my curiosity consumed me, and I went looking for Colby, taking the risk of running into Garrett. I found Colby just as he was about to enter the gym locker room.

"Hey, Colby."

"Hi, Matt."

"Can we talk for a minute?"

"Sure."

We walked into the cafeteria.

"Somebody threw mud in my locker," I said.

"Yeah." He laughed. "I heard about that."

"You did?"

"Yep. Pretty funny, huh?"

I could feel my face turning red. "I didn't think it was funny."

"Sure it was, Matt."

"It was not funny."

"Sure it was," he said. "You just take things too seriously. You need to come out of yourself."

"You know who did it?" I asked.

"Maybe I do; maybe I don't."

"Come on, Colby. We're best friends."

He laughed. I felt even hotter.

"Matt, my boy," he said, "you look mad."

"I am mad."

"You look funny when you're mad."

My teeth began to grind. I had this overwhelming desire to punch him in the face. If only he weren't bigger and faster. "Don't play games, Colby."

"Who's playing games?"

"You are! Who slung the mud?"

"I ain't tellin'!" he said.

I couldn't believe what I was hearing.

"Now what are you going to do about it?" he asked. His voice had a taunt to it.

I glared, my rage mingled with fear. I saw something in him I had never seen before, something awful.

"See you around, pal," he said and turned and went back to the locker room.

"Colby!"

He walked through the door, laughing.

I went upstairs to get ready for class. I kept grinding my teeth.

I should have beaten Colby to a pulp. Or am I afraid of . . . ?

I stopped at my locker, extracted the books, then slammed it shut.

I'm not afraid of Colby. We're best friends. I secured the locker, then entered the classroom.

Best friends? It sure shows.

Cathy was already sitting at her desk. "Hi, Matt."

Maybe she's right about Colby.

"Hi." I slumped into my chair and waited for the torture to begin.

Colby knows who threw the mud. Just think about it. He must know. Some friend.

After a minute, Wade came in the room. "H-hi, M-Matt."

Here's a great chance. Go ahead and beat him up.

"I-I sorry, M-Matt."

"Sure."

"I-I—"

"Sit down and shut up."

That was good. That showed him who's boss. Of course, who's afraid of Wade?

Wade said nothing but dutifully sat down and faced the front.

A lot of people were afraid of Colby. And that was a fact. It probably was also a fact that Colby knew who flung the mud but wouldn't tell me. My teeth continued to grind.

I am not afraid of Colby!

The bell rang. Class started. It was awful to be in school, and we all knew it. We just sat around and wished the time would fly by, but of course it didn't. We were doing time, just like inmates.

Rain fell that afternoon, light but steady. That

day I ran ahead of everybody and reached home first. I changed into sweat clothes and ran toward the dirt road, but I knew it would be too muddy and it was. I jogged back down the gravel road, past our house, turned up Tenth Street to Main Street, then jogged west to Bethel Cemetery.

The leaves of the oak tree had turned reddish brown, and water dripped off them and off the branches, too. Many of the leaves had already fallen, and these now littered the ground. I found the grave and the newly placed stone lying flat on the ground, now partially covered with wet leaves. It read simply:

Thomas Collins, 1924-1963
Beloved Husband and Father

The rain fell harder and soaked me to the bone, and the wind, though slight, chilled me. I didn't care. I knelt on the stone under the overcast sky and brushed the leaves off. The rain splattered around me and on the gravestone, too. I felt like I should cry, but I could not, not even if I wanted to; and I didn't want to because I knew I would never cry again.

"Why?" I asked.

I was kneeling on the stone, and my knees were beginning to hurt; everything was wet, and the leaves, too, were bunched and wet. The oak offered no protection from the rain, and the sky was low and gray and just seemed to fall around everything.

"Why?"

I heard only the rain and the slight wind and the water dripping off the nearby oak.

Later I got up off the stone and jogged back home. There was no answer. Not in the world of Bethel.

ELEVEN

The parade assembled at the high school, proceeded north to Main Street, moved west to Tenth, south to Church, then finally back to the school. Bethel enjoyed parades and always made a big deal out of them, including homecoming parades. The parade contained many floats on trailers pulled by pickups or occasionally a tractor, and local businesses also had entries. Many students walked in the parade. The marching band walked too, and they played loud, raucous tunes that everybody could hear but nobody could identify.

Or even cared to.

Everybody in Bethel, as well as half the county, would watch the parade. People packed the town and lined the sidewalks for the entire route. For these homecoming festivities, school let out early so students could either participate or watch. After the parade concluded back at the school, a rally was held in the football stadium.

Kids who attended Baptist churches did not go to school dances. This meant I would not be going to the homecoming dance, and I didn't know who I would ask even if I could. Since I did not play football or go to dances, I had no interest in homecoming or the game or the parade or the rally, so I took the opportunity to skip out and walk home. I left football and parading and dancing to others.

That afternoon I gave little thought when Debbie brought home her friend Julie, but had I been thinking, I would have realized something was up. Julie had dinner with us, and before it was over, the bomb fell.

"Can we, Mom?" Debbie asked.

I looked up from my plate.

Obviously Mom knew what. "Yes, you can."

"*Oh, boy!*" Debbie shouted.

Julie clapped.

Mom then looked at me. "Would you please take the girls to the football game tonight?"

"Take them?"

"Yes. Please."

"Do I have to?"

Mom sighed. "Yes, Matt, would you take them for me?"

I looked at the two.

They looked back at me, smiling in anticipation.

"We'll stay right with you," Julie said.

That was what I was afraid of.

"Please, Matt," Debbie said.

If I said no, that meant Mom would take them. For the girls to be with a brother was one thing. For them to be with a mother would be something much worse. They desperately wanted me to say yes.

Of course, sitting with them would not actually be that bad.

"I'll take them." I had no plans, not really.

They cheered again, and since it was late, Mom agreed to clean up dinner by herself. We found our jackets, walked to the football stadium, and got seated in time for the opening kickoff. The girls sat beside me and giggled and carried on and had a fine time, while I sat and watched the game without paying much attention to it or the girls or anything else.

A slap on my shoulder startled me.

"Hey, Matt." It was Colby. He was alone.

"Hi, Colby."

He pushed me into the girls a little bit to make room to sit down. Debbie and Julie moved a space, and everyone had plenty of room on the bleachers. The girls continued to squeal. Their conversation, though animated, had little to do with football.

"Surprised to see you here," Colby said.

"So am I," I answered.

"Looks like you're babysitting."

I shrugged.

"Going to the dance tomorrow night?"

I stared at Colby. He knew I wouldn't be going.

"Oh, I forgot," he said. "You don't do dances." He used the same tone as before, when he'd refused to tell me who threw the mud in my locker.

I turned back to the game and tried not to get mad.

"You need to come to these dances," he continued. "Have some fun."

Ask him about the locker, then punch him in the face and be done with it.

"I'm going with Bonnie," he said.

"Bonnie? Bonnie who?" I asked.

"Bonnie Wilson."

"The cheerleader?" I looked down on the sideline and saw her.

"The very one," he said.

"Why?" Colby was only a sophomore, and he couldn't even legally drive. Why would a senior girl go with a sophomore?

"Why? Why do you think?"

"She's a senior," I said.

"She sure is." Colby grinned.

"You're going with Bonnie?" I asked.

"Are you hard of hearing?"

Since I couldn't think of anything smart to say, I remained quiet.

"Look, Matt," he said, "you need to get with the right crowd."

I shook my head.

"What's the matter?" he asked.

"Nothing."

"Can't I have a girlfriend?"

"Well, sure."

"You have one," he said.

"No, I don't."

"Oh yes you do."

"No, I really don't," I said. He knew I didn't have a girlfriend.

"Yes, you do. She saved your hide in English class."

"You mean Cathy?"

"Sure. She's ugly; that's all."

"She's not ugly."

"I think she is," he said.

I held my tongue. Colby had changed. Until recently, I had never heard this mocking tone from him.

"She's a loser to boot," he continued. "In fact, Matt, you're becoming a loser."

"Hey, Colby, that's enough." I looked back toward the game. My teeth began to grind and my jaw felt stiff. *Go ahead. Bring up the locker business.*

"That's what I'm trying to tell you," he said. "You're becoming a loser like Cathy. And the nerd."

My head snapped back toward him.

"You hang around nerds," he said, "so you're becoming a nerd. Why you'd hang around those two is beyond me. Especially the nerd."

"I don't hang around the nerd. I just got swindled into being his locker partner."

"You do hang around him," he said. "And you're becoming like him."

My face began to feel hot.

"Pretty soon," he said, "everybody'll be calling you a nerd."

I looked back toward the game. The night was dark and murky, and there were wisps of fog and halos forming around the stadium lights. The two girls on my other side continued to giggle, completely unaware of Colby's presence.

Or the football game.

Go ahead; punch him.

"Take the World Series." Colby continued his lecture. "The Yankees have lost the first two games. You've picked the Yankees. You've picked a loser. This makes you a loser."

"That was a bad pick," I said.

"Then there's your girlfriend."

"I don't have a girlfriend." *Haven't we already been through this?*

"And she's ugly," he said.

I glared at him.

"All right, not *ugly* ugly, but she's not as sharp as Bonnie. So this makes her a loser. Then there's the nerd. He definitely's a loser. What makes this difficult is that you're becoming a loser. You hang around losers, you become a loser."

Go on. Punch him in his ignorant face.

"You need to hang around the top crowd, Matt," he said. "Leave those losers behind."

He does have a point. At least about Wade.

"Yep. Leave those losers behind."

I'd sure like to leave Wade behind.

"You know," he said, "just hang around me and you'll be with the top crowd."

That would be nice.

"We can go to parties, and you'll be at the top."

The thought was intriguing—to be with the top crowd and to go to parties.

Maybe he's right. Maybe I am becoming a loser.

At that moment I wanted to be Colby. He was not a loser. He was everything I ever wanted to be. Life had been good to Colby. Even more, he did not have to see what I had to see on that July night. Nobody should have had to see that.

"That might be nice," I said.

"See. That's the spirit. That's the old Matt." He slapped my back.

We were friends again, but my face still felt hot.

"You need to have fun," he said. "Tell you what. We'll buy you a Cubs hat and a cane, and you can go around being Garrett."

I smiled in spite of myself.

"That was funny, Matt," he said. "You make a great Garrett. And that's what I'm talking about. You know. Having fun."

We silently watched the game for a moment.

"By the way," he said, "have you seen the nerd?"

"No. Why?"

"Just wondered. Thought I might have some fun."

"Fun?"

"Sure," he said. "Since he's new to school, I thought I'd get together with him and have some fun." The tone was back.

"What kind of fun?" I asked.

"You know, fun. Fun for me. Fun for him. You know, fun."

"I see."

"You don't care, do you?"

"No. Of course not."

"I didn't think you would."

I did not know what Colby had in mind, but I really didn't want to know either. I watched the game for a couple more minutes. The other team was trouncing Bethel.

"Well, better be going," he said. "Me and Bonnie have big plans later on." He stood up. "See you around, buddy."

"See you around."

He left, chuckling as he went.

By the middle of the fourth quarter, it had become quite clear that Bethel would be humiliated. I noticed the girls had quieted down and were becoming bored, so I told them to come on. The night had become chilly, and they were tired and probably cold, so they obeyed without any complaint. We walked back home in the cold October night.

The next morning I worked at Cornett Ford. I had a lot of cars to wash, and soon I was wet and cold but did not mind because of the money.

The service area was located in the newer metal building and had large garage doors on two sides. Big Joe had been working a lot of Saturdays, so I would try to eat lunch with him, for he was always full of stories. We would never eat in the customer waiting room but instead out in the service area. We would usually sit on some folding chairs and keep our food on the concrete floor. Eating lunch in the service area was just grand.

"Well, kid," he said, "had a '47 Chevy not too long ago."

"You did?" I was stunned. "Thought you were a Ford man."

"I am."

"Well, why did you have a Chevy?"

"It was my aunt's, and she had problems with it. She lived back east. She died a few years ago, so I got it."

"So what did you think of the Chevy?"

"I hate Chevys. It had a six cylinder, a 216. I hated it."

"Why? Was something wrong with it?"

"It had a cracked block," he said. "I didn't know it either."

"How did you find out?"

"It kept losing coolant. The stuff leaked into the oil. Ruined the bearings. It had Babbitt bearings, you know."

I told him I knew, but I really didn't. I had no idea what Babbitt bearings were.

"Did you fix it?" I asked.

"No way. I wasn't going to spend a dime on that thing."

"Well, what did you do?"

"I traded it to my buddy at the machine shop," he said.

"Traded it?"

"Yep."

"What for?"

"For a Remington pump shotgun and a drill press."

"That's all?"

"Told you I hated Chevys. Was just happy to get rid of it."

Big Joe offered me a cigarette again, and I thanked him but declined. Big Joe had lots of stories that he would spin out real easy and natural-like, and I couldn't help but sit and listen. Lunches with him were always fun, and I was glad he worked on those Saturdays.

I returned to my cold, wet work, and though I worked hard, I could not finish all the cars.

"You need to come in Monday after school," Scotty said when he paid me.

"Yes, sir."

"That won't cause a problem, will it?"

"No, sir. I'll be here."

The thought of working Monday did not bother me at all, and as I walked home, I made a note to be sure and tell Mom. I thought, too, how I might just leisurely jog around town in the late afternoon instead of running down the dirt road.

On Sunday we endured church, and we endured the sermon, too. That day the Los Angeles Dodgers completed the slaughter of the New York Yankees to win the World Series in four straight games. Colby was right; I had picked a loser.

The autumn season continued its march to glory. When we walked to school, we could see that crimson and gold dominated Church Street. The days could be sunny and bright or cloudy and overcast but were usually cool and brisk. We watched leaves collect at the base of trees, then scatter with the wind from yard to yard and across streets, except of course when the leaves were wet from rain and would stay put.

Yet the glorious colors failed to penetrate into the

interior of Bethel High School. School remained dull and drab, and the classes were dull and drab too. The days were long and boring.

On Monday I watched Wade as he walked to school. I watched him struggle with the locker.

"You hang around nerds, so you're becoming a nerd."

"Pretty soon everybody'll be calling you a nerd."

"You hang around losers, you become a loser."

"Hang around me and you'll be with the top crowd."

After school I secured the locker because Wade could not be trusted with such a simple task. I took my old clothes and walked over to Cornett Ford, where I changed and began cleaning cars. To my surprise, I did not wash but instead vacuumed out cars and cleaned interiors, because clean cars sold, and we all wanted cars to sell. I could hear nothing over the roar of the vacuum.

"Matt!"

I looked up. Mom was standing behind me with Debbie. I turned off the vacuum.

"There's an emergency!"

"Mrs. Collins, there has been a terrible accident. You'll need to come with us."

"Matt! I need you!"

"What's wrong?" I asked.

"Wade's hurt," she said. "Beat up."

"Beat up?"

"Somebody cracked him on the head. Looks really bad. We've stopped most of the bleeding."

"Bleeding?" I suppose I sounded stupid.

"I'm taking him and Elaine to the hospital in the

city. I need to leave Debbie with you. Wendell said she can stay with you until you're done. Then you two hurry straight home. Mom's not feeling well today, so we can't bother her. So finish here, then get yourselves home and get something to eat. I have no idea when I'll be back. Probably late. You two will be all right."

"Sure, Mom."

Debbie stood beside me as Mom hurried toward the front of the lot. I saw her Chrysler with its rear tail fins and could see that somebody was sitting inside, but I could only guess who it was.

"Mom?" I called after her.

She turned and looked at me, her face tense.

"Is he hurt that bad?"

"It looks really serious, Matt." She rushed on toward the car.

Beat up?

That's what you wanted. To teach him a lesson. Something to get even. "Matt?" Mr. Cornett was walking toward me.

"Yes, sir?"

"Under the circumstances, you can put things away and go on home."

"Okay."

"He's taking medication for his heart."

"And he might die?"

"Elaine said there is always that chance."

I got things squared away; then Debbie and I walked home to a cold and dark house. After I turned up the furnace, we made sandwiches, though I was not hungry.

Mr. Scott was out of town on the road, so he had no idea there was any problem with his son.

Will he die?

I sat at the kitchen table with a half-eaten sandwich while Deb went into her room. The only light on was the light over the kitchen sink, and I looked into the dark dining room and at the descending blackness outside beyond the window.

I thought about Wade and how I had wanted him to drop dead, but I didn't want him *dead* dead. I just wanted to be left alone, to live in a world without him. After all, he was a loser, and he was making me a loser. But I had never wanted this.

But something else gnawed at me, deep within.

I could not shake the thought that Colby was behind it all.

TWELVE

That year Grandma Pine lived in a two-story house on Delaware Street. A flower bed surrounded the house, and there were also many rosebushes. The house was white with green trim, but the flowers were now mostly brown. A large sugar maple dominated the front yard, and there were other trees too. Though only some of the leaves had fallen, they still covered her yard, and many of these leaves were gifts from her neighbors.

Every fall our family would assemble to rake and burn leaves for her. We would rake the leaves into piles, then rake the piles between the sidewalk and the street, where we would burn them. This year was different. Debbie and I were to go to her house after school to work in the yard. This meant there would be no running in the afternoon, but I did not mind.

The morning walk to school was cool and damp. Clouds hung low in the gray sky, and the wind whispered to us that winter was hiding around the corner. Leaves littered the churchyard, and I watched the wind swirl them about some, but many were wet and did not move much. I waited at the church and watched the leaves and listened to the wind and tried not to think about Wade or Colby.

"Hi, Matt. Sorry I'm late."

"You're not late, Cathy," I said.

"Been waiting long?"

"Only a few minutes. I'm early."

Cathy had her hair tied back in a ponytail and secured by a blue ribbon that matched her blue dress. Despite the cool morning, her white jacket remained open.

"How is Wade?" she whispered.

"Still at the hospital."

"How is your mom holding up?"

"Okay, I guess. She got home after midnight. I tried to wait up for her but fell asleep."

"Did he get beat up bad?"

"Not too bad. Mrs. Scott told Mom he staggered in the house bleeding. But that's not what he's in for."

"Oh? What then?"

"His heart. Mom said it was beating wildly. They were afraid he would have an attack."

"Oh my."

"It was pretty serious. They couldn't get his heart to settle down. I guess everybody had quite a scare. Wade is not in good health."

"But now?"

"The doctors say he'll be all right."

We walked toward school and watched a rabbit shoot across Church Street and into the tree row.

"Who beat him up?" she asked.

"We don't know."

"Didn't Wade say?"

"Nope."

"I just can't imagine why," she said.

"Well, everybody hates him."

She stopped walking, so I stopped too.

"Why?" she asked. "He's so gentle. Harmless."

"He acts so weird. Nerdlike."

"Matt. That is not true."

"It is true. A lot of people call him a nerd."

"Who does?"

"A lot of people."

"You mean Colby, don't you?"

I started walking again. "Colby and a lot of others," I said.

Cathy caught up with me. "Did Colby beat him up?" she asked.

"Thought I'd get together with him and have some fun."

"Anybody could have," I said.

She started to respond but instead remained quiet. We walked toward school, and I wished the subject would change.

"Poor Wade," she finally said. "I'm glad he will be all right."

I guess.

I supposed Cathy was right for feeling sorry for him. As for me, I felt more guilty than sorry. I really hadn't treated him all that well. But on the other hand, he was awfully gross and very much a retard, and he had caused me a lot of grief.

Cathy shivered. "You think Colby beat him up?" she asked.

"I told you I don't know. Let's not worry about Wade anymore."

Cathy zipped up her white jacket and did not ask any more questions about Wade.

That day at school I did not worry about Wade. Actually I began to enjoy not having him around. There was no need to keep checking the locker or worry about some nerd embarrassment. There was a freedom with him being gone. If Cathy wanted to feel sorry, she could. But I would enjoy being free of him.

I did not run into Colby, and I decided that I really didn't want to know if he'd done anything to Wade. That was Wade's concern, not mine, so there was no reason to find out. I would hang around Colby and with his friends. Then I could forget all about locker mud and not have to think about Colby's snotty attitude.

Though no rain fell throughout the day, when Cathy and I walked home along Church Street, the clouds still hung low in the gray sky. I had forgotten about Wade and Colby, and as long as they were out of mind, guilt and fear remained out of mind too. I felt good and happy and actually felt a little silly. Not having Wade around made me happy because he was an emotional drain.

"I wonder how Wade is," Cathy said.

"Let's not worry about him," I said. "Let's talk about other things."

She raised an eyebrow. "Like what?"

I had no idea. I just didn't want to talk about

Wade. Or Colby. "Let's talk about you," I said with
a flair, bowing.

"What?" She wrinkled her nose.

"You look very attractive today, Miss Cornett."
She blushed.

"'Tis true, 'tis true," I said while positioning myself in
front of her, bowing again.

Actually, it *was* true. She did look quite attractive.
She had a simple beauty that not even Colby's Bonnie
had—perhaps it was an inner beauty.

"Well, thank you, Mr. Collins." She curtsied.

"'Tis an honor to walk with you, my lady," I said.

"What has gotten into you?"

I enjoyed her blushing, for it made her blue eyes
sparkle even more.

"Quite an honor to walk with such an attractive
lady," I said.

"You feel all right, Matt?" She still smiled.

"Haven't felt better," I said.

"Are you sure?"

"My lady's cheeks are rosy," I said.

They turned even brighter. "So are yours," she said.
My face instantly felt hot.

"You're becoming a nerd."

She then laughed and I laughed too, and we both
felt better and a little less silly.

Why do you always do dumb things?

"I think we had better change the subject," she said.

"I suppose."

We walked along Church Street. I would go home,

where I would change into old clothes, then on to Grandma's. I wanted to run but would not mind raking leaves. I loved to be outside on gray days.

"Did you talk to Colby?" she asked.

"No."

"I bet he beat Wade up."

Here we go again. "You're too hard on Colby," I said.

"Am I?"

"Yes."

"He is shallow and selfish."

"He's my friend."

"Matt, he is not a friend, not really."

"Who slung the mud?"

"I ain't tellin'!"

I shook my head. Escaping Wade and Colby was impossible, even in conversation. We reached the church and stopped.

"I'm sorry for acting silly." My face still felt hot.

"That's okay," she said quietly. "It was good to see you come out of yourself."

"You just take things too seriously. You need to come out of yourself."

She headed toward her yard.

"Oh, Cathy," I called.

She turned around and looked back.

I froze for a moment. She patiently endured the eternity.

"You are pretty," I finally said. I did not wait for a reaction but jogged down Church Street to the little gray house.

Later I began raking leaves at Grandma's house.
She had not been feeling well, so when Debbie arrived
from school, she helped Grandma with the inside work
instead of helping me outside. I began raking in the front
yard. Raking leaves was okay, but burning them was
more fun—almost as much fun as running and jumping
in them.

There would be days when Dad was out raking
leaves, and I would jump in them when he wasn't looking, but he knew, of course, what I was about to do and
never stopped me. I would jump in the leaves and sometimes help rake them back up, then jump in them again.
It would be October or November, and the air would be
crisp and damp, and there would be color everywhere
in the world along with browns and retreating greens.
I would jump in the leaves and thrash about, and there
would be leaves everywhere—in my coat and down
my shirt. It felt good to be outside and even better to
be alive. We knew there would be hot soup and grilled
sandwiches waiting for us inside, and if you thought real
hard, you could almost smell them. Everything was wonderful, for I was Daddy's little helper.

As I grew older, I wanted to also burn the piles,
because burning looked fun.

"Can I burn?"

"Are you through jumping?"

"Can I light the match? Please, Dad?"

"I don't know. Burning leaves is grown-up stuff."

"Please, Dad? It looks fun."

"Well, okay. Here're the matches."

"Don't light that yet."

"*Please, Dad.*"

"Matt? Did you hear me?"

I looked at Grandma.

"Don't light the leaves yet."

She stood several feet away from me. She had a coat thrown around her shoulders, and she suppressed a shiver. Grandma Pine barely stood five feet, and she weighed less than a hundred pounds when she was healthy. Now she looked very frail and even smaller than usual. Though she was gray, I never thought she looked old, but now she looked old and pale.

"Are you cold?" I asked.

"Yes."

"Don't you want me to burn the leaves?"

"I thought you might want to come inside for a snack first."

"Sure."

We walked inside and found Debbie sitting at the kitchen table. Grandma handed me a bottle of cold pop. Though cool outside, the pop still tasted good. She also had chocolate-chip cookies, though I did not eat any of them.

"I guess poor Wade has had quite a time," Grandma said.

"I suppose so."

"Well, thank God he's going to be all right."

"I'm glad," Debbie said. "I don't want anything bad to happen to him."

"Nobody does, honey," she said.

"I even prayed for him."

Prayed?

"And Mom told me she did too," Debbie added.

Prayed?

"That's sure sweet of you. I think we all did some praying."

Why pray? Haven't you guys learned anything from this past summer?

"I-I'll tell people they need to p-pray."

Why did they? Hadn't they learned how God operated the universe and how He didn't care what happened or who got hurt? So why pray? What was the use?

"Wade is sure sweet," Grandma said.

Sweet? Try nerdlike.

"You know," she continued, "I've been touched by how he gives thanks for everything."

"Yeah," Debbie said, "he does do that."

"We all could learn a thing or two from him."

Learn from Wade?

"Don't you think so, Matt?" Grandma asked.

"Somebody beat him up," I said.

"I know. That is so sad. Wade is harmless."

"That's what Cathy said."

"Now Cathy. There's a sweet girl. A very pretty child too."

She sure is.

"You like her, don't you, Matt?" Debbie asked.

"Well, I guess." I pushed my chair back. "It's hot in here. I'd better get back outside. There's a lot of leaves to rake."

"I appreciate you getting rid of those leaves," Grandma said.

"Sure." I stood up from the table. I still had some pop left.

"They can be a mess. Is it hard work?"

"Not really."

"They need to rake leaves at the church, too," Grandma said.

"I don't think you can get anybody together to rake leaves there," I said.

"Now, Matt."

"Everything's in such an uproar."

"We need your dad." Grandma then shook her head. "We just need Tommy."

"So what's all the fuss about?" Debbie asked.

"We have a young pastor who just tried to live his faith outside the church and in the community."

"So this is Pastor's fault?" Debbie asked.

"No. Greg is just inexperienced. And some other people took advantage of his inexperience."

"Like who?"

"Like Jack and Forest."

"I don't really understand," Debbie said.

"Well, the real problem looks like Forest Parker has done some things he shouldn't have," Grandma said.

"Is he guilty?" I asked.

"Well, I suppose we really don't know for sure," she said.

"He's causing trouble, isn't he?" Debbie asked.

"Pretty much. Then he tried to pin the blame on the pastor. This school board thing was just a smoke screen."

"Was Forest the one who did the sign?" I asked.

"We don't really know," Grandma said. "But there are some people who are thinking that."

I took the final swig of pop.

"And his business is also in trouble," Grandma added. "And I'm not surprised. I won't go in his store. Forest will cheat you. And I know a lot of other people who won't trade there either."

"Is he going out of business?" Debbie asked.

"He might. Poor Cindy. This has been terrible on her."

"I heard there's going to be a church split over all this," Debbie said. "Or at least people might leave."

"Why, mercy no, child."

"What's to stop it?" I asked.

"I would hope the good Lord would stop it."

"There have always been church splits," I said. "The good Lord hasn't stopped those."

"Matt, I would just hope the Lord would stop this," Grandma said.

"Can't Pastor stop the trouble?" Debbie asked.

"He's still young," she said. "At least he's trying."

"But he was part of the problem," I said. "By being on the school board."

"No, Matt. He isn't part of the problem."

"Just seems like it. That's all."

"No. He has done nothing wrong. The problem is

with Forest Parker. And Metzge. Like I said, Greg is just inexperienced."

"How would Dad have helped?" Debbie asked.

"Your dad was a very strong person," Grandma said. "He would not have put up with any nonsense. Besides, if he told either Jack or Forest to shut up, they would. They were a little bit afraid of your dad."

"Afraid?" Debbie asked.

"Well, not afraid. But they would do what your dad told them to do. Maybe they were just afraid not to."

"I still don't understand it," Debbie said.

I walked back outside to burn leaves. What was clear was that the head-on crash at Bethel Baptist Church that Sunday night had ejected people from their pews and left them sprawling all over the countryside. They were bloodied and dazed, and they tried to understand why but could not. They did not understand that God did not care about them, nor would He stop a church split should they decide to do so.

I lit a small piece of paper near the bottom of a pile of leaves, then continued to feed the fire by raking more leaves on the pile. Thick, white smoke rolled off the leaves, for some were damp. The fire smelled sweet and pleasant.

"*I guess poor Wade has had quite a time.*"

"*Who beat him up?*"

"*We don't know.*"

"*Thought I'd get together with him and have some fun.*"

I knew I shouldn't have wanted to beat him up or to have him drop dead or something. But now because I did, God would punish me for it. I just knew that would happen because that was the way God worked.

I continued to rake and burn; the neighborhood filled with sweet smoke.

Maybe I can make things right.

The next day after we arrived at school, I headed down to the gym locker room and waited for Colby. I hoped to clear up some doubts that would not leave me alone. Several minutes before the start of class, he appeared in the noisy hallway.

"Hey, Matt." He spoke first. "Heard the nerd got into some trouble."

"Who told you that?" I asked.

"Everybody knows. It's all around."

"What do you know about it?"

"What do you mean?" he asked.

Coach Garrett then came out of the locker room and glared at both of us. "Need you now, Colby," he hissed.

Colby looked from me to Garrett and back at me.

"School hasn't started," I said.

"Better go," Colby said. He shrugged, then turned and headed toward Garrett.

"School hasn't started," I repeated.

Colby walked toward the locker room door. "Coach says now," he said.

"Don't listen to him," I said.

Garrett stared at me before heading back toward the door.

"He's nothing," I said. "Come back for a minute,

Colby. I need to talk to you. School hasn't started yet."

Colby entered the locker room without turning back.

"You know," I said, "those who can't do, teach."

Garrett wheeled around and pounded his cane on the floor.

I whirled and beat a hasty retreat. I did not know whether Garrett called after me. I did not wait around to find out.

THIRTEEN

On Friday I walked into the kitchen as Mom was making breakfast. Every light was on, and bacon sizzled in the electric skillet; the refrigerator faithfully droned in the corner. When she pushed the bread down in the toaster, all the lights went out and there was silence.

"Oh no," she said. "We've lost electricity."

I stepped back into the dining room and flipped the switch. The dining room lights came on. "No, Mom. We've just blown a fuse."

"Now what do we do?"

She was wearing an apron over her light blue dress, and she had her hair brushed and pinned back. She was ready for work except for whatever makeup she was going to use. She had a frightened look in her eyes. Worried.

"Don't worry, Mom. I'll fix it."

"You can fix it?"

"It's only a fuse, Mom."

I opened the door to the basement stairs and flipped that switch. Luckily it was on a different circuit and came on. I went down to the basement to Dad's workbench and found his extra fuses where he always kept them—on the little shelf on top of the bench to the left. He had only one 15 amp fuse left.

I pulled the string to turn on the light that was in the corner near the fuse box and opened the panel. Dad had everything labeled, and this made it easy. I unscrewed the fuse labeled *kitchen* and took it back under the light; it was blown. I went back and screwed in our last fuse. Then I turned off the lights and went back upstairs, placing the old fuse in my pocket.

The kitchen was again lit and breakfast cooking. I turned the light off over the kitchen sink and unplugged Mom's iron, which I'd just noticed was plugged in, even though she had not yet set up her ironing board.

"Going to iron something?" I asked.

"No. Why?"

"Your iron was plugged in."

"Oh my. That was from last night. I thought I turned it off."

I looked at it and touched it. It was warm but not excessively hot. "You turned it down but not completely off," I said.

"Matt, I just don't know what to do when things like this happen."

"It was only a fuse, Mom. You know about fuses."

"I don't know how to change them or where they are or what to do."

"It's no big deal." I sat down at the kitchen table and watched her.

She looked worried as she worked. She fried eggs in the bacon grease; scooped bacon, eggs, and toast onto a

plate; and set it before me. Debbie hadn't arrived at the
table yet. "Things can be overwhelming sometimes," she
said.

I started eating.

"A lady at the bank couldn't get her car started. A
condenser or something broke, and it wouldn't start. Her
husband had to come and fix it."

"I never heard of a condenser breaking."

"She said it broke where it screwed down to something."

"Oh."

"What is a condenser anyway?" She sat down with
just a single piece of toast on a plate.

How did they explain this in class? "Cars have ignition
points, breaker points," I said. "These create a pulsating
current that then can be stepped up to higher voltage
by the coil. A condenser simply helps hold the voltage. Then it all goes to the rotor that fires each cylinder
when it's supposed to. If something breaks, then nothing
works and the car won't run."

She gave me a long, blank look. "You just made that
up, didn't you?" she finally said.

"Well . . ."

"That's just hot air. You have no idea what you just
said." She started laughing.

I had not heard her laugh in months.

"You are just full of it this morning." She laughed.
The worried look had disappeared.

"Actually, it should be pretty close to the truth,"
I finally said.

"Are you serious?"

"Yes."

"Where did you learn such things?"

"We go over this and different things in shop class."

And Dad. Don't forget all the things Dad taught you.
"Anyway, you change all that stuff—points, rotor, condenser, and spark plugs—when you get a tune-up," I
added.

She stopped laughing. "You are serious," she said.

"Yes."

"Matt, I don't know what I'd do without you." She
still smiled.

"No problem, Mom."

With that crisis solved, I finished breakfast and
got ready to leave. I made a point to keep track of the
burned fuse so I could buy extras when I got a chance.

I left the house and walked to the churchyard, where
I waited for Cathy. When she arrived, we started our
walk to the penitentiary. Cathy thought we were walking to school, but I knew the truth. We were to put in
our time, then be let out for good behavior. We had
nearly three more years to serve.

We entered the front doors about the same time Mrs.
Scott drove up with Wade. He got out of the car and
shuffled toward the building. She waited until he entered;
then she drove away. Wade carried no books, and the coat
he wore hung loose on him and unbuttoned. He made his
way inside the building and up the stairs. Other students
climbed around him, for they could move much faster
and were in a hurry. I watched Wade from a distance. I fol-

lowed him up the stairs to our locker. The right side of his face was slightly discolored, but other than that he looked the same. He struggled to open the lock without success, so I came up and opened the locker for him.

"M-Matt. H-hi."

With Wade back the old heaviness returned. I put my jacket in the locker and did not answer him.

"I so th-thankful to b-be back," he said.

"Thankful?"

"Y-yes."

"I suppose you are. Anything is better than the hospital. Even this prison."

"I so th-thankful," he repeated. "Yes-sir-ee."

I helped him hang his coat in the locker and handed him his books.

"Th-thanks, M-Matt."

"Sure."

"Y-you are g-good to me, Matt."

I closed and locked the locker. At least it was locked for now.

"God is g-good to m-me," he said.

God?

"God is v-very g-good."

I shook my head. There was no point in arguing with a moron. Or a retard. "Come on," I said, and I led the way to our seats in the classroom.

He followed and with some effort sat in the desk ahead of me.

I watched Squareface enter the room, glance at Wade, then walk over to the windows and sit down.

There goes a coward. That's why he hides behind Colby.

Cathy was already in her seat, and she was giggling with several girls behind her. I opened my notebook and awaited the start of class.

So am I a coward?

I was willing to forget about the mud in the locker if Colby would make me part of the top crowd. But was the real reason simply because I was afraid of Colby and did not want to push the issue?

Class began with the usual ritual. Life in prison thrives on routine. Miss Edmonds had finished *Silas Marner*, and we now plowed into *The Adventures of Huckleberry Finn* amid various writing assignments. Mark Twain openly mocked Christianity, and this made the book fun to read. Miss Edmonds talked at length about the two feuding families attending the same church.

I wonder if they were Baptists.

I doodled on some paper from my notebook and daydreamed about Baptists and churches and Dad.

We were always doing stuff together, and during those times we would talk about many things. One early spring day we walked through McLean's field to go fishing down at his pond. The day was warm but the ground still cold, and you could see the stubble of last year's corn and smell that fresh smell of thawing soil, especially when the damp dirt was kicked up. We reached the pond and sat down in the grass on the dam, some brown and dormant but some turning green. We cast our lines, but we didn't care if we caught anything. Everything was lazy, the sun was shining, and there were clouds, too, giant balls of cotton, high and floating and idle. We always talked about many things, but we never talked about nerds or cowards. Now we would have no more conversations, for those days were gone forever.

"Gone."

"What is gone?" Miss Edmonds asked.

I looked up.

"You interrupted, Mr. Collins," she said. "So could you please tell the class what is gone?"

"Those days."

"What days?"

My mind finally caught up. "Days of slavery," I said.

"We're not talking about slavery but about feuds."

"Yes, ma'am, I know. But those days of slavery are gone forever."

She walked toward the front of my aisle.

"I'm sorry I interrupted," I said.

This appeased her, and she returned to the feud and I to my doodling. But I was right. Those days were gone forever.

After class, I headed in the direction of Wade's second hour and waited for him to appear. I saw nobody of consequence in the crowded hallway. When Wade reached me, I stopped him. "Hey, Wade."

"H-hi, M-Matt."

"Who beat you up?"

He looked at me with that quizzical, moron look of his. "I-I d-don't know."

"You don't know?"

"No, M-Matt."

I considered for a moment. I was capable of telling a white lie, but I doubted if he was. There were many things morons couldn't do. I supposed he really didn't know.

"Well, what happened?"

"I-I don't know, M-Matt."

This was becoming frustrating. "Just tell me what happened."

"I-I was walking home when someth-thing hit me."

"Hit you where?"

"B-back of my head. And s-side."

"Who hit you?"

"M-Matt, I don't know what h-hit me."

"You got hit on the head?"

"W-with a club or s-stick. Th-they said."

"You don't know with what?"

"Or wh-who."

It was obvious he knew nothing.

"I f-fell, lost m-my glasses. Couldn't s-see."

"Then what?"

"I d-don't know. After a while, I found m-my glasses, got up, and m-made it home. D-don't remember m-much."

"Well, it was all too bad."

"Y-you know who d-did it?"

"No."

"You a g-good friend, M-Matt."

I'm not a good friend. I'm not a friend at all.

"G-good friend."

"I'm late. I need to be going."

"I-I so thankful t-to have you as a f-friend, M-Matt."

"And you're becoming like him. Pretty soon everybody'll be calling you a nerd."

"So th-thankful, yes-sir-ee."

"You're just thankful for everything."

"Th-that's right, M-Matt. I-I learned th-that."

"I'm late." I left Wade in the hall. The bell was about to ring, and the halls were nearly empty. I hurried toward my second-hour class while Wade ambled toward his.

Did Colby beat up Wade? Cathy thinks so.

Somehow it was all so amazing. Mind-boggling. Wade was the only person I knew who could get beat up and still be thankful.

Did Colby throw the mud?

No, he couldn't have. He was at the meet. But he probably knows who did, and he sure thinks it all funny.

My friendship with Colby had reached a crossroads. I so wanted him as a friend, yet if he was a friend, he should have stuck by me when mud got thrown in my locker.

I don't care what Cathy thinks. I wish I was like Colby. I don't want to be a nerd. Or a coward.

Later, after third hour, I was walking down the hallway on the second floor. Students filled the hall, and there was a lot of noise, too. I rounded a corner and ran into Colby, quite by accident. We stood face-to-face.

"Hey, Matt." He wore an impish grin. "Garrett's sure mad at you."

Ask about Wade. Ask about the mud.

"Your mouth has gotten you in trouble," he said, "and he wants to skin you alive."

"I'll stay clear of him."

"You better. He's hot."

Colby started to walk on.

"Hey, Colby."

He stopped and looked back.

"Who beat up Wade?" I asked.

"The nerd?"

My mouth suddenly felt dry. "Yeah. Who beat him up?"

"Who cares?" he asked.

"Did you? You said you wanted to have fun with him."

"Don't know what you're talking about."

"Did you beat him up?" I asked.

He scratched his head. "What's it to you?"

"Colby, leave him alone."

"Leave him alone? Why stick up for the nerd?"

Good question. "I'm not," I said. "I just don't want any more mud in my locker."

He shook his head. "You've gone from nerd to mud. You're not making any sense."

He's right. You're not making any sense.

"Is he your friend?" he asked.

"No."

"Then what happens to him is no concern of yours."

"Look, Colby, I don't want anybody hurt."

"So who got hurt?"

"Wade."

"That doesn't count," he said.

"He got taken to the hospital. He has a bad heart."

"Sorry to hear that."

"I don't want anybody hurt," I repeated.

"Nobody's going to get hurt."

"He ended up at the hospital," I said.

"Look, Collins . . ."

Collins? He never calls me Collins.

". . . I know nothing about the nerd in the hospital."

"Did you beat him up?" I asked.

Colby dropped his books and slammed a locker with the palm of his hand.

I jumped a foot. Maybe two. I backed up a step. Several kids stopped and stared.

"What I do's none of your business!" he shouted.

"Who threw mud in my locker?" I felt my face getting hot. My heart was racing.

"You're becoming a bore, Matt."

Matt Collins, you're a coward.

"Aren't we friends, Colby?"

"I thought so. But you're a little hard to get along with anymore."

"Why don't you just tell me what you know?"

"I don't like your attitude!"

We stared at each other for a moment; then Colby picked up the two books he had dropped. "So go find your nerd friend!" he said.

"He's not my friend."

"Matt, you're not rational. If he's not your friend, then don't stick up for him."

Good point.

"But get this clear! What I do's none of your business!" Colby stormed off.

I leaned against a locker and caught my breath.

Normalcy returned to the hallway as students walked in both directions and around the corner. There was talking and clattering of lockers, and classes resumed like always, and life in the penitentiary continued on, just as before.

FOURTEEN

By the first of November we would usually wake up to a frosty world. The mornings would be cold, and my room would be cold too and dark. I would dress using only the dim light from the closet. Boxes and books cluttered the floor of the closet, and my Bible was also part of the clutter, buried under a stack of debris. The Bible was leather-bound with gold-edged pages. Dad had bought it for me and had signed my name in it, along with the notation *Proverbs 3:5-6.* In July I had tossed the Bible in the closet, bending a corner of the cover along with some of the pages. Had Dad not signed it, I would have thrown it away.

So on those cold mornings I would dress, then enter the kitchen. Mom usually had the coffee on, the rich fragrance filling the house. Mom did not want her children drinking coffee, but the ex-marine did not mind, and he had given me coffee ever since I was ten. Now Mom no longer cared and would always have hot coffee in the morning, and she would sometimes pour it for me too. Nothing in life was better than hot, rich coffee on a frosty morning.

I would take my hot cup and often stand on the back

porch just outside the kitchen and look at the white world with frost hanging on everything. You could see your breath hang in the air, and you could see too the steam rising off the coffee. As long as there was no wind, I could stand on the back porch and feel toasty as long as I could sip from the hot cup.

Sometimes Mom fried bacon, and the sharp aroma mingled with the fragrance of the coffee; the smell would be delightful. The coffee was hot, the world was fresh and cold, the bacon smelled great, and for a moment I would find peace. This was the best part of life. Except for running.

Despite working at Cornett Ford, I still found time to run. I did little homework, and my superb grades of the preceding year began to show the neglect, but I did not care and Mom said little. Everything was different from the year before; everything was upside-down. Cross-country teams meant nothing and should be avoided, school was dull and horribly oppressive, and church was . . . well, church was complete madness. All that mattered was running. When I ran I felt a great peace, for I was alone and out of prison. The dirt road had no bells or crowded halls or noise or sermons.

November 2 was the first Saturday of the month. I walked back inside just as Mom was setting breakfast on the table.

"Hungry?" she asked.

"Starved."

I poured myself more coffee, and we both sat down.

She bowed her head and said prayers. I quietly watched her.

"You like working?" she asked when she looked up.

"Yes." I began to devour the bacon and eggs.

"Wendell told me last Sunday that he was pleased with your work."

I was very glad to hear that. "I try to work hard," I said.

"Well, he is very pleased."

"How about you? How's the bank?"

"Oh, the bank is all right."

"Do you have to work today?"

"No. I worked last Saturday."

I spread jelly on a piece of toast.

"I seem to have other problems to worry about," she said.

"Like what?"

"The life insurance company needs a certified copy of the death certificate. I've requested one from the state office, but they still haven't sent it."

"Why haven't they?"

"Who knows?"

"What will you do?"

"Wendell offered to drive me up to the capitol and get one if things don't happen soon."

"You can't let things worry you," I said.

"I know. But I do anyway. Can't seem to help it anymore."

"It'll all work out." I grabbed another piece of toast that was extra on a separate plate.

"Thanks for buying the milk," she said, "and those other things."

"Sure, Mom, was happy to."

"I'll be able to pay you back next week."

"Don't worry about it. You don't need to."

"But you want your money for something. What are you saving for anyway?"

"New shoes. I need some new running shoes."

"I see." She quickly finished her breakfast. She never did eat much. Little birds and petite, hundred-pound women don't seem to need much food. "Debbie told me something," she said.

"Oh?"

"She said you gave her a little money."

I looked up at Mom. She looked tired but managed a smile. I just shrugged at her.

"Thanks," she said. "That means more to me than you know."

I finished the last piece of bacon on the plate. I suspected I'd just eaten Debbie's breakfast. Oh well, that's what happened when you slept in on Saturday morning. Besides, Mom just didn't seem to realize how much food I really needed.

"I should go," I said. I pushed myself from the table.

"I made a lunch for you," she said.

"Thanks. And, Mom?"

"Yes?"

"Don't worry. It'll all work out."

"Thanks, Matt."

I grabbed the lunch and my jacket, then hiked in

the frosty morning to Cornett Ford. I arrived at the shop to discover a '63 Ranchero being worked on. Essentially the Ranchero was a car with a truck bed, and it had the look of a Falcon when viewed from the front. The Ranchero had been sold new two months earlier and now suffered from engine problems. Big Joe attempted to make some headway with this crisis.

I cleaned cars in the morning, and at noon I took my lunch and went looking for him, finding Big Joe under the hood of the Ford.

"What's the problem?" I asked. I now felt like one of the guys.

Big Joe wiped his hands and we sat down. He was always nice to everybody, including customers, and Wendell considered him a top employee. "Has a bad bearing," he said.

"So what will you do?"

"Don't know."

"You don't know?"

"Need to ask Ford."

"Why?" I asked.

"I want them to exchange the engine."

"Will they do that?"

"I hope."

"For just a bearing?"

"Well, if I'm right, there's more damage than a rod bearing. Won't know for sure until we tear the engine completely down."

"Who has to pay for all of this?"

"Ford will, one way or the other."

"That will be awful expensive, won't it?"

"They can afford it." He pulled out a cigarette and lit up.

I ate my lunch and watched him with great admiration.

"You go to Mr. Cornett's church, don't you?" he asked.

What on earth brought that on?

"Yes," I finally said.

"What's it like?"

I cleared my throat. "Like any other church, I suppose."

He puffed on his cigarette. The shop was tomblike. "I don't know about churches," he said. "Never thought they were for me."

"I don't think they are for me either," I said.

He looked at me for a moment, then stared back out into space. "Mr. Cornett has invited me to your church," he said.

"He has?"

"Several times."

The Ranchero looked like it had its mouth wide open. I noticed that the shop was getting warm.

"Do you get anything out of church?" he asked.

"No. Church is boring."

"That's what I thought."

I finished my lunch and knew I should be getting back to work. I stood up.

"I don't know," Big Joe said.

"About the car?"

"About life."

"Life?"

"My life seems . . ." He shook his head, then coughed on the cigarette. "Anyway, Mr. Cornett says I will find the answer in church. But if you don't get anything out of church and find it boring, I won't waste my time there."

I watched him put out his cigarette and walk back to the Ford and make notes on a clipboard.

"One way or another," he said, "we'll have to pull this engine."

I nodded and returned to the north side of the lot, where I had been working that morning.

By three o'clock I had finished what Scotty wanted done, so he paid me and I left. I now had twenty dollars saved, and I would go to the city the next time Mom went and try to find a new pair of running shoes.

That afternoon the temperature was in the forties. I walked home and found Mom and Deb had pretty much cleaned up the house, so I changed into sweatpants and running shoes and jogged down the gravel road.

I reached the dirt road. The road looked damp but solid. I jogged a little bit down then back and found the footing to be excellent, for there was no mud that would cling to your shoes. I desperately wanted a record run, so I stood in line of the corner hedge post, raised my hand with the stopwatch, lowered the watch, and clicked it as I leaped down the road.

The sun hid behind the low overcast on that calm

day. Autumn surrounded me, and I felt fine and ran very fast. I took control of my breathing and inhaled in two steps and exhaled in two steps. I continued this pace. My knees remained relaxed and I ran from the hips, taking large strides, lightly touching the ground. My feet were gliding along the road.

Silence dominated the dirt road except for my breathing and my shoes touching the packed gumbo. The trees stood proud and beautiful, even though they had just passed their peak. The ground was decorated with fallen leaves, yet many still clung to the trees. I ran hard and knew I was pushing everything to the limit. I attempted to inhale through my nose and exhale through my mouth but soon found I inhaled some through my mouth as well. Past the willow trees I flew, then up the gentle incline. Though I felt strong, I also knew I was pushing too hard and was uncertain how long I could keep up this pace. McLean still had a small patch of brown corn that needed to be cut, and the winter wheat was green and well established on the west side.

In two, out two; in two, out two. I ran and the stillness of the day and the cool air surrounded me and inspired the running. I hoped for a record run, but I did not bother to ask God for help because I knew it did not matter to Him. He could not be trusted for help anyway.

I ran fast and commanded the legs to record speed. I let my mind wander. I wondered about the slide in Colby's friendship and how I was a coward, but I really didn't want to be but was anyway, and—could I possibly keep up this pace?—and everybody knew Squareface was a coward, but of course Colby was not a coward, and I wanted to be like Colby, and I wanted Colby to be a great friend just like old times, and—did my heart always beat so fast?—and I really didn't like Wade but actually hated him, and why on earth did I put myself in the foolish position of inquiring about his problems, and it would sure be much better if he simply dropped dead and was out of my life.

I knew God would probably strike me dead for such thoughts. But those were my feelings. Of course He would stomp me for the poor way I answered Big Joe. Something awful would soon happen to me because that's just the way God works.

I reached the fence line, the halfway point. The stopwatch read 2:28. Joy flooded my heart. This was a record run. A five-minute pace. I had never hit five minutes. Neither had Colby. I did not know if I could possibly keep it up. My side ached and breathing was hard. Still I kept up the pace and took long strides and commanded my legs to swing from the hips.

I now ran on the level stretch between the mulberry trees. I saw no cows or tractors or anybody or anything. My arms swung in perfect coordination, and the thrill of a five-minute mile drove me onward, harder, running even faster if that was possible. I breathed deep but ran from the heart.

I had learned that the best races were always run from the heart.

I first saw the gray obstacle a little way down the final level stretch. A large elm limb had broken off a tree and fallen across the road. There were smaller branches and twigs along the limb but no leaves; the limb had probably been dead for some time.

My mind raced. I would have to hurdle the branch. This would slow me down slightly, perhaps as much as a couple of seconds. God had placed an obstacle in front of me. I had not asked for help, but for Him to hinder was grossly unfair. Yet I would overcome even this problem and still have a record run.

I approached the limb at full speed and aimed for the lowest part to vault. I reached the limb and timed my leap to clear the obstacle.

I gracefully sailed high into the air.

I misjudged.

My right foot caught one of the branches, and I tumbled out of control.

My right hand and shoulder hit the ground first, and the stopwatch soared into space. My head hit and I rolled; my back smacked against either a rock or a hard clod. I took the name of the Lord in vain as I skidded another foot.

I couldn't breathe for a moment. Pain shot all through my body. I knew that my running career had ended. I would never run again or even walk. I was probably paralyzed. But that didn't matter that much because even if my back weren't broken—and I knew it was—such a fall could ruin a runner anyway by crushing hips and wrenching knees and ankles beyond repair.

God had gotten even with me and I knew it.

My running had ended.

My life was over.

FIFTEEN

A slight breeze rustled the trees, but the gray day was mostly still and very quiet. Several leaves detached from a tree, just to drift and be teased by the breeze. I lay on my back and looked at the trees and the overcast and watched birds flying south. The birds flew under the low clouds, and I wondered what it might feel like to be a bird and be able to fly.

I knew enough not to move and wondered how long I would lie before somebody would find me and whether maggots would be crawling over me when I was found, but probably not, because the weather was too cold for maggots.

Once again I swore at the Lord for His lack of help and all the obstacles He threw in my way. Yet I knew I was being punished, for that was how God worked. I accepted my paralysis as one of those horrible things we must receive from the hands of a mean and uncaring God. Too bad Wade wasn't around to give thanks for it all.

In time my breathing returned to normal. I felt no pain. I was numb. After a while, my toes felt cold and I tried to wiggle them. I could. I then lifted up my knees. They responded as well.

I was astonished.

I rolled over on hands and knees, and though there were small aches, no sharp pain stabbed me. I stood up. I could. Balance, fine. Breathing, normal. Feet and legs responded properly. Hands and arms worked.

Am I really okay?

I stared at the limb that had nearly ended my life. Vision, okay.

So far so good.

I walked around in a small circle.

I can't believe it.

I walked down the road, picked up the stopwatch, and found it still ticking. I stopped the watch, reset it, and walked back toward the limb.

I suppose I'm awful lucky. Probably shouldn't have sworn though. Taken His name in vain.

I grabbed the limb and pulled it mostly off the road, though not entirely. Still, there was enough room for a truck to pass, and I would be able to safely run by the next time.

But why not? He ruined my record run.

I jogged back toward the gravel road. All systems worked fine. No pain, no problems. Though shaken, I obviously was not seriously hurt. I stopped jogging and resumed walking.

Colby is my friend. We've always been best friends. Wade is not my friend. I will be like Colby.

The breeze felt cold as I walked along the gravel road toward home.

Colby wants nothing to do with God. Neither will I.

I walked down one of the hills. In winter this hill would ice up, for the sun did not directly strike it. We would sometimes go sledding down this hill, and Dad would come when he could. The ice and snow would be packed from traffic, and there would be snow in the ditches and fields and on the trees. The sledding was usually good when the pack was thick enough to cover the imperfections of the road and as long as you stayed away from the edges, where most of the gravel was. Dad would come to watch for traffic—or so he said—but we all knew there would be little if any traffic and that the real reason was he wanted his turn on the sled. The days were usually gray and cold, and flurries often hung in the air. On the best days, the snow would actually be falling.

So we would take the sled and trudge toward the hill, but Dad would have to go down the hill first to make sure it was safe, but we knew he just wanted to join the fun. We were glad he came because it was always more fun with him around. Besides, we flew faster with his weight on the sled. We would keep to the center of the road as we went down the hill, and if we hit a rut or some loose gravel, we would go flying off the sled and roll in the snow. We got cold, bruised, and wet, and of course there would always be the concluding snowball fight. We had a grand time, mostly because he was with us.

Those days are gone. Forever.

I walked into the house, then to the kitchen for a drink. Mom was cooking dinner.

I will hang around Colby more. I will do what he does.

"Matt, what happened?" Mom asked.

"I tripped."

"Are you all right?"

"Yeah."

She had that worried-mother look about her.

I got my drink. "I'll get cleaned up," I said.

I had a scratch on my forehead and scrapes on my knees, shoulder, and side. But that was all. After I cleaned up and had dinner, I felt better.

I will be able to run anytime I want.

You're lucky, Matt. Awful lucky.

•◆•

The first Sunday in November, I awoke stiff and sore. We walked to church together as a family. I decided not to run in the afternoon; a day of rest was in order. We walked into church and greeted Pastor Yoshida.

"Good morning, Mr. Collins," he said.

I shook his hand.

"Miss Collins."

"Good morning, Pastor," she said.

"Good morning, Angela."

Pastor talked to Mom while Debbie and I walked down to Sunday school.

"Good morning, Mr. Collins," Harvey Wells said.

"Good morning."

He did not ask about my Bible. I no longer felt any guilt for not bringing it.

Everybody looked alert in Sunday school, and even Wade looked interested, but I tuned out the class.

Later I sat in the back pew of the sanctuary and watched everybody enter. The Metzge twins raced up and down the main aisle. Jerry tripped and fell down but quickly got back up. Or was it Jimmy?

The two ran into Wade as he shuffled in, nearly knocking him down.

"He's got cooties," one said.

"Ninny!" the other said.

Wade wore his blank moron expression.

"I'm glad I'm not like you," one said.

They laughed, then ran out of the sanctuary into the foyer.

Dorothy Cornett was sick, so she was not in attendance when church began. Instead Catherine Cornett played the piano, and she did a fine job of playing. I paid little attention until Catherine began playing during the offering collection.

Her introduction snapped me alert. She began by playing a low, melodic rhythm, interspersed with several high treble notes. The music sounded haunting, compelling, perhaps like a cold fall day in the woods with colored leaves falling, then gently blowing across the pathway. The music, striking and beautiful, grabbed the soul and demanded its attention. The introduction blended into a hymn played in the same compelling style. The church heard her play "All Creatures of Our God and King" in an arrangement never before played in Bethel Baptist Church.

My soul took control and forced my body to sit at the edge of the pew and pay the strictest of attention. The music played, and the ushers stopped their activity and listened, and everybody in the church became still. No one coughed. The Spirit of almighty God had begun to speak.

My soul awoke as if it had been in a deep slumber for many years. As Catherine played on, the words welled up—O *praise Him! Alleluia!*—and individual notes could no longer be heard but only the flow of the music. The music transcended earth and lifted all who heard it to the very gates of heaven and into the throne room of God. A thirsty soul that I did not know existed awoke within a cold heart and demanded to be touched by the Creator Himself. And Catherine, sitting in front of the keyboard, became transformed into something more beautiful than an angel. On she played, and the entire church sat spellbound, breathless, taken to the highest heaven, brought forth for the sole purpose of worship.

Then she finished. Not a breath or a sound. The notes echoed off our hearts and around the church. No one moved. All were afraid to clap or make any noise. Something extraordinary had happened, and everyone knew it.

She quietly left the piano and sat down in one of the front pews by herself. The church dwelled in the absolute beauty of holiness.

Pastor Yoshida stood up awkwardly, and the ushers snapped back to their task and completed the collection. Pastor began to speak, the spell was broken, and my soul sank back down from where it had been awakened to return to its slumber. I slouched in the pew and took a deep breath.

"Thank you, Catherine," Pastor Greg said. "Please turn to Psalm 107."

The church coughed and pages rustled too. Everything returned to normal, including the noise. Church continued on as before.

"'O give thanks unto the Lord, for he is good: for his mercy endureth for ever,'" Pastor read.

I found a bulletin and a pencil and used a hymnal for support. Pastor preached on God's mercy, a theme that had replaced the old one of judgment and God's wrath. Pastor said we all experience God's mercy.

"I'm sorry, Mrs. Collins, but your husband is . . ."

Big Joe did not come, and I knew I would be punished for all I had said and for a lot of other things as well. I would be punished because of Wade, and it was really unfair because it was not my fault he moved in next door.

Pastor continued to read from the psalm, then preached, adding many other words. I did not try to listen but let my mind wander instead.

"Mrs. Collins, there has been a terrible accident. You'll need to come with us."

"Matt! I need you!"

Greg preached about the mercy of God and how good God was, but I had not seen God in the funeral home or during the funeral. The impossible task of comforting my mother fell to me. God did not help; I saw no mercy.

I did see awful things, things never to be spoken, things nobody should ever have to see. But I did not see God or His mercy, so it was very hard to listen.

"We are gathered here . . . gathered here today . . . to say . . . to say good-bye. . . ."

I doodled on the bulletin.

In time the service ended, and I ducked outside and sat on the bench with my back to the sign. As Catherine opened the doors to the church, I jumped up and walked back up the steps to her. "Cathy, you played great. That song was . . . well . . . wonderful."

"Why, thanks, Matt."

"It was . . . well . . . it was really great."

Can't you think of something better than that?

Wade then appeared, and my opportunity was forever gone. "You play g-great," he said. "Really touched m-me."

"Why, thank you."

Wendell Cornett joined us.

"I must go now," Cathy said. They walked down the steps together and around the building to the back.

"G-good preaching."

"I suppose."

"God is g-good."

"I suppose." I continued to stare at the corner of the building where the angel and her father had just disappeared.

"H-He is m-merciful."

I looked at the retard.

"I so th-thankful."

"For what?"

"Every-th-thing, M-Matt."

We had been through this before. Mom and Debbie walked out the door, and together we walked down the steps, Wade remaining by the doors.

"Look," I said, turning around. "Haven't you ever wished things were different? looked around and maybe wished you were somebody else?"

He had that blank moron look of his. "Y-yes, M-Matt."

Well, at least he was honest. We started on our way home.

"What was that all about?" Mom asked.

"Education."

"What?"

"Wade just needs to learn a few things."

"Matt, sometimes I don't think you are very understanding of Wade."

"I understand him fine."

"Matt, I—"

"Mom, you just don't understand. Wade is sometimes just difficult. Believe me. It's okay."

She said nothing as we continued walking in the cool, overcast day toward the little gray house on Church Street.

SIXTEEN

The final bell rang, signaling the end of another day. Inmates poured out into the halls, rushing to find lockers and retrieve jackets.

"Aren't you coming, Matt?"

I collected my jacket, slammed the locker, secured the lock, then looked at Cathy. The freckles on her cheeks seemed to make her eyes sparkle more. "No."

Wade was already ambling down the hall toward the stairs. School had ended for the day, and the masses of inmates were preparing to leave the prison.

I reached in my pocket and pulled out the burned fuse. "I need to get some more of these. For the house."

She nodded. "We'll just go on without you. See you tomorrow."

"See you tomorrow," I said.

I watched her head off in Wade's direction. I went the other way, down the hall that eventually led out the north doors into the November afternoon. Once outside I zipped up my jacket and kept my hands in the pockets and started north toward the hardware store in downtown Bethel. The day was partly cloudy, and the wind was brisk and blew from the north. The afternoon lighting had a gray shade to it, and the world had that typical fall feel.

Main Street bustled with activity. A loaded lumber truck whined in a low gear westward up the slight incline of Main Street. All the angled parking in front of the post office was filled. Chief Brewer had pulled over a car, probably a speeder, and the Dodge, its red light rotating, was parked behind the embarrassed Cadillac. I crossed Main Street and saw several contractors' trucks parked on the west side of the lumberyard. A forklift was moving lumber, and a man shouted directions to somebody over its roar.

Parker Hardware was located one block north of Main Street on the east end of town next to the Bethel lumberyard. A parking lot on the north side serviced both the hardware store and the lumberyard. Many of Forest's customers used this lot and would enter his store from the back. Others simply parked in front on Maple Street and entered the store from there.

A tinkling bell announced my entrance into the store from Maple Street. I waited a few seconds for my eyes to become accustomed to the gloom. The world was strangely quiet from the surrounding commerce of Bethel. Merchandise sat haphazardly on shelves and counters, and there were partially opened boxes too, neglected in the aisles. It looked like the aisle with the nuts and bolts had not been swept for months. A fluorescent light flickered over the shelf of disorganized spark plugs. I headed for the back corner, where the electrical supplies were stocked.

I remembered coming to this store with Dad years ago when I was little and before Forest had purchased the business. Back then the counters seemed to tower to the ceiling, and merchandise loomed large and exotic. Dad was buying some wire and fixtures to wire lights in the basement. That day the store had been a wonderment of science and invention and capitalism. Anything you could possibly think or imagine was on the shelves, and you could simply build anything, any conceivable invention that you had the money for.

But the wonder had disappeared with the passing of time. Perhaps the store deteriorated as well.

Forest finished checking out a customer, then walked over to talk to Mrs. Dunlap, who was in one of the paint aisles. He saw me but said nothing. I saw no other person in the store.

Mrs. Dunlap wore a brown coat, and a white scarf covered her gray hair. She was in her sixties and had lost her husband to cancer a year earlier. She was a kind woman who volunteered at the Bethel public library. She attended another church, and everybody in town knew her.

"Is your church all right?" I heard her ask.

"Everything is fine," Forest said.

"No more vandalism?"

"No."

"That's good. We don't need things like that in our town."

"It all happened because we had a pastor on the school board," Forest said. "That was a big mistake."

"Oh, I don't know about that," she said. "Your pastor got that awful Mr. Wilcox fired. That should have been done years ago. In fact, he should have never been made superintendent. I'm kind of sorry your pastor will be leaving the board. He always spoke with common sense."

I reached the back corner in the electrical section. I found fuses scattered on a shelf. They sold for twenty-five cents a fuse or a box of five for a dollar. There were several partial boxes and many fuses scattered about. I found only one intact box of 15 amp fuses that screwed in. I compared these fuses with the burned-out one I carried. They were exactly the same. I picked up this box and looked through the automotive tune-up kits on my way to the front, but I did not pick up any of these. The flickering light was truly an irritant. With only the box of fuses, I made my way to check out.

Forest was stepping around to the register to ring up Mrs. Dunlap. She emptied her handbasket of several small cans of stain, a large can of varnish, two trim brushes, several rolls of masking tape, and a box of trim nails. I noticed that a new push broom rested against the counter near the register in the lane where customers stood.

"Find everything you need?" Forest asked.

"Yes. My daughter is helping me finish the baseboards."

"That can be quite a project. Do you have enough stain?"

"Yes. We're finishing up."

As he rang up the cans of stain, I could see the individual amount for each item appear on the cash register.

"When we are done, then we will have finished repainting everything," she said.

"Always good to finish up."

"Then I'll put the house up for sale."

"Moving?"

I watched more numbers appear as Forest continued to ring up her purchases.

"I'm afraid I have to. Ever since Earl passed away . . ."

"Sorry to hear that you'll be leaving."

Forest then leaned over the counter, glanced at the broom, and rang $9.95 on the register.

Mrs. Dunlap was fumbling in her purse for her wallet. "It's too much. The house. It's too much for me to keep up." Her hands were inside her purse, holding her wallet, but I could tell they were trembling slightly.

"That's $31.70 with tax."

She looked a little surprised. "Oh my. I'm not sure I have that much." She opened her wallet, pulled out some money, and handed it to Forest. She rattled around in her purse and found some more. This, too, she gave to Forest. "It sure adds up fast," she said.

"I'm afraid it does." The register clanged, and the drawer popped open. He gave her back her change.

She stuck this loose in some pocket inside her purse, not in her wallet.

"Sorry to hear that you're moving," Forest said.

"We've lived here all my life. Both me and Earl. He would have hated to move too."

"Where will you go?"

"Don't know. Probably to some retirement place in the city."

"I'm sure it will all work out."

She gave a half shrug. Forest put her purchases in a sack, and Mrs. Dunlap headed for the Maple Street door.

"Thank you, Forest," she said.

"Thank you."

I spoke just when she was about to open the door. "Mrs. Dunlap?"

She turned around and looked at me. "Why, hello, Matt. I didn't notice you there. How have you been?"

"Just fine—"

"How's your mother?"

"She's doing fine," I lied.

"That's good."

"Mrs. Dunlap? You forgot your broom."

"My broom? I didn't buy a broom."

Forest snapped his gaze at me, his eyes wide.

I just looked at Mrs. Dunlap. "Yes, you did. You were charged for it. Look at your receipt."

Forest came around the counter sputtering. "You didn't want the broom?" he blurted.

She fumbled in the sack for the receipt as she worked her way back to the counter. "How much was the broom?" she asked.

"It was $9.95," I said.

"You're right. There is a $9.95 charge on my receipt. I don't think I bought anything for that."

Forest stared at me. "I'm sorry, Mrs. Dunlap," he

finally said. "I noticed the broom there on the counter, and I thought you had put it here."

Why didn't you make sure she took it when she left?

"Well, I thought the bill was a little high," she said.

"I'm sorry. Here, let me refund you."

"No problem. These things happen. No harm done. Thanks for noticing, Matt."

"You're welcome," I said.

She came back to the counter, and Forest walked around to the register.

I looked at Forest. "Good thing I came along, right, Mr. Parker?"

His face was red, but he did not look at me. Rather he fumbled in the register for the cash. He handed her a ten-dollar bill. He did not refund any of the tax he had collected.

So how many times a day do you sell that broom?

"Yes, Matt," he finally said. "It was a good thing that you came along."

Mrs. Dunlap put the money in her purse.

Forest Parker made no other accounting adjustment to his register.

"I thought the bill was a little high," she repeated. "Good-bye, Forest. Good-bye, Matt. Tell your mother hi."

"I will."

She walked out the door to the sound of a tinkling bell.

Forest attempted to drill his eyes into me.

I placed the fuses on the counter. "Box of five for a dollar," I said.

"I know how much they are."

"Well, one can never be sure."

His face became redder.

There was a toothpick dispenser on the counter. I took one and began to chew on it. I folded my arms and returned his stare, much like Garrett would.

"So you think you know it all," he said.

I continued to stare him down. I placed my dollar on the counter, reached into my pocket, and retrieved three pennies for tax. I slapped these on the counter.

"That was the same problem your dad had," he continued.

He was ten times the man you are.

"I guess you're trying to be just like him."

I felt hot and considered whether to punch him in the face or just move around the counter and kick him. Or better yet, grab the broom and beat him with it. Too bad I didn't have a cane. I continued to chew on the toothpick and glare. He rang up the sale, scooped up my money, and placed it in the register.

"By the way," I said, "I don't want the broom either."

With that, I took the fuses, not waiting for a sack or a receipt, and left the store. The bell tinkled after me.

SEVENTEEN

November progressed toward winter, often cloudy and usually cold, and we would walk to school in the still mornings of Bethel. The trees had passed their peak, and there were some that had lost all of their leaves and now stood barren and stark against the gray sky. These trees looked dead, but we all suspected that this was not true. Spring always came and brought life to what looked dead, though that fall we did not fully believe this truth.

One day in the second week of November, Cathy and I walked to school without Wade. We gave little thought to his absence, for he occasionally was sick and would miss.

At school, the lights were bright in contrast to the outside world. We arrived at our lockers amid the ruckus of school, got our books, and entered homeroom.

Class began on schedule and had progressed for some time when Miss Edmonds quite unexpectedly made an announcement. "Class, we have a treat today." She looked toward the door. "Please come in, sir."

To our surprise, Wade came into the classroom. He wore a gray suit coat along with a gray hat that bore the Confederate battle flag—the cheap hats that could be found at any chain store. Typically little children would buy them, not high schoolers. He wore his toy sword, and he looked absolutely ridiculous. He carried a folder in his hand.

He stood in front of Miss Edmonds's desk and faced the class. She quietly walked to the back of the room to watch.

"W-Wade Hampton at your s-service," he stated with a slight bow. He opened his folder, removed a picture of the real Wade Hampton, then held it up for the class to see. The general had dark hair and a full beard, was of a stout build, and had a strong, though not overly stern, countenance. "I one of G-General Lee's b-best generals."

The class sat quietly, not knowing how to react.

"I-I not a soldier by t-trade. I a planter. B-born in South C-Carol-lina." Wade shuffled back toward the door and continued his presentation. "I was b-born in 1818."

You could hear a pin drop.

"F-fought in many b-battles. I important c-calvary officer."

Calvary? You mean cavalry!

"P-part of Jeb Stuart's calvary d-division."

He said it wrong again. I shook my head.

"B-Brandy Station—important b-battle. V-very important."

Wade drew his sword, held it above his head, and began his reenactment across the front of the room. "Ch-charge the Y-Yankees!" He glanced behind. "Move up the r-regiments! Ch-charge!"

He formed the fingers of his left hand into a pretend pistol and waved the sword over his head with his right hand.

"Charge! *Kuuue, kuuue, kuuue!*" He fired his finger pistol with the accompaniment of a great amount of spit. "K-kill the Y-Yankees. *Kuuue, kuuue, kuuue!*" He charged, fired, and swung his sword at the imaginary enemy. "Ch-charge!"

Wade waved up his rearward troops for the next attack. He continued to swing his sword, and his movements mimicked a contorted dance of sorts, consisting of striking, jabbing, and swinging. The battle raged amid various sound effects. And spit.

He took his eyes off the enemy and addressed the class. "I was g-gallant at Brandy S-Station. I secured Fleetwood H-Hill." He swung his sword again and jabbed wildly in the air. Then as peculiarly as it had begun, the battle ended. He scuffed his way back toward the door, turned, and faced the class again.

"A-after Brandy S-Station was G-Gettysburg. I was wounded bad at G-Gettysburg. T-took two sword wounds to the h-head."

Wade held his sword up and began the attack again. "Ch-charge! *Kuuue, kuuue, kuuue!*" He made his way across the front of the room, adding juvenile sound effects as he went. "C-calvary, ch-charge!"

Cavalry! Cavalry!

"*Kuuue, kuuue, kuuue!*" He swung and jabbed his sword in the same wild contorted dance.

The reenactment of Gettysburg bore a striking

resemblance to the reenactment of Brandy Station. I stared down at my desk.

"*Kuuue, kuuue, kuuue!*" He fired his finger and swung his sword, waving more troops into the fray. He charged the imaginary Yankees with great valor.

"O-o-o-o-oh." His sword clattered to the floor, and he put his hand to his head, knocking his Confederate hat to the floor.

With his hand still on his head, Wade walked to the center of the room in front of Miss Edmonds's desk. "I-I wounded b-bad at G-Gettysburg. Very s-serious." He rested against the front of the desk for a moment, holding his head.

The class remained spellbound, uncertain of how to react to General Wade Hampton, whether to laugh or to take all of this seriously.

"W-when Jeb Stuart d-died, I took c-command of the c-calvary."

He meant *cavalry*. Why couldn't he get it right? I stared out the windows on the other side of the room.

"Th-they made me lieutenant g-general. In ch-charge of the c-calvary."

Wade shuffled over to his dropped hat, placed it back on his head, and retrieved his sword as well. He then waged another battle against the Federal forces. "*Kuuue, kuuue, kuuue!* Ch-charge!"

To the uninitiated, the battle looked identical to the Brandy Station and Gettysburg conflicts. The problem with war is that after a while, all the battles look alike.

After several minutes, he returned to the center of the room. "W-we lost the w-war."

I could understand why.

"A-after the war, I was g-governor of South C-Carolina, and later a s-senator. I was known as the s-savior of South C-Carol-lina. I died in 1902."

Why couldn't he be somebody else's locker partner? Why couldn't he live next door to somebody else?

"I n-named after Wade H-Hampton. I n-named after a famous g-general. H-he a g-great m-man and a s-savior. H-he is my h-hero."

Wade then took off his hat and his gray suit coat and laid these along with his sword on the desk. He turned back toward the class. "Jesus Christ is the r-real S-Savior. He is m-my main hero. I-I named after Him, too. I am a Christian. H-He saved m-me. He has been g-good to m-me." With this conclusion, Wade bowed, gathered up his things, and left the room.

Miss Edmonds began to clap, and everybody else clapped too.

Wade stepped back in the doorway, gave another bow, then left.

The class continued to clap.

"Thank you, Wade, for that history lesson," Miss Edmonds said.

Squareface snickered, but Miss Edmonds silenced him with a stern glance.

A little later, Wade came back in and sat down at his desk. He seemed to suffer no embarrassment.

In time class ended, and we emptied into the hall.

I noticed Squareface and several other boys walking up to Wade.

"Hey, Nerd," said Squareface, "that was quite a show."

Wade smiled at them and bowed.

"A show like that belongs in a circus," said another.

"But you need to know," Squareface continued, "that the playground is down at the grade school."

The other boys laughed.

"In fact, you're more than a nerd. You're a . . . well, I don't know. A missing link maybe."

The others laughed harder.

"That's it. A missing link nerd."

Wade was no longer smiling or bowing.

"I didn't realize they let nerds like you in here. You know, the nuthouse is in the next county."

Miss Edmonds walked out of the class and noticed the boys.

When Squareface saw her, he walked on toward his next class. "See you around, Nerd," he said over his shoulder.

The other boys went their way too. I could not be sure whether Miss Edmonds had heard the taunts, but her unexpected presence broke up the party. She stared in the direction of the boys but made no comment.

Wade had his typical blank look about him, possibly unaware he had been insulted. He showed no emotion.

I took a different route to my second-hour class, walking in front of the main office.

"Hey, Collins." It was Squareface. "Your nerd friend is cute."

I stared at him.

"Word has it you're a nerd too."

"I think you've said enough." I continued to stare at him.

He took a step backward. I always knew Squareface was a coward, and cowards were easy to scare. "Just thought I'd let you know," he added.

Coach Garrett opened the office door unexpectedly and walked out into the hallway into the stream of students, stomping his cane as he walked.

"I hadn't better find any more mud in my locker," I said at that instant.

Garrett stopped, looked at me, then back at Squareface.

"What mud?" Squareface asked.

Garrett stood still, resting on his cane, studying the situation.

"Because if I do, I'll come looking for you," I said.

Squareface slithered away.

"And another thing." I pressed my advantage. "Be careful who you call a nerd."

Squareface glanced at Garrett before shouting at me, "I heard you do a real good imitation of Garrett. Stomp around and swear and everything. I heard that you look just like him. A carbon copy. A Garrett copy. That's great, Collins. You'll have to show me sometime." He disappeared in the crowd moving down the hallway in the opposite direction.

Garrett glanced after him, then glared at me.

I turned and walked to my second-hour class. I had nothing to fear from a cripple.

EIGHTEEN

That afternoon I went running, and I did not return home until evening, when it was cold and dark. I walked up the front steps and through the door of the little gray house on Church Street.

Mom sat at the dining room table, the place she had established as a work area for the family's business. The drawer of the bureau where she was keeping important papers was open, and she had many papers in front of her.

"What's for supper?" I asked.

"Haven't started yet," she said.

Oh no. That means a late meal.

Debbie was sitting on the floor in the living room in front of the television set, consumed by some program. She had the volume down low so as not to bother Mom. From my angle, I noticed dust on the top of the television.

"But it came today," Mom added.

I walked to the archway that divided the living room from the dining room. "What came?"

"The death certificate," she said. "The certified copy of the death certificate. It finally came in the mail today."

She looked tired sitting at the table in a sea of

papers, but she also looked relieved, as if some unseen burden had been lifted from her.

"This means a lot," she said. "A whole lot."

"I knew you were worried about it."

"Yes." She slowly exhaled. "Now we will be able to collect the life insurance."

I pulled off my stocking hat and sweatshirt.

"Have a good run?" she asked.

"It was just a leisurely jog. Around town. It's calm out there."

"The company refused to pay until they received this," she continued. "Once we get the money, we will be able to pay off all debts, including the house. With no debt, we will be able to live off what I make at the bank."

This was good news, even though I did not fully understand the exact dollars involved and how everything would fit into place.

"But it is more than that," she said.

I sat on the floor and took off my running shoes. She was looking directly at me.

"I have been praying for this," she said. "It's like God is again hearing our prayers. This is truly an answer."

God? Answering prayer?

I studied her. She was smiling, and it looked like some of the natural color had returned to her cheeks. "That's great," I said. I smiled back at her.

"I am getting this ready to mail tomorrow. When I'm done, I'll start supper."

"No hurry. I'll just get cleaned up."

"Maybe we can go to the city and get some shopping done."

Debbie was engrossed with the television and had not heard Mom; otherwise she would have jumped and squealed with joy. She loved to go shopping.

"I need some new shoes," I said.

"Shoes?"

"Running shoes."

"Oh yes. I remember you mentioned that. Well, we will plan a day and go. Maybe this Saturday."

"That would be great."

She returned her attention to the papers on the table. "An answer to prayer," she repeated.

I went to my room and collected clean clothes, then headed for the shower.

An answer to prayer?

"I'm sorry Mrs. Collins, but your husband is . . ."

It was kind of like praying that your city would be spared during wartime, and then the enemy flying bombers over and carpet bombing it. All that is left standing is one wall of one building, and you climb through the rubble to the lone standing wall and claim this is proof that God answers prayers.

Still, the arrival of the death certificate was good news, and I did not want to take anything away from it.

•◆•

That Saturday Scotty did not need me at Cornett Ford, for business had slowed. Mom organized her shopping trip, and all of us, including Grandma, wanted to go. So first thing in the morning we assembled in the Imperial, headed east out of Bethel, and began the thirty-mile trip to the city. Debbie and I sat in the back of the car and looked out the windows.

"Feels awfully cold," Grandma said. She sat up front with Mom.

"Even looks like snow," Mom said.

"Sure does."

"I hope it holds off till we get back."

"Oh, I'm sure it will, dear."

The Chrysler had four doors, and both the front and rear seats were very wide and comfortable. Debbie could sit by her window and I by mine, and there would be nearly a mile between us. The Imperial had power windows, but the driver also had individual buttons to all four windows. We rode out of Bethel, and we heard the muffled sound of the engine and also the low purr of the heater motor.

"Do you think it will snow, Mommy?" Debbie asked after a moment.

"It might," she said. "I'm afraid it looks like it. But this is the only chance we have to go to town."

"I hope it does," Debbie said. "I want it to snow."

"Not until we get back."

There were no shifter or turn levers around the steering wheel of the Chrysler. The transmission was simply engaged by a vertical row of push buttons on the left side of the dash. The turn indicator was activated by a lever above the row on the upper left side. A matching row of vertical push buttons was located to the right of the wheel, and these controlled the heater and air-conditioning functions.

"I sure appreciate you taking me, Angela," Grandma said.

"No problem. I need to get some things. So does Matt."

"Matt?"

"He wants to buy some running shoes," Mom said.

"Why? Make him run faster?" Grandma looked back at me and winked.

"He thinks so," Mom said.

"Well, if he thinks they will help, then he must get them."

I had twenty dollars—a fortune. Of course, running shoes cost a fortune.

I looked out the window and watched the country-side. We were heading east along the blacktop highway. The dark, gray sky indeed held the promise of snow. The cold had a raw feel to it.

The highway was blacktopped and smooth and well built with a very nice shoulder. We drove by the spot at the top of the hill just east of Bethel. The very spot. It had been a dark night, and Dad had been west-bound. When he reached the very top of the hill, there was the other car, and instantly there was the crash and . . .

We could only guess the rest.

Dad never had a chance.

"Mrs. Collins, you need to pick out a coffin. I'm sorry, but this should be—"

"Matt?" Grandma turned around in the front seat.

"Yes?"

"How long have you been running in those worn-out shoes?"

"They're not really worn out."

"They look like it to me."

When did she ever get a good look at my running shoes? "They're not too bad," I said. "I can still use them. In fact, I will on muddy days. I just need a better pair."

"Well, I hope you find them."

"I hope so too."

We continued to drive, and I watched the cold, brown countryside pass by. I wondered what Dad's last thoughts had been when he saw a car directly in front of him.

"I'm sorry, Mrs. Collins, but we need to do this. Is there somebody we can call? Do you have a priest or a pastor?"

Yes, we have a pastor. He thinks he knows about the love of God, but actually he is completely ignorant on the subject.

In time we arrived at the shopping district in the city, and Mom parked the car in a large parking garage. Grandma and Debbie walked to a department store while Mom and I stuck together. We first stopped at a fabric store, where Mom bought several yards of material plus several dress patterns for both her and Debbie.

We then walked to the sporting goods store. We saw racks of golf clubs, bowling balls, fishing tackle, and every imaginable item. We walked over to where they sold shoes.

"May I help you?" a clerk asked.

"I need some new running shoes."

There was a row of chairs for you to sit in while you tried on shoes. Mom sat in one of the chairs while the clerk measured my foot.

"What kind of shoes do you want?" he asked.

"Good ones."

"You run track?"

"I have."

"Are you going to in the spring?"

"I haven't decided."

He looked at me for a moment. "But you want good shoes?"

"Yes."

"Will they be used on regulation tracks," he asked, "or just training?"

"Both."

"You'll need an all-around shoe. I might have just the thing for you in your size." He went to the back room.

Mom waited patiently. I walked up and down the aisles looking at shoes.

Presently the clerk returned with a box of shoes. "Try these on," he said.

I sat down, slipped them on, and laced them up. They felt good. Real good.

"Do you like them?" he asked.

"Very much."

"They'll be good on all kinds of tracks."

"Even dirt tracks?" I asked.

He looked at me. "They'll do all right on dirt. If you run on dirt, you might want spikes."

"Can't have spikes. One pair will have to do everything."

"Then this is your best choice."

"How much?"

"They're $24.95."

I took a deep breath. I only had twenty dollars. Mom really did not have any extra money to spend on such things. I knew that. I looked at her anyway. She knew I only had twenty dollars. "Mom, can you help out?"

I held my breath while she looked at me without answering.

"Mr. Cornett still needs me," I said. "I'll pay you back."

"Matt, I'm not sure."

"Mom, this is . . . well, this is important."

"Can it be that important?" she asked.

I looked into her troubled eyes.

"Yes," I said.

The word fell flat, blunt. It was the truth. No need to embellish.

"This is a lot of money to pay for just shoes," she said.

"I know."

"Are you really sure?"

"Very sure."

It looked like she was trying to read my thoughts. I had nothing to hide.

"Then let's get them," she said.

"We'll take them," I said.

The clerk smiled and boxed them up while I put my

street shoes back on. We went to the counter and paid for them. They cost $25.70 with tax. I counted out my twenty dollars on the counter, and Mom counted out the rest. I knew she had every dollar accounted for, and this would mean she would have to do without something on this trip. I felt bad, but I knew I needed the shoes. I also knew I should be able to pay her back. Anyway, I helped her out with milk and other small things from time to time.

We walked back outside in the raw November day and saw several snowflakes fall. We'd known this might happen, so we walked over to the department store and met Grandma and Debbie as they were leaving.

"Get what you need?" Mom asked.

"Not really," Grandma said. "How about you two?"

"Some of it," Mom said.

"Matt?"

"Mission accomplished." I had the box of shoes tucked under my arm.

"Do we have time to look any more?" Grandma asked.

"I don't think so," Mom said. It was now lightly snowing. "We don't want to get caught in snow."

"We sure don't," Grandma said.

Debbie jumped up and down. "Oh, boy, snow."

"I think we should head back," Mom said.

"Well, let's go then," Grandma said.

We drove back to Bethel, and the flurries blew across the highway and swirled around the roadside but did not accumulate. By the time we dropped Grandma off at her house and parked the car at home, the snow had stopped.

That afternoon the temperature remained below freezing. I laced up my new shoes and took a leisurely jog down the gravel road to the dirt road. The ground was frozen solid. I jogged down the dirt road. The countryside was still. I heard the shoes lightly touch the road, and I heard my breathing too. Everything else was silent except for the north wind, a raw wind that rattled the nearly bare branches of the trees. The shoes felt good as they glided along the road, and they hardly needed any breaking in.

That evening I proudly placed the shoes back in their box, then stacked the box on top of some books in the closet. The Bible rested at the bottom of the stack.

•◆•

On Sunday morning when we walked to church, I could only think about the new shoes. I had no desire to go to church. God did not need me and I did not need Him. The morning was cold and frosty. I liked cold, frosty mornings. All I wanted to do was go running.

"Good morning, Mr. Collins."

I nodded and shook Pastor Yoshida's hand.

"Good morning, Miss Collins."

"Hi, Pastor," Debbie said. "Frosty morning."

"Certainly is."

"Sometimes I like cold mornings," she said.

"Sometimes I don't. Matt likes cold days. But I'm not so sure I do."

"Does Matt like this cold morning?" He then looked at me. I had reached the top of the stairs and was about to descend to the classrooms.

"I think so," she said.

"And how about you?"

"I think I like this morning too," she said. Debbie passed me and skipped down the stairs to her Sunday school class. I watched Debbie disappear but still lingered at the top of the stairs.

"Good morning, Angela. How have you been?"

"Better. How's Paula doing?"

"She's been having some trouble," Pastor said. "A lot of pain and discomfort."

"She doesn't have much longer now, does she?"

"Over a month. She's due December 25."

"Do you think you'll have a Christmas baby?"

"Probably not," he said. "But that would be interesting. Nice. Certainly different. But for now, I just want a healthy baby."

"I've been praying for all of you," Mom said. "Especially Paula. She's sure had a time of it."

"Thanks. That means a lot to me. To us."

I started down the stairs.

"How's Matt?" Pastor Yoshida asked.

I stopped halfway down the stairs. Neither of them knew I was there. They obviously believed I had gone on to my class.

"Matt worries me," Mom said.

"He hasn't been the same after the accident, has he?"

"No, he hasn't."

"Angela, these things often take time. He'll be all right. You'll see."

"I hope so."

"Sometimes . . . well, sometimes God needs time to work; that's all."

"I'm still worried about him," she said. "Something strange happened yesterday."

"What?"

"We went to buy him running shoes."

"What happened?"

"He didn't have quite enough money. Yet he needed the shoes."

"But he's not running, is he?"

"On his own," Mom said. "Yet he said he needed the shoes."

"So what happened?"

"He asked me to help him out."

"Did you?" he asked.

"Yes."

"Why would that worry you?"

"You don't understand. I saw something."

"What?"

"In his eyes. A passion. An intensity. It frightened me."

"Frightened you?"

"Maybe not frightened," she said. "He just took me back. You see, he was not to be denied. He would accomplish his goal no matter what."

"Matt is a very strong person."

"Yes, he is. But I saw something. . . ."

"What did you see? What bothered you?"

"Oh, I'm not saying this right. You just should have seen him. You should have seen his eyes."

"His eyes?"

"They were . . . they were piercing. He had that same intense look that . . . well, that Tommy always had."

NINETEEN

"**I**-I like Th-Thanksgiving."

We were sitting in English class and listening to Wade announce his opinion. He stood by his desk while I doodled on some notebook paper. I wished he were not my locker partner and hoped he would just get out of my life. Thanksgiving was less than a week away on this Friday, November 22, 1963.

"Th-Thanksgiving is m-my favorite holiday."

"You like Thanksgiving better than Christmas?" Miss Edmonds asked.

"Y-yes."

Wade was always saying stupid things. In fact, every time he opened his mouth something stupid fell out. He was a retard indeed.

"Why is it your favorite?" Miss Edmonds asked.

"W-we have so m-much to be th-thankful for."

"That's why you like Thanksgiving?"

"Y-yes. B-besides, Thanksgiving is m-more sincere."

"You can be thankful even though bad things happen?"

"*I'm sorry, Mrs. Collins, but your husband is . . .*"

"Y-yes."

"That's interesting," she said.

Bad things happen, but they are supposed to happen to somebody else. Yet in the final analysis, bad things catch up with us all. Nobody escapes. Nobody gets out of life alive. I did not fully understand it back then. I supposed I would live forever.

"Thank you, Mr. Scott. Anybody else prefer Thanksgiving? Mr. Kindle? How about you?"

"I prefer Christmas."

"So do I," somebody said.

"Thanksgiving is all right," another boy said. "We get out of school and all."

Several students clapped at this.

"But Christmas is the best," he concluded.

"And why is Christmas the best?" Miss Edmonds asked.

"Because of the presents."

Several students clapped again.

Catherine stood up. "I prefer Thanksgiving," she said.

I dropped my pencil, turned around, and looked at her. For Wade to have a stupid opinion was to be expected. For Catherine to have the same opinion, well, I'd never given the question any thought until this morning.

"Why?" Miss Edmonds asked.

"Mr. Scott is right," she said. "Thanksgiving is more sincere. There is no phony pretense about it. A proper holiday. And besides, we do have a lot to be thankful for."

"I'm sorry, Mrs. Collins, but . . ."

"We are greatly blessed." Catherine sat back down.

This was going to be the first Thanksgiving without Dad. I did not look forward to the holidays, with Mom sighing and crying, with the feeling of something missing.

"I prefer Thanksgiving."

"W-we have so m-much to be th-thankful for."

I just shook my head. Somehow I could not feel thankful.

The bell finally rang, ending class, and we walked out into the hall.

"Hey, Nerd," Squareface said.

Everyone stopped and looked first at Squareface, then Wade.

"I know why you hate Christmas."

"I-I like C-Christmas. Jesus—"

"You hate Christmas because nobody gives you any presents." Squareface forced out a laugh.

Wade wore his usual blank expression

"Nobody would give a nerd anything." Squareface then sauntered by without saying anything else.

Everybody dispersed in the direction of their next class, and after a moment, Wade also headed in the direction of his.

Life in the penitentiary continued its routine. Outside a light drizzle fell on Bethel, and the day was dark and cold and gloomy. It was early afternoon, and we were sitting in class when the announcement was made.

The words crashed through the entire school over the intercom: *President Kennedy has been shot.*

It was a radio newscast, and the announcer jabbered and was very excited, and we all just sat and listened and looked at each other in a stupid sort of way. The gloom moved from outside to inside the building as we listened to the news and tried to grasp the meaning of the words. We could see the drizzle outside and hear the water gurgling down the gutters, and we could hear, too, the crackle of the intercom and see the numb, brainless sort of expressions that we were all wearing. For some reason we all felt strangely cold. They turned the intercom off, but shortly after that they announced to the entire school that the president of the United States had died.

President John F. Kennedy dead. Assassinated in Dallas.

Some of the teachers cried. Many of the girls cried too.

"I'm sorry, Mrs. Collins, but your husband is . . ."

Dead. The president is dead.

That afternoon we walked home in a cold, wet world that was falling apart. The drizzle continued to fall, and we were cold and wet, but we said nothing to each other. There was silence except for our walking and the drizzle. In truth, there is nothing you can say when the world is out of control and nothing makes sense.

Once home I put on my old shoes and went running down the county road. I knew the dirt road would be muddy so I did not even attempt it. I ran down the gravel road, then ran back, my mind numb, my body wet.

That night the TV was full of the assassination, and

the country was in an uproar and full of wild rumors. At that time we had no idea whether our enemy was outside the country or simply one of us. We suspected that the Russians were behind it and feared that they truly were.

We did know that we had a new president, Lyndon Johnson. We were certain of little else.

The TV droned on while Mom fidgeted and circled in and out of the living room, hesitating each time in front of the set. In time she began crying in earnest and could not stop and ultimately retreated to her bedroom, where the tears continued.

We remained glued to the set and watched as our world changed from something predictable and secure to a world more ugly, more violent. In a strange sort of way, this tragedy seemed to make our personal catastrophe of 1963 complete.

❖

The cold drizzle in Bethel continued into Saturday. Big Joe commandeered me to help clean the shop in the morning, after which several used cars were driven in to have their interiors cleaned.

Big Joe appeared somber, and I was melancholy too. He directed me as I swept the shop, but he said little else. He was still quiet when we ate lunch together.

"You know, kid," he said at last, "I still can't believe it."

"You mean about Kennedy?"

He nodded. "He's just gone."

I still couldn't believe it either.

"I saw pictures of him riding in the car. He looked

healthy and happy. A few minutes later, he's dead. Gone." Big Joe shook his head.

I didn't know what to say.

"I guess everybody dies," he said after a while.

"Yes, they do."

"It just was so sudden."

"*Mrs. Collins, you need to come with us. . . .*"

"I remember Lloyd Watson," he said.

"Who?"

"Lloyd. He was out racing on some gravel roads with some of the other guys. He was driving a '37 Ford coupe, a thrifty sixty. Those were tiny V-8s and were underpowered. Some of the guys didn't think it could go fast. Anyway, Lloyd got the puppy up to speed, then lost control on the gravel. He left the road, snapped a fence post, wrapped barbed wire around everything, and wedged the car between two trees. The front door popped open; he got jarred partially out, then was pinned in the door when the open door smashed against a tree. He was crushed between the door and the car body."

We were alone in the shop. Big Joe ignored his lunch, lit up a cigarette, and continued talking, more to himself than to me. "Death came real sudden that day too. Unexpected like."

"*I'm sorry, Mrs. Collins, but your husband is . . .*"

"I always wondered about Lloyd," he said. "What it might be like to be dead."

I ate my sandwich in silence.

"Is there really a God, Matt?"

"I suppose."

"And a hell?" he asked.

"I guess."

"You're not sure either, are you?"

Me and God have not been getting along too well lately.

"I'm sure," I said. "There's a God." *A cruel God. No mistake about that.*

"What's it like to be dead, Matt?"

Why is he asking me? "I don't know," I said.

"Mr. Cornett has been talking to me about it," he said. "About Jesus and all."

"I see."

"We don't think about it, but all of us are going to die someday." He nervously crushed out his partial cigarette and closed his lunch box, leaving his lunch uneaten.

"Yes, we are," I said.

"But I don't think about it. I mean, I just act like I'll live forever."

"I think like that too."

"But it's not so," he said. "You're going to die. I'm going to die. That's hard to believe."

"I try not to think about it," I said. Until that year, I had never given the matter any thought.

"But it's true."

"Yes, it is true."

"So how can you be sure it's all true?" he asked.

"What's all true?"

"You know, the Bible. Salvation. All the stuff Mr. Cornett has been telling me."

Good question. How can you be sure? Are you sure of anything right now?

"You need to talk to Mr. Cornett," I said. "Not me."

"You're a Christian, aren't you?"

Yes, I'm a Christian. Being a Christian keeps you out of hell. But me and God have not been getting along too well lately. God is a very hard taskmaster. I promised to leave Him alone if He would only leave me alone.

"You need to talk to Mr. Cornett," I said. "I've been asking a ton of questions myself lately."

He considered me for a moment. "I guess you have."

We were silent as I finished my lunch.

"I just can't believe it," he said.

"Me either."

"It was just so sudden."

I stood up and went back to work. I finished the cars, and after that there was no more work. They sent me home.

We were quiet Sunday morning, and everybody was quiet in church too, even the Metzge twins. I half expected Pastor Greg to lapse back and preach another one of his wrath-of-God messages. He did not. Ever since the blowup, he stayed away from that topic. The church had planned to have a Thanksgiving meal after the morning service, but Pastor Greg canceled the meal after several of the older ladies asked him to. Church quietly dismissed at noon, and we returned home.

That afternoon things began to quiet back down. Quiet down, that is, until Oswald was shot.

Then everything exploded again. The television coverage became crazy and refocused on the national tragedy, and the country plunged once more into turmoil.

Sunday night service was poorly attended, and the service quickly ended. The country had forever changed, and we knew it.

"I'm sorry, Mrs. Collins, but the funeral needs to be a closed casket. . . ."

Kennedy, too, had a closed casket. And there were pictures, many pictures. We saw Jackie in her blood-stained dress and Johnson being sworn in and little John saluting. We also saw flags and caskets and soldiers and caissons. But there was something we didn't see then, and we wouldn't see until years later, after many other terrible things happened in our country. We would look back and see that all those terrible things had their beginning on that awful November day.

So that year there was another funeral, and we watched it, for we understood funerals and closed caskets.

We understood little else.

TWENTY

"**Y**ou've what?"

"I've invited the Scotts over for Thanksgiving dinner." Mom held the door open for Grandma, who carried a box covered with a towel. The aroma of the turkey baking filled the house.

"Why?" I asked.

"They have no family near, and we . . . well, we . . ." Mom had her faraway look.

I couldn't believe my ears. Grandma walked into the kitchen, then returned with her coat, which Mom hung up in the front closet. Debbie struggled with the tablecloth on the dining room table.

"When are they coming?" I asked.

"Around noon. Elaine is baking some pies."

"Noon?"

"Yes, around noon. The turkey will be ready to eat at one."

"I can't believe you invited them."

"Matt, what is the problem?"

"No problem." I left the house and stood outside. *Why the Scotts? Can't I have one day without him?*

The day was cold though the sun was shining. After

a moment, I walked back in the house, where the smell of turkey soothed me. I hid in my room.

At twelve o'clock sharp I heard a knock.

"I'll get it," Debbie said. "Hi. Come on in."

"Hi," Mrs. Scott said. "Hi, Angela."

"Happy Thanksgiving."

"Howdy." Arthur Scott's low voice reverberated throughout the house.

"Where's M-Matt?" Wade asked.

"You'll find him in his room," Mom said.

Rather than be invaded, I walked out to meet our company.

"Howdy, Matt." Mr. Scott greeted me with a hearty handshake.

"Hi, M-Matt."

"Howdy," I said. That seemed to be the greeting for the day.

"Smells good in here," Mr. Scott said.

"Very good."

"I l-like Th-Thanksgiving."

"Thanksgiving seems to be Wade's favorite holiday," Mr. Scott said.

"So I've heard," I said.

"I've so m-much to be thankful f-for."

"We all do, Son. We all have much to be thankful for."

Perhaps they did. But my day had taken a turn for the worse.

The women chatted incessantly in the kitchen and dining room, and they scurried about with dishes and food. Before long, Grandma carved the turkey, and we were seated and ready to begin.

"Matt, will you please pray?" Mom asked.

Me and God have not been getting along too well lately.

"I think we should let our guest have the honor," I quickly blurted. "Mr. Scott, would you please say the blessing?"

Surprise covered Mom's face.

"Why, I'd be happy to," he said.

We folded our hands and bowed our heads.

"Lord, we praise Your most holy name and give You thanks for the many blessings You have given us. We thank You for the country we live in and the freedom we enjoy . . ."

"President Kennedy has been shot in Dallas."

". . . and for Your love, mercy, and protection on us. . . ."

"I'm sorry, Mrs. Collins, but your husband is . . ."

"We thank You for the friends and family we enjoy in Christ . . ."

"You hang around nerds, so you're becoming a nerd."

". . . and for the abundant feast You have provided. We thank You in the name of our Lord Jesus Christ and for His sake. Amen."

"Amen," they echoed.

We passed food around the table and began our feast amid the clinking of silverware on china.

"I guess we have a new president," Grandma said.

"Yes, we do," Mr. Scott said.

Mrs. Scott shook her head. "Wasn't it awful?"

"My heart goes out for Jackie," Mom said.

Mrs. Scott nodded.

"Who is Lyndon Johnson?" Grandma asked.

"Well, he's from Texas," Mr. Scott said. "He was Senate majority leader before vice president."

"Is he any good?"

Mr. Scott just shrugged.

"Did you vote for him?" Grandma asked. "I mean for senator when you lived in Texas?"

"No," Mr. Scott said.

"I don't know much about him," she said.

"I guess we'll soon find out," Mom said.

"Funny," Grandma said, "but I can remember when McKinley was shot."

"That was before me," Mr. Scott said with a grin.

"Really. I can remember. I was a little girl then."

"Actually," Mrs. Scott said, "I've read about someone who was alive when Lincoln was shot."

"It was a terrible thing," Mr. Scott said.

"It all makes you wonder if God is really in control," Mom said.

I looked at her. She had that faraway look again.

"We all wonder about that at some time," Mrs. Scott said.

Mr. Scott passed the bowl of mashed potatoes to me.

"He obviously allows some things," Mrs. Scott continued, "but we still sometimes wonder."

"God is innnn c-control."

"Yes, Son," Mr. Scott said. "The God who created all things can still control His creation."

"God is very g-good."

"Yes, He is."

"W-we have so m-much to be thankful f-for."

"I'm sorry, Mrs. Collins, but your husband is . . ."

"Yes, we do."

"God is so g-good to us."

"I wanted you to know that the gravestone is now in place. . . ."

Wade attempted to eat a spoonful of cranberry sauce but smeared some of it around his mouth. He then concentrated on the mashed potatoes. "I so th-thankful for my s-salvation."

Must he always preach?

"True," Mr. Scott said. "If God did nothing else, salvation would be more than sufficient."

"God is g-good." Part of his spoonful of mashed potatoes made it successfully into his mouth, but the rest fell in his lap.

"It is good to take one day," Grandma said, "and give thanks to God for His blessings."

"Amen," Mr. Scott said.

Wade spilled his milk, partly on himself, the rest on the table. "I s-sorry."

"I'll get some towels," Mom said.

"Scoot back, Son," Mrs. Scott said. She helped him move his chair back.

"I s-sorry."

"That's okay," Mom said, returning from the kitchen. She handed Mrs. Scott one of the towels, and together they attacked the mess.

We just sat and watched the drama and Wade's feeble, comical attempt to wipe himself up.

"Pretty soon everybody'll be calling you a nerd."

When she was done cleaning up, Mom carried the towels back to the kitchen and dropped them in the sink.

"This meal is delicious, Angela," Mr. Scott said.

"I had a lot of help," she said as she sat back down.

"We appreciate being invited over," Mrs. Scott said.

"We are happy to have you."

"We think it is wonderful that Wade has found such a good friend in Matt," she said.

Though Mr. Scott was right about everything being delicious, Wade would ruin your appetite if you watched him for long. I tried hard not to look at him.

I sat as long as I could stand it. "May I please be excused?" I asked.

"Why, Matt," Mom said, "you haven't had any seconds or dessert."

"I'm hot. I need to go outside for a few minutes."

"Don't you want any pumpkin pie?"

"Maybe later."

"Well, all right then."

I carried my plate to the kitchen counter before stepping out the back door. I walked around the house to the front porch, where the sun was shining, then sat down on the steps. They were cold, but everything around me was peaceful, and I felt better sitting outside. Thanksgiving had not been the same. Something was definitely missing.

Is there a difference between being murdered on the highway and murdered with a gun? Either way you're dead.

We had talked of many things, but we never talked about car accidents or assassinations or death or even that much about war. He would talk about his war experiences but would say very little about the gore and the killing. We once had a black dog, and one autumn evening the dog got hit by a car driving into town. We had heard the thunk of the impact, and we heard too the piercing yelps. We ran outside and found the dog, crying and whimpering, her rear end destroyed, entrails squashed in the gravel and in a growing pool of blood, and there was blood coming out of her mouth. The evening was cold, and we could see our breath, and we could feel the darkness begin to settle in around us, and everything was quiet except for the yelping and whimpering and gurgling. Debbie was inside crying, and Mom was with her. Dad ran inside and returned with his revolver. He aimed and fired. Once. The crack shattered the cold stillness, then echoed throughout the neighborhood. I jumped a foot, ears ringing. Then the darkness began to creep around us again and settle, and everything was cold and quiet and still, and the dog was quiet and still too. Dad asked if that bothered me, and I said it didn't, but of course it did. He then said it was a whole lot better than killing Japs. That had been the first time it ever occurred to me that he had killed people.

"I had never thought of it before."

"Thought of what?"

I looked up. Grandma had just stepped outside on the porch. She had her coat on, and she carried mine.

"Oh, nothing," I said.

"Anything you want to tell me?"

I shook my head.

She tilted her head, still gazing at me. "Want to walk me home?" she asked after a moment.

"Isn't Mom going to take you?"

"I prefer to walk."

"Sure. I'll go with you."

"Besides, I don't have to carry anything home."

Grandma handed me my coat, which I put on, and we started toward her house.

"Aren't you leaving early?" I asked.

"Maybe a little. I suppose I just need a walk."

"It's cold, but it's a nice day for a walk."

We reached the end of our drive and began walking on the street.

"Is there a problem?" she asked.

"A problem? With me? No. I just needed to cool off."

"Is that all?"

"I guess I needed some quiet."

"Does Wade bother you?" she asked.

"Sometimes."

"He does take a little getting used to."

That was great of her to say that. Perhaps she understood. I knew Mom didn't. We walked north to Delaware Street.

"How come you left early?" I repeated.

"They just started talking about Kennedy again," she said.

"Does that bother you?"

"A president has been murdered, Matt. That bothers me very much."

"I just meant the talk about it."

"The country is reeling from it. In ways we probably don't even know yet."

"I suppose so."

We headed east along Delaware Street to her house. It was clear that the head-on crash in Dallas, Texas, on November 22, 1963, had ejected people from their security and left them sprawling over the countryside. They were bloodied and dazed, and they tried to understand why but could not.

"I worry about your mother," Grandma said. "How this will affect her."

"She was upset by it."

"But more than that. It seemed to drag up all the hurt from the summer again."

I knew the feeling. It was like you got hit in the gut by a bully, and it hurt real bad. Then several days later you're in another situation, and you're about to get hit again. The expectation always makes the second blow hurt more than it would have just by itself.

We reached Grandma's house, and I walked her to the front porch.

"Will it ever end?" I asked.

"What?"

"All the hurt. All the turmoil in the country."

Grandma looked at me sort of quizzically. I knew I was a bit ambiguous. "Only the good Lord and time heal hurts, Matt," she said.

"Oh."

"Do you want to come in for a minute?"

"No, I'd better be getting back."

"Well, thanks for walking me home."

"Sure."

"Good-bye, Matt."

"Good-bye."

The sun hung low as I loafed back home. My hands and ears were cold, but that was all.

Maybe time would help with hurts, but I questioned whether the Lord would do anything. As for Wade, well, he took a lot more than just getting used to. I wished I could cut him out of my life. I just wished I could be free of him.

I wanted to be like Colby. I wanted to be *with* Colby. I supposed I wanted to *be* Colby.

I made a decision. I decided to do whatever it took to restore a strong friendship with Colby. Just like old times.

TWENTY-ONE

"You coming with us, Matt?" Cathy asked one rainy December afternoon.

"You go on. I'll catch up later. I need to check something out in the library first."

"And you will catch up?"

"If you're with Wade, I'll catch up. I'll only be a moment in the library."

"Well, we will go on then. It is sure gloomy outside."

Cathy put on her gray coat, which was nearly as long as her dark blue skirt, then locked her locker and went looking for Wade. He was probably shuffling around at the other end of the hallway. I walked in the opposite direction toward the library.

In the library I found the encyclopedias and pulled out the *H* volume. I looked up Wade Hampton, but the article was quite small and gave little information. It did not contradict what Wade had presented, yet it did not confirm his talk either. I was hoping to find . . . I don't know what I was hoping to find. Maybe some glaring error in Wade's presentation or perhaps some great flaw in this heroic Wade Hampton, this savior of South Carolina. Anyway, the encyclopedia was of no help.

I put the volume back and checked the card catalog. Nothing.

I left school. The rain had diminished to a drizzle. I walked near the tree line on the south side of Church Street, taking my time. The trees stood as black silhouettes against the dark sky; wet leaves were matted on the ground and mixed with mud.

I could see Cathy and Wade ahead of me but had no desire to join them. Nobody else was in sight. I lagged behind and watched the fog from my breath hang in the damp air, then slowly dissipate.

Life is like that. Hangs for a moment, then is gone.

I crossed the ditch, walked along the trees where I could not be easily seen, and kicked through the wet, muddy leaves that messed my shoes and pants with mud. I stopped to pick up a fallen oak branch. The stick was straight, over three feet long. It had been dead for a while, and the earth was attempting to reclaim it, though it was not yet rotten. I idly broke off the twigs and threw them onto the muddy ground.

A scream snapped me back to reality.

A scream sounded so inappropriate. Screams should not be heard on a damp, peaceful street. I heard it again.

Cathy?

I hopped back to the street and sprinted west almost two blocks. I found Wade sitting on the ground near the tree line with mud on his face and the front of his brown jacket. Cathy, standing nearby, had mud on the side of her coat too. Squareface and Colby stood together in the street.

I ran between Cathy and the attackers. She had tears on her face. I paid Wade no attention, but seeing mud on Cathy made me mad. I whirled toward Colby and Squareface, still holding the stick. "What's going on?" I roared.

"We're just having a little fun," Colby said. "Did you come to join us?"

"I think you've had enough fun!"

"Has he come to stop us?" Squareface asked. His hands were muddy. Colby's were not.

"He's not that stupid," Colby said. "There's two of us."

I quickly tried to figure out a course of action. Colby was right. There were two of them. I had no desire for a fight. But I saw tears on Cathy's face, and I remembered mud in my locker and Colby's attitude about the mud. I was hot and getting hotter. I needed a plan. A plan for one against two.

"Maybe he's come to join us," Colby repeated.

With both hands on the stick, I pointed it straight out in front of me and aimed it at Squareface. "You need to go home, you coward!"

His mouth opened slightly, and he took a step backward.

"I've wanted to drop you for a long time," I said. "You'll be first."

For an instant, he either forgot he was with Colby or questioned whether Colby would help him in a fight.

"Go on home, you coward!" I shouted. "This is just between me and Colby!"

Squareface backed up another step.

"This is between old friends," I said, "and you're not invited!"

Squareface glanced at Colby, who was watching me. Colby's failure to immediately respond seemed to unnerve the coward even more.

I took a step toward Squareface. "Go home! Scat! This is between me and Colby! Doesn't concern you! Scat! Before you get hurt!"

Squareface turned and ran, then stopped and looked back at Colby.

Colby merely stared at me.

"Scat!" I said. "You'll just get hurt."

Squareface ran down the road and up Fourth Street, for he obviously had no desire to see what I might do. He never looked back.

I knew how to handle cowards, being one myself. I turned and pointed the stick at Colby. His mouth was half open, his face red. "This isn't fun anymore, Colby!"

"What's gotten into you?" he asked.

"I've had enough!"

"We're not hurting you none."

"I don't like your idea of fun."

"What are you going to do about it?"

Good question. "I'm going to stop it," I said.

"Are you threatening me?"

"I want the mud stopped," I said.

"So, you're choosing the nerd over an old friend?"

"I'm sick of mud, Colby! Mud in the locker. Remember? I'm sick of it!"

"There hasn't been any more mud in your stupid locker," he said.

"There was."

"And it stopped."

"Squareface do it?"

"Yes."

"Why didn't you stop him?"

"I wasn't there. There was a meet. Remember?"

"So you two beat up Wade the first time?" I asked.

"Squareface did."

"So you're doing it again?"

"He was. What's it to you?" he asked.

"I don't like it," I said. "I don't like mud in my locker."

"You have a thing about mud," he said. "Maybe you need to see more mud!"

"Let's see it, Colby! I'm ready!"

"You're a nerd, Collins. A nerd. Do you hear me?"

"I hear you fine."

"You have nerd friends. And a nerd girl."

"Leave them out of this. This is between you and me."

"All right," he said. "You're a nerd. We were once friends but not anymore. Friends don't threaten each other."

"A friend would tell about mud in a locker."

"I still can't believe you would choose a bunch of nerds over an old friend."

"I can't believe you would throw mud at a girl."

"What's eating you, Collins? Is it because you all go to that same church?"

"Church has nothing to do with this."

"That's it, isn't it?" Colby asked. "You all go to the same church, and you guys think you're better than everybody. You all think you're goody-goody."

The drizzle increased to rain, and almost instantly the rain became heavy—a truly Baptist rain that soaked all of us. Wade remained sitting. The rain washed mud off his face. Cathy silently watched us. Rain soaked Colby's hair and clothes.

"We're not goody-goody," I said.

"That is it. You've got religion, and you think you're better than everybody."

"No."

"This is some Christian thing."

"There's no Christian thing."

"Oh, but you have Jesus. That's what you said."

"That was a long time ago."

"So you don't have Jesus now?" he asked.

The rain was falling in sheets, and it splatted and bounced off the street. I rotated the stick in my hands.

"This is between you and me!" I finally shouted. "Leave Jesus out of this!"

Colby swore, using both *God* and *Jesus*.

"You don't need to talk like that!"

"What's it to you?" He unleashed another flurry, concentrating more on Jesus this time.

"Leave Jesus out of this!"

"Garrett's right. Your church is stupid. Your friends are also stupid. You're stupid." Colby started walking around me, like a wild animal watching its prey. He was mad too.

I continued pointing the stick directly at him. "Colby, if there's anything you want to settle, settle it now!"

"You're a nerd, Collins!" He then swore, calling me many names. He kept walking in an arc.

I kept facing him, uncertain what he might do. More uncertain what *I* might do. Rain continued to fall. The afternoon was very dark. The world was even darker. "I thought we were best friends," I said.

"We *were* friends. Not now!" Colby unleashed another foul torrent.

"I said leave God out of this!"

"Does that bother goody-goody Collins?"

"This is between you and me. Not God."

"What are you going to do about it?" he asked.

"I want it stopped!"

"Do you think you can take me?"

I was too mad to think clearly or feel anything. I kept the stick pointed at him. "Do you think you can take *me?*" I echoed back at him.

"I'll take you, Collins, when I feel good and ready."

"No. If you want to do something, do it now!"

"I'll do it when I'm ready," Colby said.

"I want all accounts settled now!"

"Matt, my boy, since you like mud so well, we'll just have to find you some more mud."

The cold rain poured. Wade was sitting in mud. The shallow ditch filled with water. Cathy shivered.

"No more mud, Colby."

"We'll see."

"Take me now if you want. Settle everything now!"

"I'll take you when I'm good and ready," he said. Colby turned and started walking along Church Street, then headed up Fourth Street. "This finishes everything between us, Collins!" he yelled back at me.

I watched him walk up Fourth Street until he was out of sight. I had wanted to be with him. I had wanted to be like him. I had wanted to be him. Now, in a fit, I had ruined everything.

"Only Squareface threw mud," said Cathy. "And only at Wade. I guess I just got in the way." Her face was wet with rain, and I could not tell if there were any more tears. Her wet hair was plastered to the side of her face.

After a moment of struggle, Wade managed to stand up.

I stormed down Church Street, stomping through the water; they followed.

"Matt," she said, "I want to—"

"Leave me alone!"

"Matt?"

"Don't talk to me! Leave me alone!" I threw the stick. It flew against a tree and shattered into several pieces. The stick would not have helped much in a fight.

"M-Matt?"

"Can't you hear? Leave me alone!"

We reached Bethel Baptist Church, and Cathy stopped. "Matt?"

I wheeled around.

She trembled. I could tell she was cold. She moved her lips, but no words came. "Thanks, Matt," she finally said. She spun and left us, then fled to her backyard.

I resumed my stomp toward home. Wade trudged behind me.

I began shaking. From cold. From rage. Maybe other reasons. It took extreme effort to control the shaking. I was thoroughly soaked. I had reached the little gray house when he called my name.

I looked back at him. He stood at the edge of his drive.

"Leave me alone!" I shouted.

"M-Matt?"

I turned and marched back across our yard toward him, still shaking. I hated God. I hated Wade. I liked Colby. Now in a twisted turn of events, I'd ruined my friendship with Colby and defended both Wade and God. My fury increased step by step. "Leave me alone! Just leave me alone! Why can't you and God just leave me alone?!"

He watched my approach, started to slosh up his drive a few steps, then hesitated again. "M-Matt?"

"What do you want, you retard?"

He considered, then shuffled up his drive toward the house.

"You know I lost my best friend?"

He stopped and looked at me.

"And it's all your fault!"

"M-Matt, I-I—"

"I bet you are! I lost my best friend, and it's all your fault!"

"M-Matt—"

"I hate you, Nerd! Do you understand? I hate you!"

He looked at me with his blank look.

"You've ruined everything! You've ruined my life!"

The cold rain continued to fall unabated. We stood in the rain as if we had no sense.

"I hate you! I wish I never saw you!"

He turned and slopped along his drive toward the house.

"I wish you would drop dead!" I was standing at our property line. "Just drop dead!"

He did not look at me.

"I wish you were killed at Brandy Station! I wish you died at Gettysburg! I wish you were killed at Iwo Jima!"

Iwo Jima?

"I hate you, you retard!"

He continued toward his house.

"Do you know what it's like to lose a best friend?"

He did not respond.

"You know, I always wanted to be like Colby. Did you ever want to be like somebody?"

Wade stopped and faced me.

"Have you ever wished you were like your best friend? Do you even know what it's like to have a friend?"

"I w-want to be like you, M-Matt. You run f-fast."

He then turned and continued up his drive.

"What do you know about anything?"

He shuffled through the collecting water toward his house.

I stood at the edge of our yard in the mud, in the rain, screaming, "I hate you!"

Wade reached his front porch.

"You're stupid! You're a nerd! I wish you were dead! Just drop dead and get out of my life!"

He opened the outer storm door.

"What do you know about anything? Tell me! What do you know about life?"

He stared at me for a moment. Then he opened the front door and went inside.

TWENTY-TWO

The Christmas season had officially begun the Friday after Thanksgiving, so by the first week of December, the season was in full swing. Bethel also suffered from the malady of Christmas. Businesses up and down Main Street installed lights and decorations. People descended upon those businesses to fulfill their shopping responsibilities. Duty permeates the lifeblood of Christmas.

The season promoted itself as a time of peace on earth and goodwill toward men as the birth of the Savior was celebrated. Yet the Christmas season could be a bitter time for families who had recently suffered loss. There could be no peace on earth when there was no peace in the heart.

On Thursday, the day after the mud slinging, I sat eating at the breakfast table while Mom watched the coffee percolate. The aroma was strong, and I was looking forward to a cup.

"I don't really want to go," she said.

I looked up at her. "Go where?" I asked.

"To the party." She glanced over at me and must have seen my blank look. "The bank is having their Christmas party Friday night. Everybody will be there."

She sighed and looked back at the coffee. "With their spouses," she whispered.

The coffee continued to percolate; the dark liquid spewed into the clear bulb of the pot.

"It will be at Homer's house," she added after a moment. She then unplugged the pot and poured two mugs without waiting to remove the grounds. "I don't know if I will—"

The phone rang.

Mom answered. "Hello? . . . Yes. . . . Oh, hi, Elaine. . . . Oh no. . . . You did? When? . . . How is he? . . . Is it that serious? . . . Oh my. . . . Yes, I'll call Greg. . . . Is there anything we can do for you? . . . We'll be praying for you. . . . Where's Arthur? . . . He's in town? That's good. . . . All right. . . . We sure will. . . . Good-bye."

She hung the phone up and turned toward me. "They had to take Wade back to the hospital."

"They did? When?"

"Last night."

"What's the problem?" I asked.

"His heart is racing. They can't control it."

"Is it serious?"

"Very serious. The medication they have been giving him may be causing some of the problem. They're trying to find something better for him."

Mom handed me some coffee. It tasted hot and rich. I finished eating my breakfast.

"He also has a very bad cold," she said. "Apparently he got chilled yesterday."

"He did?"

"Do you know anything about it?"

"It was pouring when we walked home."

"Well, if it turns into pneumonia it could be . . ."

"Be what?"

She just stared in my direction with that faraway look of hers.

"Mom? How critical is this?"

"Very."

"Can he . . . can he die?"

She nodded. "We need to pray for him."

I took my plate over to the sink and gulped the rest of the coffee. I then gathered my coat and left. Mom was on the phone with Pastor Greg.

It was not raining, but the December day was cold and damp. Water dripped off the trees, and the streets and sidewalks were wet. The temperature was near freezing.

What if he dies?

I did not wait for Cathy but hurried on to school. I had no desire to see or talk to anybody.

"I w-want to be like you, M-Matt."

I had calmed down from yesterday and felt greatly embarrassed by everything. I supposed that the feeling was similar to the embarrassment felt by the church after the blowup meeting.

If he dies it will be my fault. I'll be a murderer.

I wanted to find Colby and apologize but knew that was probably impossible. My friendship with him had been destroyed forever. Wade, in his bumbling way, had turned my life away from Colby. I had never wanted this.

It won't be my fault if he dies. I didn't throw mud at him.

I may not have thrown mud at him, but I had wished he were dead. Moreover, I had clearly said it. And if that was not enough, I had announced it at such a volume that the whole world, had it wanted to, could have heard. Some neighbor I turned out to be.

He won't die, will he?

The cold usually did not bother me, but this day it drove me faster toward school. It felt like ice gripped my spine, refusing to yield to any heat.

Somehow it all seemed unfair. I never requested that Wade would move in next door. I didn't decree that he would get hit with mud. It wasn't my fault that he was in poor health. But because of the way things worked out . . . well, God would squash me for the way I'd acted. I just knew it because that was how God worked.

I entered the school and found my locker. As I hung my coat up, I wondered whether Colby would deliver more locker mud. I closed the locker and made doubly sure it was locked.

"Hi, Matt."

I turned around. "Hi, Cathy."

"You guys were not there this morning," she said. "I was worried."

"Wade's in the hospital."

"Oh my." She turned a little pale.

"They took him in last night."

"Is it serious?" she asked.

"Yes, Mom said it's very serious. For his heart problems, mostly."

"Mostly?"

"And from getting cold and wet. They're trying to find a different heart medication that will work better."

"I would have slapped that Colby and Squareface if I had half a chance."

"What happened, Cathy?"

"We were walking home when Squareface and Colby jumped us."

"They jumped you?"

"Well, they were hiding in the tree line, and when we got near, they jumped out and threw mud."

"*They* threw mud?"

"Well, like I already told you, only Squareface threw the mud."

"What did Colby do?"

"Nothing, really. He jumped out with Squareface, but he didn't throw any mud."

"How did you get hit?"

"Well, they jumped out, and the first mud ball hit Wade in the face. This knocked him down. He then managed to sit up. I walked over to him and was surprised he still had his glasses on. When I was by him, I got hit. He was actually the target, I guess."

"When did you scream?"

"Did I scream?" she asked.

"I heard you."

"I suppose I did."

"Do you remember when?"

"Not exactly. Anyway, after I got hit, you showed up."

"Wade only got hit once?"

"I think so."

"He was awful muddy."

"He fell down in mud," she said. "I guess he was kind of a mess."

"Did you tell your mom and dad?"

"Yes."

"Are they going to do anything?"

"I don't know. Maybe not. At least, not until they talk to you."

"Talk to me?" I asked.

"You broke it up, Matt. You saved us. Thanks."

I could feel my face getting hot.

"I mean it, Matt," she said. "Thanks."

"We better get to class."

"Yes, we should."

We had started to enter the classroom when I noticed Squareface walking up the hall. I let Cathy go in by herself as I headed over to him. "Well, Squareface, you got your wish."

I could see panic in his eyes.

"Wade's in the hospital," I said. "And you did it."

"I didn't do anything." He took a step back.

"Yes, you did," I said. "You hit him with mud. Now he's in the hospital."

"Mud don't hurt nobody," he said.

"It does if you have poor health. It does if you have a heart condition."

"He has a heart condition?"

"Yes. But don't worry. He may die."

"You're lying."

"That's what Mrs. Scott told my mom this morning."

He turned pale. Of course, you'd expect as much from a coward.

"You did a good job, Squareface," I said. "I hope you're proud of yourself."

I knew he didn't care about Wade, but he didn't want to be blamed for killing him either. I walked to class and left him to think about it. There was more than enough guilt here to spread around.

I did not see Colby that day, and I did not know what I would have said or done if I had. He had officially pronounced me a nerd. I did not like the title. I always assumed Wade did not really care when he was called a nerd. He acted like he didn't care. But maybe down deep it did hurt.

My thoughts tormented me for the rest of that day. Yet throughout it all, I felt no desire to pray; prayer was useless.

On Friday the overcast remained over Bethel, and the temperature continued to flirt with the freezing mark. Much of the grass had turned brown, and the trees stood barren and black. Some of the oaks tenaciously held on to their brown leaves, but most leaves had fallen and turned into nasty wet clumps now mingled with mud. We went to prison as usual and dutifully went to each class in the prison as usual. We saw the same people as we usually did. Except for Wade.

Wade remained in the hospital with no change in his condition.

TWENTY-THREE

"I'm not sure I'm ready for Christmas," Mom said.

It was Saturday, and we were at the kitchen table eating breakfast and getting ready for work.

I just nodded.

"I wish I hadn't gone to the party last night," she said.

I didn't know what to say, so I said nothing.

"Everybody was there with their spouse. They were all laughing and having fun. There were a lot of jokes. Since I was single, they treated me like I had leprosy."

"Was it that bad?"

"Seemed like it."

"Didn't anybody talk to you?"

"Yes. I guess the truth was that a lot of people tried to talk to me and include me in things. It just didn't work. I was the odd one with leprosy."

"What did you do?"

"I smiled. I left early. I came home. I cried. What else could I do?"

I looked down into my half-filled mug of coffee.

"I'm not sure I'm ready for Christmas," she repeated.

I wish there were no such thing as Christmas.

But there is a Christmas and it comes whether we are ready or not. On that Saturday the Salvation Army band played in front of the First State Bank of Bethel. They placed their kettle near the main door and played carols and collected donations. People smiled and nodded to one another and wished each other a merry Christmas. There were signs around the band that read Joy to the World and Peace on Earth.

But despite the optimism, joy did not exist in the country. President Johnson had renamed Cape Canaveral as Cape Kennedy, as if we needed another reminder that a president had been murdered. Clearly there would be no joy this Christmas season.

And not only was there no joy; there was no peace. Peace did not exist in the little gray house on Church Street.

I noted the festivities and the carols and the singing as I walked to work, and I watched as people stuffed bills and dropped coins into the army's kettle. I wished there were no Christmas season. I wanted to be left alone, left alone by Christmas and by God.

The band played "God Rest Ye Merry, Gentlemen" as I crossed Main Street and walked east toward Cornett Ford. The day was still overcast, but the streets were dry, and this fueled the hope for better weather.

During the past few days, the dealership had received a '60 Chevy and a '57 Pontiac as trades toward new Fords. These cars had been parked on the north side of the lot facing Maple Street. Scotty was not there that morning, but I understood what I needed to do. I uncoiled the hose and began to wash the cars. I got wet and cold, and my hands felt numb.

"Hey, kid." It was Big Joe.

"Hi."

"How many cars do you have to wash?"

"Just these two, I think."

"Looks like the Chevy's done," he said.

"Just finished."

"I was told I could have you for a while."

"Okay."

"You wouldn't mind working inside, would you?"

"No, sir."

"You look cold," he said.

"I am."

"Well, come along. We'll warm you up."

I followed him inside the shop.

"We weren't able to clean up last night," he said. "Get a broom and sweeping compound and begin."

"Yes, sir."

I sprinkled the compound around, especially on the oily places, then began sweeping. Two mechanics worked today. One was working on an older Studebaker and the other on a '54 Ford. I enjoyed watching mechanics work on cars, but I did not tarry too long. I had overheard Big Joe telling Mr. Cornett that I was a hard worker, and I did not want to lose that reputation. The overhead furnaces blew hot air, and soon I dried out and felt warm.

After I swept, I carried boxes of parts from the back door, where they had been left yesterday afternoon, to the parts room behind the service area. I then swept the showroom floor and emptied wastebaskets. I paused at the Model A.

Big Joe went home by late morning and the mechanics went home too, so I ate lunch alone. Only Mr. Cornett and several salesmen were left on the lot.

After lunch I went back outside to wash the Pontiac. The day had grown darker, and I became cold as I hosed down the car. The Pontiac was quite dirty, so it took a great deal of scrubbing to clean it up. Traffic up and down Maple Street was light, and I paid no attention to it.

"Hello, Matt."

I looked up. Pastor Greg had left the main building and was walking toward me. I half waved, then returned my attention to the Pontiac to complete its final rinsing. I did not notice the slow-moving car on Maple Street until I heard the door open. I turned around in time to see a bucket of soupy mud splash on the Chevy. Before I could react, another hit the Pontiac. Then a third bucket of slop hit the Chevy again.

"Matt, my boy, you've done a very poor job of cleaning these cars." Colby gave me a big grin. "You need to get these cleaned up."

The driver of the car let out a hearty laugh. I noticed that it was Colby's older brother. Colby got back in the car, and they drove off.

The mud had splattered both cars. Mud was everywhere, even on several nearby cars. The Chevy got nailed bad—the windshield, the driver's side, the roof, and the hood. The Pontiac was not as bad.

I was relieved I had not been the target. Very relieved.

I took the hose and rinsed off the Pontiac and the other cars, getting most of the mud off. However, the Chevy was a different matter. I was able to hose much of it off, but I would have to wash the rest off and wipe the entire car down again. I was handicapped by not yet having the power sprayer available to me, and I would not have that until the remodeling of the detail area was complete.

"Looks like you have a little trouble," Pastor Greg said.

I merely sighed.

"Here. I'll help." He took the bucket of water and began wiping the mud off the Chevy that refused to be hosed. "That's Stanley, isn't it?"

"Yes."

"Haven't seen him for a while."

After a few minutes, Greg stood back from his work. "Hose it off. I think we've got it."

I hosed and the car came out clean.

He checked the Pontiac. "This one seems all right," he said.

"We now need to wipe them down." *We? Did I say we?*

"All right," he said.

He took a rag and began on the Pontiac while I worked on the Chevy for the second time that day. I had a nagging feeling that Colby would find his way back with more mud and more work. I kept watching the traffic on Maple Street.

"Think they'll come back?" he asked.

"Maybe."

"You can't worry about such things," Pastor Greg said.

"I am worried."

"If they come back, we'll call Chief Brewer. We know who they are."

I kept watching Maple Street as I wiped the Chevy.

"Were those the two who threw mud on Wade?" he asked.

"Stanley was one of them. Squareface was the other."

"Who?"

"Squareface," I said. "Ronnie Kindle."

"Oh. You've brought Stanley to church. I don't believe I know Ronnie."

"How do you know about the mud on Wade?" I asked.

"Wendell told me."

"What did he say?"

"Just that two boys threw mud on Wade. I found out from Elaine that the incident was what put him in the hospital."

"Do you know how he is?"

"They think he'll be just fine. I was there this morning and saw him. The doctor is talking about letting him come home tomorrow. He may go to school on Tuesday or Wednesday."

"So he's not going to die?"

"No, Matt. Though he might have. Between that incident and his medication, we almost lost him."

"But he's going to be all right?"

Pastor Greg stopped working and looked directly at me.

"Yes, Matt," he said after a long pause. "He should be fine."

I knew I should feel happy for Wade, but I did not feel anything. I did not feel happy, relieved from guilt, angry he would be alive to bother me again, happy that he still had life, thankful, or any other feeling. I only felt cold and numb.

"I'm glad to hear it," I said.

I finished wiping the Chevy, turned the wash bucket upside down, then sat on the bucket in front of the car and watched traffic on Maple Street.

Pastor Greg squatted beside me. He wore good slacks that were now wet and spotted with a little mud. "Looks like we both have had our share of mud," he said.

"How's that?"

"You have mud on cars. I have mud on people."

"You mean all the church turmoil?" I asked.

He nodded. "It was all so unnecessary."

"I guess."

"Had I just resigned from the school board before the meeting started, maybe . . ."

"So what really happened?" I asked. "What was going on?"

"What was going on?" He scratched the back of his head. "What was going on was that almighty God was rebuking His little, immature pastor."

"You mean Jack and Forest weren't the problem?"

He stood up and stretched. "I didn't say that," he said. "I said God rebuked His pastor."

"I don't understand."

He looked down Maple Street, even though there was absolutely nothing there to hold anybody's attention. "When I was little, I lived in an internment camp. Manzanar. It was for Japanese Americans. During World War II. Established by the USA. Established by that government of the people, by the people, for the people. It was an awful experience. My family lost everything. My father became a broken man. He never recovered. When I was little, I vowed to go into politics. Make things better. Maybe even become president."

"So what's wrong with that?"

Pastor Greg squatted back down and looked at me. "Nothing's wrong with that. It's just that when I was in high school, I became a Christian. And later I knew God had called me to preach. That's why I went to Bible college and seminary."

"So it's wrong for Christians to get into politics?"

He shook his head. "It's not wrong. I believe it is essential for Christians to get into politics. I believed it when I preached it then, and I believe it now."

"So it's wrong for pastors to get into politics?"

"Not at all. Pastors may get into politics if God calls them into politics."

"Well, what was the problem then?"

"The problem was me. I had lost my focus. I was more interested in the political process than the gospel.

The school board was just going to be a stepping-stone for me. For greater things."

I scanned Maple Street. I didn't want to be caught flat-footed by more mud.

"I should not have run for the school board," he said.

"'Caesar over Christ'?"

"That one hurt. Maybe I would say that I just let my past get in the way of the present. Regardless, there was truth in the charge."

"So Jack and Forest were right?" I looked at him.

Pastor Greg glanced back down Maple Street with that faraway gaze. He then looked back at me, shaking his head. "Remember when Joseph's brothers sold him into slavery, and afterward they were under his authority in Egypt? And even though his brothers had meant evil against him, remember how Joseph told them that 'God meant it unto good'? That verse has application in this situation. In fact, that verse has application in any situation where bad things happen."

"I don't understand."

"Regardless of why Jack and Forest did what they did, God used the incident to get me back on the right track."

"So what about you?"

"What about me?"

"I mean, what can you do about it all? The mess and everything."

"I pray. I give God time to change hearts. I repent of what was in my heart. I tell people what I did wrong. I ask for forgiveness. I love people more. I serve them more faithfully. You see, I was upholding doctrine higher than people."

"And that's wrong?"

Pastor Greg smiled. "If I have all knowledge and all faith but have not love, I am nothing."

"I still don't understand. I thought Jack and Forest caused all of the trouble. I saw Forest try to cheat Mrs. Dunlap in his store."

"I'm not saying Jack and Forest are faultless. What they did that night was wrong. The hurt they caused was . . . was awful."

The bucket felt uncomfortable, but I did not move. I scanned Maple Street again.

"I should have stopped that as well," he added. "But you must understand—my rebuke was not from them. Or from the church. It was from God."

"Is he guilty?"

"Who?"

"Forest. Is he guilty of . . . ?"

"Matt, I'm not at liberty to talk about any of that," Pastor Greg said.

I suppose not.

We sat quietly for a minute—or rather I sat while he squatted. We watched a lone Rambler drive down the street.

"When Christians don't act Christlike," Pastor Greg finally said, "it damages the name of Christ among non-Christians. Let me give you a for instance. Let's say you witness to somebody in town about Christ, but they are not interested because somebody in your church did something to them. How would you handle it?"

"Did something? Like what?"

"I don't know. Stole something or lied to them or something."

"Or they were having an affair with."

He looked directly at me.

"Or were having an affair with," he finally said.

Since God doesn't care, why should I?

"I don't know what I'd do," I said at last.

"Well, obviously they need to focus on Christ, not us fallible church people. The claims of Christ are true regardless of how we live. Regardless if we even believe them or not. Christ is still true."

"So is this what happened?"

"Matt, that was just a for instance. I just wanted to show you that it is an awful thing when Christians don't act Christlike. There are terrible consequences. Consequences beyond the immediate sin. Consequences that affect people in ways you don't even realize."

"So what really happened?"

"Like I said, what really happened is that a pastor was too preoccupied with school politics to handle a problem that was brewing within his church. The result was a mess with a lot of hurt people. A lot of mud."

I shivered. It was not wise to sit cold and wet.

"And about Forest," Pastor Greg added, "I will tell you what I already have publicly said. Whatever rumors there are, they are just that. Rumors. They should not be repeated. No proof has ever been presented and should not be repeated. I am sorry they have circulated around the community. I am very sorry all of this boiled over."

Greg stood back up and stretched. "I sure miss your dad. And his marine ways. He would not have been intimidated by any of this. Especially by Forest and Jack. He would have kept this from happening."

"He would have?"

"Oh yes. Your dad always said that the Christian life is true. It will make the impossible times possible. He always believed in a down-to-earth Christianity. He lived it. And he would have kept all this from getting out of hand."

I looked up Maple Street.

"As for me," he said, "I'm afraid my days are numbered here in Bethel. I may have survived a vote. But my ministry suffered a setback. In case you haven't noticed, a few people have left the church. If any more go or ask me to go, I'll have to."

"Why? You still have a large majority."

"I can't destroy the body of Christ over this. I'm the expendable one here."

"You shouldn't let this get you down," I said.

"No, I shouldn't," he said. "I should be like Wade. He doesn't let things get him down."

"I suppose he doesn't."

"You know, Wade has sure taught me a lot of things. In fact it's as if God sent him here for the sole purpose of teaching us a few things."

"What could he teach? He's kind of dumb." I instantly regretted having said that.

"He's not dumb," Greg said.

I did not look at him but I felt his stare. "I didn't mean it that way," I lied.

"Wade is right about being thankful. He sure has taught me quite a lesson."

"Yes," I said. "He is thankful for everything."

"Yes, he is."

"Or so he says."

"No," Pastor Greg said, "he definitely is thankful. And that's quite a testimony."

"A testimony?"

"Sure. With his past and all."

"What about his past?" I asked.

"You know, about how he got the way he is."

"What do you mean?"

"You don't know about his past?" he asked.

"What about it?"

"The injury. The adoption."

"What are you talking about?"

"I'm sorry, Matt. I thought you knew."

"About what?"

Greg stretched again and rocked on his heels. "Wade was born a perfectly healthy baby. Did you know that?"

I took my eyes off Maple Street and looked back at Pastor Greg. "No, I didn't know that."

"Well, he was. He was born perfectly healthy. Do you know about Elaine and Arthur?"

"I guess not."

"Elaine and Arthur had been married for many

years, but they could not have any children. Elaine
had problems."

I had never heard this.

"Elaine Scott worked as a registered nurse in a hospital in San Antonio," he continued. "Well, Wade was
born a healthy baby. One month later he was admitted
back into the hospital. He had been beaten by a drunken
father and suffered serious brain damage. They thought
he would die. He has suffered from cerebral palsy ever
since. No charges were brought against the father, though
everybody knew what happened. The family had been
in trouble for various other things, so they willingly gave
the boy up for adoption if the authorities would leave
them alone."

"Wade is adopted?"

"Yes. The Scotts immediately offered to adopt him."

"They adopted him, knowing he had brain damage?"

"Yes, they did."

"I didn't know."

"Well, his given names were Wade and Hampton.
The Scotts saw no reason to change them, so they
didn't. Apparently Wade Hampton was a very capable
Southern general in the Civil War. As Wade grew older,
he took a keen interest in the general and apparently has
read a great deal about him."

"Does Wade know he is adopted?" I asked.

"Yes. Wade knows all about his past."

"And he is thankful for it?"

"Absolutely. Hasn't he ever told you about it?"

"No."

"Well, growing up, he had a hard time with his handicap. His injuries made him dull and slow. And on top of everything else, he had heart problems and poor health, possibly a result of his injuries. Who knows? Anyway, he would watch other kids, and he would long to be able to run and play like them. He said he would give anything to be normal."

"Have you ever wished you were like your best friend?"

"I w-want to be like you, M-Matt. You run f-fast."

"So he just had a hard time with everything. Arthur and Elaine took him to church, but he did not respond to the gospel. So one night a few years ago, their pastor went over to visit. He asked Wade if he wanted to receive Christ as his Savior. Wade said no. The pastor asked why. Wade said that Christ could have kept him normal, but He didn't.

"The wise pastor showed him the Scripture that says, 'in everything give thanks.' He then explained to Wade if he had not been injured, he would never have been adopted by the Scotts. And if the Scotts never adopted him, he'd probably never have been taken to church. And if he had never been taken to church, he might never have had the opportunity to receive Christ. The pastor asked him if he would be willing to suffer any handicap just to receive salvation plus all Christ had to offer him.

"These were very tough questions for a handicapped boy to understand. But Wade did understand them. He received Christ as his Savior that very night. And starting that night, he has given thanks for everything, including his handicap, the very thing in his life that hurts the most."

"So we're supposed to give thanks for everything?"

"Actually, Scripture says 'in everything give thanks,' not *for* everything. You give thanks that Christ is your Lord and Savior, in spite of your circumstances. I thought you knew about Wade."

"No," I said. "I didn't know this."

"Well, it's quite a testimony. I'm embarrassed to say he has taught me a great deal."

"I'm glad he's all right," I said.

"Did you know he believes he has been called to preach?"

"Yes. He has mentioned that."

"You have too, Matt."

I stood up. "Things have changed that."

"I don't think anything has changed God's call in your life."

"I don't want to talk about it," I said.

I gathered up the bucket and rags, carried them over to the outside hydrant, unhooked the hose, coiled it up, then carried everything back inside. I just up and left Pastor Greg outside. I went to Mr. Cornett's office and knocked on his open door.

"Come in, Matt."

"Is there anything else for me to do today?"

"No. That's fine. Did Pastor Greg find you?"

"Yes. He even helped clean the cars."

"He did?"

I explained what Colby had done and how Pastor Greg had helped.

"Don't worry about it, Matt. If anything else happens, I'll take care of it."

"Thanks."

"Are you in a hurry?" Mr. Cornett asked.

"Yes." I really wasn't.

"Well, sometime I want to talk to you about all of this. You know, the mud throwing at Cathy and Wade."

"Yes, sir."

I had worked Tuesday, and Mr. Cornett paid me for the week. I now had more than enough money to pay Mom back, and I intended to do so that very afternoon. I glanced out the back before I left but did not see Pastor Greg. He had probably walked home, for the Baptist parsonage was located just two blocks west of the dealership on Maple Street.

Traffic was light on Main Street. The Salvation Army had left because the bank closed early on Saturdays.

"I don't think anything has changed God's call in your life."

I did not feel like running or doing anything, so I walked home, where I took a hot shower. Later I just sat in the living room and looked out at the gloom.

TWENTY-FOUR

On a Sunday morning in the December of that year, we walked to Bethel Baptist Church. The day had a raw feel to it, but inside the church felt warm, and there was a musty smell from the furnace stirring up mold and dust. We looked around and saw Christmas decorations, but we did not see Pastor Greg.

Wendell Cornett greeted the saints that morning.

"Where's Pastor?" Mom asked him.

"At the hospital."

"Why?"

"Paula started bleeding in the night. She's having trouble with the baby."

"Oh no. And the baby?" Mom softly asked.

"Don't know. Just don't know about either of them."

"She's had a hard time with the baby," Mom said.

"Yes, she has."

"Poor dear. She's early. Oh my." Mom put a hand to her mouth. She looked like she was about to cry.

"I'll ask the church to pray for them. Pastor called me early this morning and asked me to preach. We didn't have time to find a substitute. I'm no preacher, but I'll try to give a message. Mostly we'll just pray." Mr. Cornett turned to me. "Good morning, Mr. Collins."

"Good morning, Mr. Cornett." I shook his firm hand.

"How are you this morning?"

"Just fine, sir."

I walked down to my Sunday school class and pondered the news. Whatever faults Pastor Greg had—whether it was immaturity, greenness, or whatever—I would at least concede that he was sincere and loved God.

Is there any reason to pray? God has such a poor record of taking care of those who serve Him.

After Sunday school I took up my usual place in the back of the church. I was quite content to merely observe how God was going to handle this new crisis with one of His servants. Prayer was pointless; it had already proved itself ineffective.

The saints assembled for Sunday morning service; Forest and Cindy Parker were not present. Grandma Pine sat with Mom and Debbie near the front. A hushed, somber mood hung over the church. Mr. Cornett kept his promise. After the singing of several hymns, he gave a ten-minute message on the need for salvation, basing his text on John 3:16. After the message, he asked several men of the church to pray for Greg, Paula, and the baby. Wendell then canceled Sunday evening service, and church was dismissed. The time was 11:40.

We all walked home, somber and quiet. Mom had earlier prepared a roast, and dinner was ready in no time.

"Glad you could join us," Mom said to Grandma.

We sat at the table, ready to begin.

"I always enjoy dinner with you and the kids," she said.

"I like having you," Debbie said. "Mom, can I pray?"

"Sure, dear."

"Let's all bow our heads," Debbie said. "Dear Lord, we thank You for our food, and please help Pastor and Mrs. Pastor. Please have everything go all right and the baby be all right too. Please, dear Lord. Amen."

"Thank you, Debbie," Mom said.

Later in the afternoon, the sun attempted to break through the overcast, but the day remained cold and crisp. Even though the temperature was a few degrees below freezing, the dirt road was soft. I wore my old shoes and ran down the road, but mud would cling to the shoes, then fling off. Mud made the shoes heavy and slowed me down. I ran the best I could all the way down the road, then all the way back. I jogged back home on the gravel road.

When I reached the pavement of Church Street, I saw the Scotts pull into their driveway. Mr. Scott, Mrs. Scott, and Wade all got out of the car. Mr. Scott helped Wade up the front steps and into the house.

So Wade's all right after all.

I suppose he is.

That evening, after a light meal, the phone rang and Debbie answered. "Hello? . . . Hi, Grandma. . . . Just a minute. Mom? Grandma's on the phone."

Mom hurried into the kitchen and grabbed the

phone. "Hi. . . . She did? . . . Praise the Lord. . . . Well, good. . . . How big? . . . What's his name? . . . I sure will. . . . She will? . . . Wonderful. . . . Okay, bye."

"What was that about, Mommy?" Debbie asked.

"Paula had her baby."

"Well, tell us!" she squealed.

"She had a boy. Five pounds, two ounces. They named him Benjamin."

"They had a boy?"

"Paula's doing great," Mom said. "She's doing so well that she may even get to come home Tuesday."

"Will we get to see him?"

"Probably not right away."

"Oh, Mom."

"Be patient, dear," Mom said. "You'll get to see him."

"And hold him?"

"I'm sure."

"Isn't it great, Matt?" Debbie asked.

"I suppose."

"Matt?" Mom asked. "Is something wrong?"

"No," I said. "I'm glad it turned out all right for them." I then went to my room.

Can you beat that?

I shook my head. There was no accounting for how God might work. Some come home from the hospital. Some do not. Wade came home. Paula and Benjamin would come home.

"I'm sorry, Mrs. Collins, but your husband is . . ."

Others do not come home.

❖

Wade did not go to school on Monday or Tuesday. I was glad I did not have to see him.

Rain fell on Tuesday—cold rain. Debbie caught the flu and had a very rough time of it. Mom stayed home from work to be with her. After school, I worked at Cornett Ford and did not get home until nearly six o'clock.

"Is it raining?" Mom asked when I walked into the kitchen.

"Not at the moment."

"Good. Can you take this basket over to Greg and Paula's? Please? I want to stay with Debbie."

"Sure."

"Come right home. I'll have a hot dinner for you."

"All right."

The basket contained hot food for the Yoshidas to help them out since Paula and Benjamin had just come home. The ladies of the church always coordinated meals when a new baby arrived.

Or when somebody died.

"And, Matt?"

"Yes?"

"Be sure to get a complete report on the new mommy and baby."

"Okay." I grabbed the basket and headed to the parsonage. The night was cold and dark, and by the time I crossed Main Street, a drizzle began to fall. I reached the parsonage and knocked.

Pastor Greg answered. "Hello, Matt," he said.

"Here's a meal for you."

"Why, thanks."

"You probably need to heat it up some," I said.

"No problem."

"Mom wants a complete report on everybody."

"Can you come in for a minute?"

"I'd rather not. A hot dinner is waiting for me at home."

"Tell her everybody is just fine."

"I sure will."

I started off the front porch, back out in the drizzle.

"And, Matt?" he said.

"Yes?"

"Tell everybody thanks for praying. Thank you for praying."

"I didn't pray." I knew I shouldn't have said that. Perhaps I was tired, cold, and hungry. Perhaps I could only speak the truth. Yet for whatever reason, I did say it.

"What?" he asked.

"I didn't pray."

Pastor Greg walked out onto the porch, still holding the basket, and closed the front door behind him. "I'm curious, Matt. Why didn't you?"

"Why should I? I mean, nothing personal, but isn't God going to do whatever He wants? What good is my prayer?"

"Your prayer does a lot of good," he said.

"Oh? I can change the mind of God?"

I had him. Pastor took a deep breath. "Prayer does

not move God," he said. "Prayer moves us. Prayer moves us out of the way so God can work. Prayer helps to conform us to God's will. God does not need prayer. We need prayer. Anyway, we are to cast our cares on Him."

"And what good will that do?"

He shook his head. "Matt, ever since the accident, you have been very confused about God."

"No, sir. Ever since the accident, I have seen things very clearly."

"We pray because we have a very loving heavenly Father," Pastor Greg said.

"We may have a heavenly Father, but *loving* is not the correct word."

"We all need a loving heavenly Father."

"I don't need anybody," I said. "I don't need God anymore. He certainly doesn't need me."

"Matt!" He set the basket down on the porch under the light and took several steps toward me.

I took several steps along the sidewalk.

"Matt!"

I turned around. The drizzle turned into a gentle, cold rain. Pastor stood on the top step of the porch. The rain fell on him, too. I could tell he was trying to collect his thoughts. Probably from some sound wisdom he learned in seminary that made excellent sense in the classroom but had no bearing in the real world of Bethel. Perhaps seminaries are really prisons also, just like high schools.

"You're not the only person who has ever suffered," he said. "Everybody—"

"Tell me this," I said. "Dad was a good man. He tried to serve God, but God let him die. So why? Tell me why."

"I don't know—"

"That's the first correct thing you've said. You don't know."

"I don't know all the reasons. But I do know some things." I could tell his great education was failing him.

"No. You tell me why my dad had to die. What wonderful divine plan did he have to fulfill by dying? Tell me."

"Maybe you're asking the wrong question."

"I think I'm asking a very good question."

"Maybe you should ask, why don't we all die? Why aren't we all consumed in a moment? We all are sinners. We live in a fallen world. We all deserve—"

"No! Tell me why he had to die!"

"I—"

"You don't know," I said. "Just don't tell me God is loving. I know better." I took a couple more steps toward Maple Street. I could see sheets of rain in the streetlights.

Pastor Greg walked down the steps to the sidewalk. "God is kind and loving," he said.

"Tell me where the love of God was that night!"

"Matt, I don't—"

"I was there! You were not there!"

"God was there."

"I was there! God was not!"

The rain fell harder. I could see Pastor Greg was about to be soaked to the skin.

"Matt—"

"Have you ever had a highway patrolman wake you up in the wee hours of the morning? Have you?"

"No. But I've had—"

"I have. How would you like to hear, 'Mrs. Collins, there has been a terrible accident'? I heard that! I was there!"

We both were soaked, but we kept standing in the rain as if neither of us had good sense. It fell hard. At least I had a coat on. "They said, 'Mrs. Collins, there has been a terrible accident. Could you please come with us?' It was awful. 'Matt!' she called. 'Stay with me. I need you. We'll take Debbie to Grandma's.' And there was more. 'Mrs. Collins, we need you to identify the body.' I heard all of that. I was there!"

"God was there too," Greg said.

"God was not there! I did not see God! But I did see the body! Did anybody ever tell you what that looked like? We couldn't recognize him. He had been thrown from the car. It was awful! I saw it! Mom threw up all over everything. I thought I would too. It was a mess. Do you know what it smelled like? With puke over everything? She threw up, and I just knew I would too. I don't know how I managed not to. I was sick enough to. I was there that night, Pastor. Tell me where God was. Tell me!"

He stood there silently. I thought he might be crying, but I could not tell.

"Then Mom passed out. I was holding on to her arm, and a good thing because she just gave way. Her legs gave out under her. I kept her from hitting the floor.

They had to help. Puke everywhere and she passed out. I was there! God was not!"

I walked to the street. He did not follow.

I turned back around. "I heard a lot of other things that night. They said, 'closed casket.' Do you know what that means? They said, 'I'm sorry, Mrs. Collins, but this needs to be a closed-casket funeral.' This meant that Dad was in such poor condition that they couldn't make him look presentable. How would you like to hear those words? Say them, Pastor, if you dare. *Closed casket.* Say them! How would you like to hear those words at three o'clock in the morning?" I was shouting now.

He merely stood and listened.

"Hell exists, Pastor. I was there. I was in it."

"Hell is far worse than that night."

"Are you saying this from personal experience? Were you ever there? I was! I was there that night."

"Matt," Greg said, "you can't just shake your fist at God."

"Oh yes, I can!"

"You're missing something. About God."

"I'm not missing anything. I saw it all that night!"

"God loves you. That's why Christ died for you. For us."

"I saw no love that night."

"So tell me then: why are you a Christian?"

"Good question. I don't know."

"Do you wish you weren't?"

"I don't know!"

He stood there in the rain, probably trying to gather

his thoughts to pontificate theology. However, his Christian theory had never been put to the test of the real world.

"The love of God was there that night," he finally said, "and Jesus Christ offers you peace."

"Peace?"

"Just a prayer away. Matt, sometimes it takes courage to pray."

"Pray? Can't you see? God can't be trusted!"

"Maybe you became a Christian for the wrong reason. Did you become a Christian so you could have an accident-free life? Or did you become a Christian because Matt Collins was a sinner in desperate need of a Savior? Maybe you have also been praying to the wrong God. The God of the Bible does allow bad things to happen. The God of the Bible does not save us from bad things but rather saves us in spite of bad things. But the God of the Bible promises to be with us through the bad things."

"I was there! I saw the body! It looked worse than hamburger. The smell, the mess—everything! It was awful. God was not there!"

"Matt," he said, "peace is reaching out to you. Just reach out and take it."

"What do you know about peace? What do you know about life? Has your mother thrown up all over you? Do the words *closed casket* mean anything to you? 'I'm sorry, Mrs. Collins, but your husband is dead'! Dead! Gone! Forever!" I turned and headed back in the direction of Main Street.

"You have to look at life from the cross," Pastor Greg called. "If you don't, then nothing makes sense."

I kept walking.

"At the cross," he said, "you see Jesus for who He is, and you see yourself as you truly are."

I think he said many more things, but I could no longer hear, for I was well on my way home. I could see there was no need to continue the conversation. Pastor Greg did not live in the real world. His training did not prepare him for what actually happens. I was happy his wife and new son were all right. I wished them all well. But I also knew that he did not have to hear the words I'd had to hear or see the destroyed body I'd had to see or witness the devastated lives around me or smell the same things I'd had to smell or be puked all over. So how would he know? How *could* he know?

The rain continued to fall, and I was entirely soaked and cold. I jogged back home to a warm shower and a hot meal.

Later that night, when I went to bed, my troubled soul would not allow me to fall asleep. Increasingly I was having more difficulty sleeping.

Peace on earth?

Peace was a word that I knew the meaning of but did not have any firsthand experience with, at least none I could remember. Peace did not exist in my life.

TWENTY-FIVE

The rain stopped on Wednesday, and the temperature dropped below freezing. Ice clung to utility poles and street signs and covered the brown grass. The trees, too, were covered with ice, and they looked frozen and barren and dead.

Wade returned to school that day. He looked a little paler than usual; otherwise he seemed the same. He scuffed into English class just as the bell rang.

"Good morning, Mr. Scott," Miss Edmonds said.

"G-good m-morning."

"It is good to see you back."

"I'm th-thankful to b-be back."

After class I said nothing to him but checked to make sure the locker was secured. Now that Colby was in the mud business—or worse—security had to be tight. I did not even attempt to communicate this to Wade. He truly lived in a world all his own.

He did not go back to the locker where I was but shuffled on toward his second-hour class.

I did not feel bad for what I had said to him, at least not bad enough to apologize. I wondered what it might be like to be born healthy, then through no fault of your own be beaten into a serious handicap. Perhaps no different than to be an excellent driver and through no fault of your own meet a drunk driver head-on at the top of a hill.

Squareface avoided both of us, and that was just fine. Perhaps Wade's serious hospital stay had changed Squareface, too. Perhaps not. A coward can be hard to predict.

I kept a sharp lookout for Colby in the halls. I often saw him, but I kept my distance to avoid any confrontation.

The school's annual Christmas dance, to be held Saturday, December 21, was the major topic buzzing throughout the school. Baptist kids don't dance, and I normally would not have given the event any thought. But this year was different. I looked the girls over in all of my classes. If I could go—if I even wanted to go—who would I ask? Who would I want to go with?

I knew the answer. She was attractive, had blue eyes, often wore a ponytail, and had a peaceful heart. I had gone to church and school with Catherine my whole life. I began to look at her in a different way. If I could ask a girl to the dance, I'd ask Cathy.

So one week before Christmas, at the end of the school day, I was approaching my locker when I realized I had left my notebook in my last-hour class. I stopped and tried to decide whether to go back and get it now or just get my coat out of the locker, fetch the notebook, and carry it home. I was debating and did not notice the crowd around the locker.

"You want to see me, Nerd?" The voice snapped me back to reality. It was Colby's.

"Y-yes."

"What do you want? What's so important?"

I reached the edge of the crowd. Colby was there, along with Squareface and perhaps a dozen other students.

Wade looked up and saw me, then faced Colby. "W-want to b-bet?"

"Bet?" Colby looked irritated.

"I b-bet twenty d-dollars that M-Matt can outrun you."

My heart stopped.

"Twenty dollars? Where did a nerd like you get twenty dollars?"

Colby asked a good question. Where had Wade got twenty dollars?

"I bet M-Matt is f-faster."

"Collins? Faster? You've lost your mind."

My mouth hung open. I couldn't believe this was happening. I simply could not believe it.

"I bet M-Matt is f-faster. Twenty d-dollars."

Colby looked puzzled, uncertain how to take this challenge.

"Two m-miles. Down the d-dirt road and b-back."

"Two miles?" Colby waved his hand at Wade and turned to walk away. "You're a waste of time."

"Twenty d-dollars."

Colby stopped and considered. Twenty dollars was a small fortune.

"You n-not s-scared, are you?"

"No way," he snapped.

"You have t-twenty dollars?"

"Of course. But I won't need it. You will need yours. How do I know you have twenty dollars?"

"I-I have the m-money. You b-bet?"

Colby hesitated.

"You s-scared, aren't y-you?"

"No way!"

"You'll r-race, then?"

"I'm in."

"How b-bout it, M-Matt?" Wade turned toward me.

Colby looked and saw me for the first time.

Everybody turned and looked at me.

"M-my twenty d-dollars against Colby's t-twenty dollars."

I stared at all of them, frozen.

"Two m-miles. Down the d-dirt road and b-back."

"What's the matter, Collins?" Colby taunted. "You yellow?"

"No."

"You in? Of course, it'll be like taking candy from a baby. Or in this case, a nerd."

"Wade," I began. My mind went entirely blank.

"Th-that's okay, M-Matt. I-I have the twenty d-dollars."

"Look. Collins is yellow."

"I'll race. When?"

"S-Saturday."

"Saturday is a bad day," Colby said. "The dance and all. Make it Sunday."

"Sunday?" I said.

"Or are you goody-goodies too goody good to race on Sunday?"

"S-Sunday w-will be f-fine."

I stared at Wade. I couldn't believe him. Wagering? And on Sunday?

"O-one o'clock, after ch-church."

"One o'clock. At the dirt road. See you there, Collins. You too, Nerd. And anybody else who wants to be there. And don't forget your money, Nerd." Colby walked off, and Squareface followed.

The rest of the students dispersed. I saw Cathy near her locker. She looked a little pale. I probably looked a lot paler.

I walked up to Wade. "Have you lost your mind?" I asked.

"N-need in the l-locker?"

"What are you thinking? Have you gone mad?"

"You r-run fast, M-Matt."

"You dummy," I said. "I've never beaten Colby in my life."

"You r-run a lot. H-he doesn't. H-he said he's tired of r-running."

I grabbed Wade's shoulders and stared him in the face. He wore his usual blank look. "You're nuts."

"No, M-Matt. You r-run f-fast."

I grabbed my coat, then slammed the locker. I couldn't believe this.

And you felt bad for wishing him dead?

I wheeled back toward him. "Should I stomp your face here?"

He said nothing.

"Maybe I should count to ten to cool off some, then stomp your face."

He began to shuffle toward the stairs.

I glanced at Cathy and stormed off in the opposite direction to retrieve my notebook.

Now what? Calm down. I can't beat Colby. This is a setup for disaster. Take a deep breath.

I stomped down the stairs and headed toward the cafeteria.

"Collins!" It was Coach Garrett. "Come here!" he hissed.

Oh no. I walked over to the open gym locker room door, where he was standing.

"You going out for track?" he asked.

"Track? I haven't decided."

"What do you mean you haven't decided?"

"I just don't know."

Garrett leaned on his cane and scrutinized me.

"I've got to go," I said.

"Not so fast," he said. "You're coming out for track."

"I said I don't know."

"I said you are."

"You can't make me," I said. "Besides, you don't need me. You have Colby."

"You need to break five minutes this spring. You can do it. Easy."

"Five minutes? No way. Colby can."

"Colby probably won't."

"What do you mean? Colby is your best runner. You have him."

"You're a better runner than Colby."

Better? "I've never beaten Colby in my life," I said.

"Colby is good. But he thunders. He runs like a freight train pounding by. He's not going to get any better. He has reached his peak. He doesn't even like to run. You're different. You have grace. You glide. Colby pounds."

He stood there, resting on his cane, his Chicago Cubs hat failing to conceal gray hair at his temples. He definitely wore at least two days' growth of gray beard. He reached in his shirt pocket, pulled out a toothpick, and began to chew it. I stared at him in disbelief.

"You're the better runner," he said. "By the time you graduate, nobody will remember Stanley Colby. Matthew Collins will hold the school records."

"No way."

"Listen, bud, I know what I'm talking about."

"What do you know about running? You're a cripple."

"What do I know?!" Garrett roared. "What do I know?!" He stood up straight and pointed his cane at me.

I backed up several steps.

"What do I know about running?" He slammed his cane behind him against the gym lockers. The crash sounded like a bomb explosion.

"What do I know?!" Garrett slammed his cane again; the racket was tremendous.

My heart skipped a beat.

"Get in here!" He then hobbled toward his office door. He turned back toward me. "I said get in here!"

I obeyed, too unnerved to do anything else. Death awaited me, and I knew it. This was where he would kill me. I entered the gym locker room.

Garrett took his cane and violently jabbed his office door open. The door swung open, slammed on the doorstop, and came wildly swinging back. He hit it again with his cane, and the door bounced off the stop again but this time came back only halfway. "Get in here!" He limped into his office, stomping his cane as he went.

I obediently entered his office of death but stayed in the doorway. It looked like a tornado had struck the place. Stacks of paper covered his desk, plus many stray pages that obviously had no home. Paper littered the counter behind him too, along with the residue from several lunches, his coat, and several towels.

Garrett walked to the counter, opened the cabinet above it, and pulled out a trophy. He then turned back to his desk, knocked a pile of paper onto the floor to clear off a space, then set the trophy down on the desk. "Read it!"

I walked over to the trophy. "'Leonard Garrett, Fastest Mile, State Champion, 1939.'" I looked up at him, attempting to absorb all the details.

"What do I know?" he growled. He slammed his cane against the counter, knocking off a dirty plate that shattered and another stack of papers. "I know a lot, Collins. A whole lot."

His office was in shambles. There was no possible way to make it look worse.

"And you—you are fast," he hissed.

I looked at the man before me and considered. His eyes were red, and I could not tell if he had been drinking. I looked back at the trophy. State Champion, 1939. "What happened?" I asked.

"What happened? The war, bud. The war. World War II. Ever hear of it? You know, the one your old man was in?"

I looked at him blankly, probably the same stupid look Wade used all the time.

"I was fast. Really fast. Probably faster than you. Some said I might break a four-minute mile. In those days that had never been done. And I might have too."

Garrett picked up the trophy and lovingly placed it back in the cabinet, then closed the door. He hobbled back and stood in front of his desk. "But then there was this war. I was a coward." His voice quieted. "I was a coward. Just like you."

I could feel my face getting hot.

"I was afraid to be a soldier," he said. "I was afraid of the draft. I joined the navy. I figured it would be safer. Cowards always do the safe thing."

He hobbled over to a shelf on the other side of his desk and picked up a plastic model of an aircraft carrier. Behind it was a can of red spray paint, missing the lid, with dried paint down the side. "Have you ever heard of the *Yorktown*, Collins?"

I looked back at the model and nodded.

"What was it?" Garrett asked.

"An aircraft carrier?"

"Good guess. Looked like this." He placed the model on his desk. "I met your dad once at a meet."

I took my eyes off the model and placed them squarely on Garrett's gruff face and red eyes.

"He never was on the *Yorktown*," he said. "But he was on other carriers. Now your dad—he was a coward too, I found out."

I was getting angry.

"Everybody's a coward."

I thought about kicking him hard.

"But your dad—he learned about courage. You see, bud, all courage is, is to recognize you are a coward but do the task anyway, regardless of how you feel. That's all courage is. Your dad found it. He told me about landing on Iwo Jima. He was afraid. In fact, he was terrified. Do you know what he did? He grabbed his rifle, and when they said to hit the beaches, he hit the beaches. When they said move out, he moved out. That's courage."

I looked back at the model.

"What do you know about the *Yorktown*, Collins?"

"Not a lot. It got sunk, didn't it?"

Grunting, Garrett picked up the model and placed it on the counter where there was room. He then returned to his perch in front of the desk. "Ever hear of *Coral Sea*? I was a seaman on that carrier during the battle." He gestured at his model.

"Those—" He caught his word. Everybody knew that if he said just one more foul word, he'd be fired. "They almost sunk us," he amended. "They shot us up bad."

Garrett pointed his cane at me. "Do you want to know what fear is? I know what fear is. Firsthand. Every Jap plane in creation came down on us. I was terrified. They almost sunk the ship."

"What happened?"

"We limped back to Pearl Harbor. I was overjoyed. I was alive. I knew it would be months and months before she could ship again. You have no idea how happy I was to reach Pearl."

He lowered his cane. "But guess what?" he hissed. "They stopped the worst of the leaks and shipped us back out. To Midway. I couldn't believe it. That's—" He caught himself again. "That's tough for a coward."

I stared at the floor. Trash and corruption were everywhere. I glanced back at the can of red paint.

"Well, at Midway they hit us again. Twice. This time we weren't so lucky. The ship sunk. I got hit. Chunks of steel in my leg and back. Five operations, bud! I had five operations! They said I'd never walk again. Well, I can walk some. But I have one short leg and one normal leg. My running was over. Forever."

"I'm sorry."

"Me too," Garrett said. "But what do I know about running? I know a lot about running. And a lot about cowards. And a lot about churches."

"Churches?"

"Your church destroyed my home."

"My church? Destroyed?"

"Yeah, your church. Your stupid church. That Jap pastor of yours. Came around looking for my wife. Can you imagine? He broke up my home."

"Pastor Greg?" I asked.

"I'll kill him if I get a chance."

"Pastor Greg?" I repeated.

"The little yellow belly gets paint on his sign, then tucks his tail between his legs and runs. Resigns off the board. Coward!"

I looked back at the can of spray paint.

"First the Japs destroy my life," he said. "Then they destroy my home. And they even keep me from getting a raise."

"His wife just left him. She may have been having an affair."

"Adultery! Forest Parker is guilty of adultery!"

"Let's say you witness to somebody in town about Christ, but they are not interested because somebody in your church did something to them. . . . Or were having an affair with. . . ."

Garrett's wife? With Forest Parker?

"I think you have it all wrong," I said.

"I have nothing wrong."

"Yes, you have Pastor Greg all wrong. He did not destroy your home. He was trying to save it."

"I don't have him wrong," he said. "Or your stupid church. The only thing I had wrong was you."

"Me?"

"Yeah, you. You were supposed to be different.

When you first came to this school, everybody told me to watch Matt Collins. Matt Collins is a good kid. Matt Collins is a fast runner. They said Matt Collins was a Christian. His dad was a deacon at Bethel Baptist Church. That was before I knew the truth about your stupid church. Then your dad got killed. That was bad. So I watched Matt Collins, the Christian. I watched to see if it made a difference. I watched you in the halls. I heard the things you said. I watched how you acted. I watched how you treated people. I watched to see if being a Christian would make a difference. You know what, Collins?"

Garrett pointed his cane back at me. "Your religion didn't make any difference! You flunked Christianity!"

My gaze snapped up to meet his red eyes head-on. His indictment cut through me like a sword.

"You know what your religion is? Your religion is nothing but a pile of—" He caught himself again. "Excrement!" he finally hissed. "Worthless!"

He then slammed the desk with his cane. "Your Christianity is worthless! There is no difference between you and me! We're alike!"

He slammed the desk once again. "Worthless! And so is your church. And so is your pastor. You all stink!" He hissed his indictment like a demon might.

I took a step backward.

"Have a good pair of shoes, bud?" he asked.

I nodded.

"You're out running all the time, aren't you?"

I did not answer.

"I know more about you than you know about you. You run because you want to. You run because you love to. You run because you have to. You can't do otherwise. You're probably out running all the time."

I looked back at the shelf, at the *Yorktown*.

"So, Collins, I know a lot about running. And a lot about cowards. After the first of the year, you get your running shoes and you get your . . . get yourself over here. I'll show you how to run so by the time you graduate, you'll be flirting with four minutes. I'll even buy you good shoes if you need them."

"I have good shoes."

"Then I'll run your feet off. Now git!"

I backed out of his office and walked toward the locker room door. I stopped for a moment to regain my breath; then I tiptoed back to where I could see him. He had the cabinet door open and was gazing at the trophy. I left the locker room, found my notebook, and slowly walked home.

I did not have the nerve to ask about the can of red spray paint. In retrospect it did not really seem to matter. There were greater issues to consider.

He had truly misunderstood Pastor Greg. That was clear. But he had not misunderstood me.

Something very terrifying had just happened. It was not the crashing or shouting. It was a face. I may have been looking at Leonard Garrett, but what I saw in those bloodshot eyes was the future Matt Collins.

Then there was the race. No doubt Wade had truly set me up to get even with me. Well, I deserved it.

But something else weighed me down. Perhaps the greatest crisis of my life. Life had handed me a major test unannounced, and I had flunked. I hadn't even known I was taking a test, and I had no idea that others were watching me take it.

I had royally flunked the test.

I had flunked life.

TWENTY-SIX

So that December we braced ourselves for the onslaught of Christmas. Stores and houses in Bethel displayed Christmas decorations, and at night the lights could be seen throughout the town. You could see too the other accoutrements of the season, from cards in the mail to multiple Santa Clauses.

The church also prepared for Christmas. Mrs. Metzge planned the Christmas pageant and held practice every Sunday evening. The pageant included a Nativity scene, complete with costumes and speaking parts. Debbie was in the pageant; I was not.

We also decorated for Christmas. Though I did not want a Christmas tree, Mom and Debbie did, so they bought one. The house smelled of pine, and I watched Mom and Debbie hang lights and fragile ornaments.

Debbie threw some tinsel at the tree. Mom corrected her. Debbie then threw some tinsel at Mom. Mom responded by throwing tinsel back at her. Within seconds the two of them were giggling and throwing tinsel at each other and making a mess.

I let them play. I sneaked into the kitchen to boil

water for hot cocoa. They would want some and I would too. The two of them continued to squeal and giggle, and the smell of pine filled the house just like Christmas past. They did not notice I was missing, and I was glad, for I did not want to decorate or play. In spite of everything that had happened, both of them had a measure of the season's joy that transcended all circumstances; I did not. We had all been given an unexpected test. They had handled their tests reasonably well and passed. I had flunked mine and did not know what to do about it.

Though I flunked, it was not all my fault. God had created the problem. He needed to admit fault in this too. Yet the simple, harsh, inescapable fact was that I had failed the test.

Is life over after you flunk the test?

I returned to the living room as Debbie placed the small manger scene on the mantel and candles on either side of it. She lit the candles, and we all looked at the baby Jesus in the manger with Mary, Joseph, wise men, and shepherds standing around.

"This is what it's all about," Debbie announced.

"Yes, it is, dear," Mom said.

When the cocoa was done, we sat in the living room sipping the hot drinks and looking at the decorations. I half expected Mom to start crying, but she did not. She and Debbie just sat around and enjoyed their hot cocoa, even though both of them must have been quite warm from their romping around.

"We really have much to be thankful for," Mom said.

She noticed my questioning look. "Many things," she continued. "We've received the insurance money. Homer helped me retire the mortgage. Our money crisis is now a thing of the past."

She was sipping her drink, flushed from romping. She looked . . . well, she looked sort of pretty. And peaceful.

"God has led us through this," she whispered. "We have much to be thankful for."

Later that night, I lay in bed staring at the ceiling, but I could not sleep because of troubled thoughts.

"I've never beaten Colby in my life."

"You r-run fast, M-Matt."

"I was a coward. Just like you."

"All courage is, is to recognize you are a coward but do the task anyway."

"You're the better runner. Matthew Collins will hold the school records."

"Look. Collins is yellow."

Thought after thought continued to churn, and my mind continued to agitate and torment the tired body and prevent sweet sleep.

Christmas dance is Saturday. If you could ask a girl to the dance, who would you ask?

"I watched you. Your religion is . . . worthless!"

"You flunked Christianity!"

I'm so smart; I've never flunked a test in my life.

But I'd flunked this one. This was one test that I'd flunked with flying colors.

●◆●

The next day I tried to push out thoughts concerning the race. I said nothing to Wade and did not even see Colby. Wade had a doctor's appointment, so I walked home alone with Cathy. We approached the church, where she would cut through to her own backyard.

"You are awfully quiet," she said.

"I suppose."

"Have a lot on your mind?"

I nodded.

"Penny for your thoughts."

I wasn't entirely sure how to receive that invitation but decided to tell her anyway. Wasn't that courage? "There is something I'd like to ask you," I said.

"Sure. What is it?"

My mouth instantly became dry. I wasn't sure I could do it. But I had to say it. "This is going to sound silly," I said.

"Oh?"

"I mean, real silly."

"Matthew Collins, just say it."

"Well, I know you don't go to dances."

"True."

"And I don't either."

"Yes."

"Being Baptists and all."

"Well, there is more to it than being Baptists."

"There is?"

"Sure," she said. "But go ahead."

"Well, you don't go to dances, and I don't go to dances."

"Yes. You said that."

"But if we could go . . . I mean, if we did go . . ."

Cathy stopped walking and looked at me rather quizzically. We were in front of Bethel Baptist Church.

"I mean, if we did go and could go and it was no big deal and all . . ."

"What are you trying to say?" she asked.

"I mean, if we could go, and I know we can't and won't. But if we could go, I would . . ."

"You would what?"

"I would like to ask you to go to the dance with me," I said, "even though I know neither of us can go."

"What?"

"Even though I know we can't go, if we could go, I'd ask you to go. I just want to tell you that you'd be the girl to ask to go with me. I mean, the girl I'd ask to go with me."

She smiled slightly, her cheeks tinted, and her eyes were moist.

"I told you it would sound silly," I said.

Boy, that was stupid.

I started to walk on.

"Matt?" Cathy walked up to me.

"Do you understand what I mean?" I said. "I mean, do you know what I'm asking? Do you know what I'm trying to say?"

"Yes," she whispered, "I know what you're saying." I noticed her cheeks begin to color more.

"You'd be the girl I'd ask."

Cathy cleared her throat. Her cheeks were now full color. "Let me tell you something." She spoke barely above a whisper. She took a deep breath and paused. "If you asked me, and we really wanted to go and it was all right, I would be more than happy to accept. I would be right proud to go with you."

"'Right proud'?"

She laughed and wiped at an eye, though I saw no tear. "I read that somewhere."

"You would go with me?"

"Sure." Her eyes were very moist and full. "And, Matt?"

"Yes?"

Cathy took a deep breath. "Thanks for asking." It was almost a whisper again.

"I wanted you to know that. Even though I really wasn't asking, being we can't go and all."

She smiled.

"But, Cathy?"

"Yes?"

"Thanks for accepting."

She grabbed my right hand and pulled it out of my coat pocket. She gave it a hard squeeze with both of her hands. "Bye, Matt. See you tomorrow." She whirled and hurried to her yard.

I watched her for a minute, then headed on home. The day was cold and calm, but my hand felt very warm.

I arrived home, changed, and jogged down to the dirt road. The ground was frozen and hard and the air

crisp and still. I sprinted down the dirt road, then back
up as fast as I could. I'd forgot my stopwatch, so I did
not know my time, but I knew it would have been good
because I felt strong and fast. Though the air was cold, it
did not burn my lungs, so I pushed myself hard and I ran
well.

The next morning was dark and frigid when I walked
to school. A light fog hung in the air, and the trees were
frosted white. Though it was cold, the day felt good
and everything was beautiful. I left early so I could walk
alone. I needed solitude and did not want to have to talk
to Wade.

Once at school, I wandered around before going to
the locker. I saw Wade go into class by the time I finally
reached our locker. And, wonder of wonders, he had
secured it properly. I had hung my coat and grabbed my
books when Catherine came up to me.

"Well, Mr. Collins."

"Yes?"

"I have been instructed to offer you an invitation,"
she said.

"What?"

"You are officially invited to the Cornett home."

"Officially invited?" I asked. "What are you talking
about?"

"Would you like to come to my house tomorrow
night? We'll be baking Christmas cookies," she said. "A
family tradition. For the party at the dealership. Also,
Dad wants to talk with you."

"Baking cookies?"

"Sure. And eating them, of course."

"What kind?"

"What kind? Sugar. And some chocolate chip."

"I don't eat many cookies."

"Maybe we can make some popcorn, too."

I finally realized what she was asking. "Your dad wants to talk to me?" I asked.

"That's what he said."

"What about?"

"He didn't say."

I could guess. "And it's okay with him to come over?" I asked.

"It was his idea. So you'll come?"

"Sure."

"You know, it won't be fancy or anything like the dance."

"I don't mind. I'd be happy to come over. What time?"

"Well, the dance starts at seven. So, how about seven?"

"Seven will be fine."

"Great. See you then."

And she did see me then. At three minutes before seven o'clock on Saturday night, I stood on the front porch of the Cornett home and rang the doorbell. The porch light was on. They truly were expecting me.

Catherine answered the door. "Hi. Come in." She wore a pink dress and a pink ribbon held her ponytail. She also wore a full white apron.

"Hi."

I took off my coat, and she hung it in the closet by the front door.

"We're putting you right to work," she said.

"Work?"

"Follow me."

We walked through the living room. The upright piano stood in one corner with sheet music of Christmas carols scattered across it. A heavy Oriental rug partially covered the wood floor. A color television set sat against the far wall. We entered the kitchen, where her parents were working.

"Help has arrived," Cathy announced.

Mr. Cornett, working at the counter, looked up, his hands covered with flour. "They caught me," he said. "Looks like they got you, too."

"Got me where?"

"Cookies, I'm afraid. We need to make cookies. Millions of them."

"Most of these are for you, Mr. Ford," Dorothy said.

"I always take cookies for everybody at Christmas," he said.

"And it takes lots of cookies for that crew," Cathy said. She then looked at me. "Don't look so awkward, Matt. Here. Pour flour in the canister."

I obeyed.

They continued to measure and roll and cut and bake. I tried to help where I could, but I had problems cutting out cookies. The dough of Santa Claus's boots would break off at the ankles and stick in the cutter. So did the star on the Christmas trees.

"Use more flour," Cathy said. "On the cutter."

I don't care how much flour was used on the cookie cutter, dough still stuck inside. Despite my efforts, I felt useless.

"Relax, Matt," Cathy said. "Don't look so embarrassed."

"I'm not, just hot."

"The oven does make the kitchen hot."

Wendell glanced at me. "Let's escape," he said. "Come on, Matt."

I followed him to his den, where it was cooler.

He sat down behind his desk, and I sat in front of it. "I appreciate what you did for Cathy," he said.

"What I did?"

"Running Colby off after they threw mud."

"Oh, that. I got mad when I saw they hit her with mud."

"Thanks, Matt. I appreciate it."

"Sure."

"I want to call the school about the incident," he said. "And some parents as well. Wanted to talk to you first, though."

"I'd rather you not call anybody."

"Why?"

"Parents have a way of making things worse."

"So you don't want me to call the school?" he asked.

"No."

Mr. Cornett stretched in his chair and scratched the back of his neck. "I've been hearing a lot of things about you," he said.

"You have?"

"Good things. You are well liked around the shop. You are a very hard worker. And you sure have helped me out. By the way, Big Joe likes you a whole lot."

"He's fun to work with."

"He's a good employee. He's also been asking a lot of questions lately about church and Jesus and life."

"Yes," I said, "he has."

"I've been talking to him about his need for Christ. I think it's great that you're working with him, and if he asks you anything, you'll say the same things I've been telling him."

"If Big Joe is going to hell, I might race V-8 Fords with him."

"You have a good testimony, Matt," he said.

"Probably not that good, sir."

"You flunked Christianity."

"Nonsense," he said. "You're a good testimony. Just like your dad."

Good testimony? "I'm afraid I can't compare to him."

"Why would you say that? You're just like him, Matt."

I squirmed in the chair.

"That was the same problem your dad had. I guess you're trying to be just like him."

"I can't compare to Dad," I said.

"Matt, you most certainly can compare. Why, when your dad was your age, he wasn't even a Christian. He'd be proud of you."

There were many sales awards from Ford Motor

Company framed and hanging on the wall to my left. There was a picture, too, of Edsel Ford and Frank Cornett. Though I was looking at the wall, I still felt Wendell's gaze.

"Perhaps," I finally said.

"What I want to ask you is whether Colby has been bothering you."

"No, sir. I should apologize for the mud on the cars. It was intended for me."

"I realize that."

"I hope there was no harm."

"No," he said. "Everything is all right."

"He never came back, did he?"

"No."

"Is there anything else?" I asked.

"Are you in a hurry?"

"Just helping with the cookies."

He laughed. "I appreciate you looking after Cathy. That means a lot."

"You're welcome." I stood up to leave.

"So leave this Colby mud thing alone?" he asked.

"Yes. Please."

"All right."

I walked to the door, then turned around. "Mr. Cornett?"

"Yes, Matt?"

"I appreciate what you've said. But you need to know—I have not been that good a testimony. You have been the good testimony. Both at church and at your dealership."

I walked down the hall before he could respond. I may have been a worthless coward, but at least I could be a truthful one.

I returned to the kitchen, where Cathy and her mother were baking cookies. I tried to help again, but because I felt so silly, I ended up sitting in a chair supervising the operation. I did keep the canisters full of flour and sugar. I also sampled an occasional cookie and rendered judgment. After a while, they finished.

"Want some popcorn, Matt?" Cathy asked.

"Sure."

Cathy started making the popcorn at the stove while I sat and watched. Mrs. Cornett wiped the counters, then started the dishwasher. It droned low and steady. I had never seen a dishwasher in action before. Mrs. Cornett finished cleaning up the mess and went into the other room.

"Have a nice talk with Daddy?" Cathy asked.

"Yes."

"He's impressed with you."

"I'm not impressed with me."

Cathy did not seem to hear. The sound of staccato popping filled the kitchen. She glanced back. "Well, I sure appreciate the way you stuck up for me and Wade."

"Like the way you saved me from Miss Edmonds?"

"This was different," she said. "I was scared."

"I was scared of Miss Edmonds too."

"Matt, I'm serious. I was terrified when Squareface and Colby jumped out. It was about to turn into something ugly."

"It was bad," I said. "The whole thing was bad. I wish it never happened. Maybe more so than anybody else."

She jiggled the popcorn into a large bowl, the aroma filling the kitchen with delight. "Well, I was sure glad you came along," she said. "Thanks, Matt."

"You're welcome."

Cathy melted some butter and stirred it into the bowl. "You sure scared poor Ronnie away," she said.

"That's really not too hard to do," I said.

"Maybe. But the way you looked. You can look through people sometimes. You have sharp eyes. And a piercing look."

"What?"

"Oh, I don't know. Piercing. Penetrating. You know, powerful green eyes that can look right through people. Or into them."

"I've never heard that before."

"He had that same intense look that . . . well, that Tommy always had."

"It's true," she said. "You have beautiful green eyes."

"Nobody has ever commented on my eyes."

"They don't miss anything. And yet they conceal a lot too. A storm is brewing within you. I can tell."

"Are you now an expert on eyes?"

Cathy gave a little smile as she finished salting the popcorn. "Let's go in the other room," she said.

She carried the bowl, and we sat together on the couch in the living room. She still wore her white apron.

A pole lamp with three lights lit the room. The house smelled of pine and also fresh cookies and popcorn. Their Christmas tree stood in front of the large picture window. The drapes were open, and the lights of the tree reflected off the dark glass of the window. A large painting of mountains hung above us over the couch. I did not know where Wendell and Dorothy were.

"You've been tense," she said. "Worried about the race tomorrow?"

"Maybe."

"You shouldn't be."

"I've never beaten Colby in my life."

"You have an advantage that Colby doesn't."

"What's that?"

"You can pray away that worry."

"Pray?"

"Sure," she said. "You're a Christian. Colby is not. You have the privilege of praying to your heavenly Father."

"I don't know. Me and God have not been getting along too well lately."

"You can change that in a moment by praying. Peace is just a prayer away. Prayer will calm any storm you have."

"Did you ever get the feeling that your prayers don't do any good?" I asked.

"Occasionally. I suspect we all think that sometimes."

I looked into her eyes.

Thanks for being honest.

"Well, I don't think my prayers do any good," I said after a moment.

"But they do, Matt."

"I don't know. Did you ever get the feeling that life handed you a test, and you royally flunked it? Big time? So what do you do after you flunk the test? Is there any life after you've flunked?"

"You can change all of that by praying," Cathy said. "Prayer is what changes things. Prayer can straighten things out if you really think you have flunked some test."

"I don't know."

"You've thought this way ever since the funeral, haven't you?"

"Yeah."

"You still haven't gotten over it, have you, Matt?"

I stared at the piano with all the music scattered about. I suspected that she could play Christmas music real good too. "I suppose not," I said.

"You frightened me."

"Frightened you?"

"At the funeral," she said.

"What do you mean?"

"Well, I was crying my eyes out. Everybody was crying. Everybody except you. You did not cry."

"So?"

"It was unnatural," she said. "It wasn't right. It hardened you somehow. It frightened me."

"It frightened you that I didn't cry?"

"When you don't cry, you keep everything bottled up inside. Matt, all that stuff is poison. It is eating you up. You have to get rid of it."

Ask her to play some Christmas carols.

But I didn't. I stared at the large grandfather clock and listened to the soothing ticking that filled the room. I didn't want to hear Christmas music anyway.

"Can I ask you something?" I said.

"Sure."

"Do you think I'm like Garrett?"

"Mercy, no."

"I'm not like Garrett?"

"No. Garrett is a very bitter man. Where did you get an idea like that?"

"That's funny, Matt. You make a great Garrett."

"From him," I said.

"From him?"

"He said I was just like him."

"Well, you're not."

We sat on the couch and ate popcorn and talked away the remainder of the evening. Later, the grandfather clock began to chime.

"Whose idea was it to invite me over?" I asked.

"Whatever do you mean?"

"Was it really your dad's idea?" I asked. "Or your idea?"

"Matthew Collins! A girl is not supposed to answer such questions!"

"I thought so."

"Matt! You're awful!" She wrinkled her nose, and I thought her face had a tinge of pink.

"It's eleven o'clock," I said.

"I know."

"I suppose I need to go."

"Yes, you probably should be going."

"Thanks for asking me."

"Thanks for coming."

We got up and walked toward the front door. She set the empty bowl on the coffee table.

"I can talk to you, Cathy. You're a real friend. Better than Colby ever was."

"I should hope."

"You were right about him."

She nodded and opened the door of the entry closet, where my coat hung.

"It's just hard," I said. "We were best friends from day one. Collins always sat behind Colby."

"You were looking the wrong way, Matt."

"The wrong way?"

"Collins may have always been behind Colby, but . . ." Cathy took my coat off a hanger.

"But what?" I asked.

"But Cornett was always behind Collins," she whispered.

Cornett? Behind Collins?

She handed me my coat, and I slipped it on. Her face was definitely pink. "Let me get a few cookies for you to take home," she said.

She turned to go to the kitchen. I immediately stepped behind her and wrapped my arms around her waist. She turned around in my arms.

I panicked.

She looked surprised, and I felt stupid, and I didn't

know what to do, but I didn't let her go nor did she try
to pull away.

She wrapped her arms around my neck and kissed
me, then let me go. Her face was now very red, and my
face felt quite hot.

"Good night," I said.

"Good night," she whispered.

I stepped out into the cold, still night. My coat hung
open, but I was very warm. I could have taken it off and
still been comfortable had I wanted to. The frigid night
was clear, and I could look deep into the heavens and
see many constellations. I found the Little Dipper and
the North Star.

I dawdled along and thought about cold hearts and
how there could be no peace if you were bitter, and I
thought too about how love just warms everything up
and how that feels very nice. Then I remembered how
I had resolved never to love again because if you loved
somebody, God would take them away from you, and
nothing was worth such horrible pain.

Or was it?

Love carried great risk. That much was clear.

As I shuffled home at what Wade's pace would have
been, I watched the plumes from my breath dissipate. I
wore no hat or gloves, and my coat remained on but was
open, and I felt very toasty, and I did not think about life
or worry about the race. I only thought about Cathy, and
I did not think of anything else.

TWENTY-SEVEN

In that watershed year I came face-to-face with the fact that I knew little about God or life. Death and love were entirely new ideas I had never before considered. I held incorrect concepts about Christianity. Yet I did realize that life had handed me a test and that I had failed. I also knew that because of this failure, there was nothing left but to die. I was convinced that death now awaited me.

So on the morning of the last day of my life, I noticed that white frost clung to the trees and covered the ground. The brown grass and dark trees became transformed by whiteness, and the morning was sharp and cold. Sleeplessness had dominated the night, and death now dominated the morning. The warm feelings of the preceding night at Cathy's now belonged to some distant, cold, forgotten past.

Dread hung over me like a black cloud, for I knew this was the last morning of my life. I did not want to race Colby. I did not want to face Wade. I wanted to crawl back into bed and let the whole world pass by. But death was now beckoning to me, and death was something that would not be denied.

The thought did not alarm me; it was merely one of those facts that simply needed to be accepted. I wrote down a few of my last thoughts, then inserted the paper into my Bible, which had been hidden in the closet. I left the Bible out on my desk where it could be easily found.

I considered what it would be like to be dead and see Jesus. I had failed my test, and I knew this was the reason why I would die today. When I met Him face-to-face, I would present my case but probably lose for some reason I did not presently know. That did not matter. Before the day was over, I would see Dad once again. That was comforting.

I hoped they would bury me beside Dad. That would be nice and would make me proud.

I ate a hurried breakfast ahead of Mom and Debbie. "Mom, I'm going early to church."

"You are? Why, Matt?"

"I need to be alone for a while; that's all."

I think she said something, but I did not hear it because I was already out the door and heading for church. The cold day nipped at me, and my breath poured out in white streams that dissipated into the surrounding frost. The feeling of precipitation hung in the air, and this made the day—just one month after the death of the president—a very fine day to die.

What would Dad say to me?

I walked inside the cold church believing I was the first to arrive. I was wrong.

I heard noise in the room off the baptistery. I hid

behind the foyer door and watched. The Metzge twins
appeared, then left by way of the back door, carrying all
the costumes for the Christmas pageant.

I entered the sanctuary and sat in my usual place in
the back row. The antics of the twins did not bother me.
If God was so powerful, He could take care of His own
things. He did not need me.

So what sort of man was Dad?

He was merely a man but a great man, an ex-marine
who had seen war and would become emotional when
he viewed that famous picture of soldiers raising the
American flag on Iwo Jima. He was a mere man who had
become a Christian, then faithfully followed his Lord.
He was a man who stood tall in the church, and he
encouraged everyone he met.

Being a marine was part of who he was, and the war
he endured defined the core of his life. He would read-
ily talk about his war experiences, though he would say
little about the gore and the killing.

He would say little, that is, except when he gave his
testimony.

He would tell about landing on Iwo Jima and how
he had faced the full terror of war. The landing had been
horrid, the terrain was horrid, and the advancement
was horrid. He told about how his buddies had fallen on
the right and on the left, bloodied, sometimes mangled.
There was the roar of battle that often left you temporar-
ily deaf. And then there were the smells. The smell of
sulfur. The smell of battle. The smell of death.

Dad's unit had been advancing when he was hit.

He fell and felt the blood flow, warm and sticky, and he knew this was the end. His terror transformed into a hyper panic, and he cried out to God to save him. Then everything swirled around him and went black.

The next instant he awoke to find himself in sick bay on board a ship, coming out of the morphine, and he knew that God had miraculously spared his life.

When the chaplain dropped by, Dad trusted Christ as his Savior, and his life was completely and eternally changed. The absolute worst event in his life, the horror on Iwo Jima, had been in reality the greatest thing that had ever happened to him.

So what would you say to me now? Even after that July night?

Silence.

Yet I could guess. He would probably still try to gently lead me back toward Christ, just as he had everyone else he came in contact with. In spite of all that had happened. Because that was who he was.

You did not fail your test. All who watched you spoke well of you.

They had come from everywhere, filling the church and then some, and they all spoke of how Tommy had touched their lives. This ex-marine who had known battle and death had led others to Christ, had encouraged, had helped, had been a leader, had been a blessing. People we had never before seen descended upon us. They had tears in their eyes, and they hugged us and wept, and they had told us how they were better people because of him. They told us stories of long-ago events in faraway places, and they spoke of recent events that occurred within our county. And they spoke with respect and admiration of a great man.

On that awful day, we were all hot and sticky, and we gagged from the pungent flowers and the flies were buzzing, and I wished I could have been anywhere else doing anything else. Yet in spite of it all I was stunned, impressed, at the sheer number of people. I was amazed how one man could have touched so many.

But I had failed my test. What will they say at my funeral?

I sat quietly.

I did not pray.

But after awhile I began to think that it might be wise to settle accounts, considering I was about to die.

Okay. Look, God, I flunked the test. I admit it. But You're to blame for some of this too. It's not all my fault.

Silence.

God made no attempt to settle accounts.

Later Mr. Cornett arrived to turn up the thermostat, and soon I heard the furnace come on. He left without seeing me. I didn't hear anything else until Pastor Greg sat down beside me.

"May I join you?" he asked.

"I was just leaving."

"Matt, I'm sorry about that night in the rain when you came over."

"So am I."

"I mean that I owe you an apology."

"No, you don't."

"I believe I do," he said. "I was placing doctrine over people again. I never realized how badly hurt you—"

"Some things needed to be said. Anyway, I was rather ugly myself. I'm sorry."

"Matt . . ."

"It's okay." I stood up.

"What I wanted to say—"

"You don't need to say anything."

"You have to look at the cross," Pastor Greg said.

"I need to go."

"You have to look at life from the cross. If you don't, then nothing makes sense. Life becomes madness."

I got up and walked out the other side of the pew.

"If there is anything I can do to help," he said, "please let me know."

I left Pastor Greg sitting in the sanctuary. By this time, a steady stream of people began to fill the church. I walked back out to the foyer, then down the stairs to Sunday school class.

I paid no attention to either Sunday school or church service. I knew I was going to die. I could not shake the thought. I spoke very little to anybody.

Mrs. Metzge came unglued between Sunday school and worship. Somebody had stolen all the costumes for the evening's pageant. Note—they were not moved, misplaced, or missing. They were stolen. She whipped the church into an uproar. I noticed her twin boys grinning, but I said nothing. I would not be alive in the evening anyway. Other things were more important than costumes.

We walked home after church. I did not want to race. I did not want to go. Yet I had to. This was something I had to face. And I knew it.

"I'm not going to eat."

"Why not, Matt?" Mom asked.

"I'm going running."

"Running? Surely not!"

"I'll be running. Colby will be there. We'll run."

"Oh. That's good. You guys must be getting along better. You'll be running together just like old times."

"Just like old times."

I changed into sweatpants, a heavy shirt, two pairs of socks, and the new shoes. I wore a stocking hat and pulled on a hooded sweatshirt. I put my stopwatch in my sweatshirt pocket, stretched, and limbered up, then left the house. I jogged down the gravel road. I saw Wade and Catherine up ahead, and they arrived at the dirt road first. We were alone.

Wade wore an old brown coat, blue jeans, and a red stocking hat. Cathy had not changed from church. She still wore her blue dress, nearly covered by her navy blue coat. The hood of her coat covered her head. She wore gloves on her hands, and her arms were folded. She stood with her black shoes together, and she looked like she was freezing.

"H-hi, M-Matt."

I glared at Wade. "I suppose you're thankful about all of this."

"Y-yes."

I glanced behind and saw Colby and Squareface riding their bicycles toward us.

"I-I try t-to always g-give thanks," Wade said.

"So I've noticed."

"Innn everything, M-Matt."

I pointed at him. "I have this desire to stomp your face right now. Will you give thanks for that?" I was mad at him, and I meant what I said.

"I g-give thanks. G-give thanks for the th-thing that h-hurts. The very th-thing."

"You're thankful because you're cold, right?"

Cathy looked very cold, but I could not tell if she was thankful.

"M-Matt, it's C-Christmas."

"Christmas?"

"Yes. C-Christmas."

"What does Christmas have to do with anything?"

"C-Christmas is when God m-made peace p-possible."

"Peace? What do you know about peace?"

"P-peace between God and m-man. That's the m-meaning of C-Christmas."

We watched Colby and Squareface arrive.

Colby hopped off his bicycle. "Bring your twenty dollars, Nerd?"

Wade nodded.

"Prove it."

Wade pulled his right hand out of his pocket, the twenty-dollar bill held tightly in his fist. He wore no gloves.

"Let's see yours," Cathy said.

Colby snorted. "Well, Collins, decide to show up?"

"I'm here."

"Surprised to see you."

"I'm here," I said again.

Nobody else from school had showed up. For this I was extremely grateful. Of course this would not interest any of them. The only reason even Colby was here was because of the twenty dollars.

"Well, let's begin," Colby said.

We lined up along an imaginary line with the hedge corner post. I lined up in the right wheel path, Colby the left. Squareface rode his bicycle past the starting line a little ways ahead of us.

The temperature was cold, maybe twenty degrees, the wind from the north between five and ten miles an hour, the ground completely frozen. Sleet began to lightly fall. Cathy shivered. We stood at the edge of the world and looked down the road toward the willow trees, now dead looking. I knew death awaited me down this road. I had known it all day.

"*On your mark!*" Squareface bellowed.

The race set before us began at the hedge corner post, ran the entire length of the dirt road to the drainage tube at the south end, then all the way back, a distance we arbitrarily agreed to be two miles. Ditches and fences lined the dirt road, and an intermittent line of barren trees followed the fences, with frozen pastures and fields beyond the trees. We would often race down the dirt road, even in winter, for the road was frozen and the footing good.

"*Get set!*"

A lump formed in my throat. My stomach tied itself into several knots. The stakes for this race exceeded a mere twenty dollars. The stakes would be for life itself.

I looked down toward the willow trees. I knew I was about to die.

Sleet fell around us.

"*Go!*"

TWENTY-EIGHT

Colby exploded into the lead.

Squareface sped his bicycle toward the south end of the dirt road.

Colby set the pace. I tried to keep up. The pace was too fast. Too fast for two miles. Too fast for me.

Silence engulfed the frozen world around us. Silence except for feet pounding the road and our heavy breathing. Silence except for the gentle, sizzling sound of falling sleet. We ran down the frozen road toward the willow trees. The world was brown, dormant, dead.

"I've never beaten Colby in my life."

I felt stiff. My legs refused to obey. They cried in pain. My side complained also. I was breathing too hard. Too fast. The cold air stung my lungs. I gulped air through my mouth but could not get enough. I was pushing too hard and falling farther behind. I would not be able to keep this pace.

"You have an advantage that Colby doesn't. You can pray. . . ."

The sleet fell and rebounded. Our feet pounded the

frozen earth. Colby pulled farther ahead. Sleet bounced off McLean's frozen pond. We reached the willow trees.

Why pray? You can't be trusted.

We ran up the incline and headed toward the woven fence line at the half-mile point. I continued to gulp air. I could not get enough. The cold stung.

We made a deal. You leave me alone; I'll leave You alone. I don't need You.

We could not feel the wind. It blew from behind us and not that hard. Colby passed the fence line. My pain increased. I realized death would occur because I would push too hard and die. I passed the fence line.

You don't need God? Well, Matt, you must be doing a whole lot better than it looks.

I wanted to run faster. I tried to run harder. My legs would not obey. The stiffness intensified. This was a terrible running day.

"Matt, peace is reaching out to you. Just reach out and take it."

I longed for peace. More than anything else.

"C-Christmas is when God m-made peace p-possible."

I pushed myself faster. My feet struck the frozen road. Sleet continued to fall.

"G-give thanks for the th-thing that h-hurts. The very th-thing."

My side hurt. Everything hurt. I pounded after Colby. He increased his lead.

"Peace is just a prayer away."

We ran between the dark, barren mulberry trees.

"Me and God have not been getting along too well lately."

The sleet sounded like grain pouring out of a sack. Fields and pastures lay dormant. The gray sky lowered. We saw no cows.

There is no mercy.

I ran past the large limb that had tripped me once before. The limb lay broken up in the ditch.

Oh? There is no mercy? Can you not walk? Are you not running?

This was not a good day. I was very stiff. Why couldn't we have raced two days earlier? That had been a good day.

I'm going to die. You're going to kill me.

I would have to make a decision. Either let up the pace or die.

"Your religion is . . . worthless!"

We ran through the frigid countryside. The cold air continued to sting my lungs. Sweat formed underneath my stocking hat. Sweat trickled down my face. I saw Squareface on his bike at the end of the road. Colby rapidly approached the end. He had a good lead.

I pulled my stopwatch out of my pocket to check the time. It read zero. I had forgotten to start it.

Couldn't You have helped in this one little thing? Couldn't You have made sure I started the watch? Was that too hard to ask?

This was a bad run and I knew it. This run was better left untimed. It did not matter.

Remember? You made a deal. You leave God alone;
He'll leave you alone. You don't need Him. Remember?

I glanced at the still hands of the stopwatch. I kept it
in my hand. The end of the road loomed ahead.

Colby turned around and headed back.

Did he reach the end?

I could not be positive from where I was. But I was
reasonably sure that he turned around too soon.

As we passed, Colby had a big grin on his face.
Squareface also had a grin. He had the type of grin that
made you want to punch him in the face.

I reached the tube and crossed with both feet. I
clicked the watch, then headed back. Squareface took
off on his bike back up the road. Colby and I ran back in
the same wheel paths we ran down.

"*You can pray. . . .*"

The wind and sleet now stung our faces as we
headed north. The sleet continued to bounce off the
frozen road. The sleet was not a factor for the feet.
Only the face.

"*You know, Wade has sure taught me a lot of things.*"

It felt like my heart was about to burst. I gasped for
air. I could not get enough. My pace was too fast.

"*What do you know about life?*"

Death was about to overtake me. All day I'd known
I would die. Now I knew how.

What do I know? I know I flunked the test. So You're
going to kill me, aren't You? Just like You killed him.

I ran into the gray, frozen world. The wind and sleet
stung my face.

"G-give thanks for the th-thing that h-hurts. The very th-thing."

Well, I'm not going to give thanks. Just kill me. Kill me like You killed him. He was my daddy and You killed him.

"You killed him," I gasped as I exhaled. "You killed him."

You didn't have to kill him. After all, You are God. You could have thought of something to save him. Maybe a flat tire two miles back and he would have been off the road. Maybe he could have been late leaving work. Or early. Maybe You could have already killed the drunk. Or given him the flat tire. You could have done something. You are God. But no, You didn't.

"You killed him," I panted.

I knew I was about to die. In my agony I began to cry. I could not stop.

"You killed him! You killed him! You killed him!"

I ran and cried and tried to run faster and felt like I would die. The sleet stung my wet face. The crying became deeper. I could not stop crying.

"You killed him! You killed him!" I tried to scream, but I was short of breath. I could only gasp it out in short, hissing, guttural sounds.

The crying changed into a wailing, then finally something deeper, almost animal-like, something only from the deepest hollows of the soul. I cried and wailed and ran and demanded that my legs push to their last full limit. I wanted to die, and I knew that I was about to. I could no longer see ahead, and I knew I was falling farther behind. It seemed like some awful poison bubbled from the depths of my soul.

I'd thought I would never cry again. But on that road, I did cry and I could not control it. I cried and wailed bitter tears. I wailed for what seemed like hours, possibly an eternity.

But the wailing wound down to crying, and after that the crying ceased.

"You killed him!" I gasped.

My eyes began to clear, and I regained control once again. My side still felt like it was about to explode and my heart as well. The eternity probably lasted mere seconds. We were still a long way from the half-mile fence line. The sleet let up.

You killed him!

I felt like stopping. I wanted to give up. Instead I pushed onward. Faster. Into the arms of death.

"And that even though his brothers had meant evil against him, 'God meant it unto good.' . . . That verse has application in any situation where bad things happen."

My feet hammered the frozen road. The mulberry trees stood stark against the winter sky.

"Actually, Scripture says 'in everything give thanks,' not for everything."

I'm not going to give thanks he was killed. I'm not going to do it.

The crying had made me feel weaker.

"You give thanks Christ is your Lord and Savior in spite of your circumstances."

I'm not going to do that.

So you want what you truly deserve?

I felt awful. I could not understand why I just didn't fall over dead.

Did it ever occur to you to give thanks for the years you had with him?

What?

Did it ever occur to you to give thanks for the years you had with him?

No.

That thought had never occurred to me.

It was a strange thought.

Foreign.

I pushed legs that would go no faster. I continued to gulp for air that did not satisfy.

After all, he could have been killed on Iwo Jima. That could have easily been arranged. Where would that have left you? You had him for fifteen wonderful years. Can you give thanks for that?

I didn't know. I had never considered.

"You have to look at life from the cross. If you don't, then nothing makes sense."

I gulped and pounded after Colby. Uselessly.

"At the cross you see Jesus for who He is, and you see yourself as you truly are."

I knew my face was red and wet from crying, but it was also red and wet from running and sweating. I knew by the time I reached the finish line, nobody would know.

"Did you ever get the feeling that life handed you a test, and you royally flunked it?"

"Prayer can straighten things out if you really think you have flunked some test."

Colby approached the fence line.

"Matt, peace is reaching out to you. Just reach out and take it."

I longed for peace.

I partially raised my left arm. This upset my rhythm slightly. "Oh, Lord . . ."

I could not pray. I lowered my hand. I still held the watch in my right hand.

"Peace is just a prayer away."

I'd do anything for peace.

I raised the arm again. I reached for peace. Wade had taught me what to do.

"Thank you." I could hardly breathe. The words came out in a gasp.

Colby reached the fence line.

"Thank you for the years we had." My feet hammered the frozen ground. I desperately wanted peace.

"You have to look at life from the cross."

Colby ran downward toward the willow trees.

Thank You for being my Savior.

My hand returned to my side in rhythmic motion.

There. I said it.

I approached the fence line.

Oh, Lord, have mercy on me. Please help me. Please.

I had no right to ask anything of God, yet Greg was right about the love of God. Deep down I knew He had been there on that awful night. He had seen it all.

I thought I might cry again but did not.

Just before I reached the fence line, I noticed I no longer gasped for air. My breathing felt solid and under control. My lungs filled with air that satisfied. My legs no longer hurt, nor my side. My chest no longer felt like it was about to explode. The stiffness had left.

Weird.

One moment I was about to die. The next I felt . . . well, I felt good.

I tried to take a longer stride. I did. I concentrated on running from the hips, taking even longer strides. I could. I ran faster. My feet no longer pounded the road but rather lightly touched the frozen surface. My movements became fluid. I felt warm, strong.

"Colby is good. But he thunders. He runs like a freight train pounding by. . . . You're different. You have grace. You glide."

I passed the fence line and raced down the slight incline. My running became graceful; my legs felt strong. I gained on Colby. Was it possible to overtake him?

"You're a better runner than Colby."

Down the incline I raced, gaining.

Lord, please.

I ordered my legs to take longer, faster strides. They obeyed. I no longer ran but began to fly. Colby reached the willow trees. I flew down the incline. The gap between us shortened. I touched the ground lightly, silently. The sleet started again, in earnest, masking my approach. Yet I no longer felt the wind or the sleet on my face.

Colby started up the final stretch to the hedge corner post, the finish line. I reached the willow trees.

Jesus, please.

Colby looked back and saw me, his eyes wild with surprise. He pounded harder toward the finish line.

I started up the final incline and continued to fly, even though the wind was in my face. I watched him pounding onward.

He glanced back again. I was gaining. We raced onward. I closed his lead to ten steps. Then five.

We approached the hedge post. I saw Squareface on his bike. His mouth hung open. Wade and Cathy looked on. Colby ran in the right wheel path; I ran in the left.

Jesus, please.

I was maybe two steps behind him. The hedge post rapidly approached. Maybe one step behind. He pounded. I flew. I stretched for all I was worth.

We crossed the finish line, and I clicked the watch.

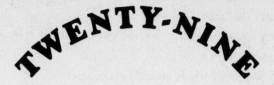

TWENTY-NINE

Colby won. By half a step.

Colby fell to the ground, gasping and wheezing.

I took several steps, then bent over slightly with my hands on my knees.

I knew I couldn't trust You. I knew You would let me down.

But I didn't mean it. I knew I didn't mean it, and God knew I didn't mean it. There was no venom in the words. The poison had left my soul. Something had happened back on the road, and we both knew it.

I glanced at my stopwatch: 4:55.

I couldn't believe it. I stared—4:55. Without resetting, I placed the watch back in my pocket.

I had broken a five-minute mile after first running a bad one. The record was set despite sleet and wind. Miracle. And I knew it.

God had touched me.

I had not died. I was alive and well. Instead of death, He gave me a second wind. A second chance.

My breathing returned to nearly normal. Colby still lay on the ground, holding his sides, groaning, panting.

Wade stood watching, a look of surprise on his face. "W-wow," he said. "W-wow."

Cathy smiled at me as she unsuccessfully tried to suppress a shiver.

A second wind. A second chance.

I took a few steps toward Colby.

"Get away from me, Collins!" He struggled to his feet and backed up several steps. His eyes looked wild.

I stood in front of him and watched him gasp for air.

I then turned toward Squareface. He sat on his bicycle, also looking surprised. His mouth hung open. I pointed at Squareface. "You cheated. You both cheated."

His eyes grew wide, and he almost fell off his bike.

"I won fair and square," Colby answered for him. "Now where's my money?" He still fought for air.

If there was going to be a fight, I would easily win. I could kick the snot out of Colby, and we both knew it.

"Cheaters better ride off," I said to Squareface. I still pointed at him. "There'll be no more of your little stunts. No more mud. Never again. Now git!"

He did not answer but took one look at Colby, a final look at me, then headed east on the gravel road.

"Where's . . . where's my money, Nerd?" Colby gasped, his eyes still wild.

Wade held out his hand clenching the twenty-dollar bill.

Colby staggered over to him, ripped the bill out of Wade's fist, and attempted to give Wade a shove. The effort was feeble and did not even jar Wade off balance. Colby, though, staggered several steps backward.

I took another step toward him.

"Keep away from me, Collins!"

"You cheated, and we both know it."

"I won fair and square."

I stood straight, my breathing normal. Colby was still gasping.

"Want to race again?"

Panic crossed his face. "I won. . . ."

I felt too peaceful to start a fight but felt Wade's money should be accounted for. "Tell you what, Colby. You can keep your money."

He held the bill in a tight fist. "You bet I will. . . ."

I walked back to Wade and placed my hand on his shoulder. "I pronounce you Wade. From now on, you will only be called Wade. Nothing else."

Colby stared at me, his eyes still wild.

"Understand, Colby? You'll call him Wade from now on."

He nodded.

"And you're through with mud too."

He nodded slightly.

"Now git!"

He glared for a moment, then staggered over to his bicycle and got on.

"Don't forget to remind your sidekick. No nerds. No mud. Got it?"

Colby rode off without answering, his bicycle wobbling some.

"I won't be so nice next time," I called after him.

Snow completely replaced the sleet and began to

accumulate on the fields and road. Cathy shivered vio-lently, her gloved hands now in her coat pockets, her face flushed.

"Let's go home," I said.

"Yes-sir-ee," Wade said. He shuffled ahead of us, his feet having minor difficulty on the road. "Yes-sir-ee."

"I hope you're not too upset for losing twenty dollars."

"Yes-sir-ee." He walked on without looking back.

"I think he cheated, but I can't prove it."

"W-wow. W-wow."

I ran ahead and faced him. "What's gotten into you?" I asked.

"S-something h-happened. Yes-sir-ee." Wade then moved around me and continued on his way.

"What?"

He stopped and glanced back, then headed onward. "W-wow."

"What are you talking about?"

"Y-you know."

"No, I don't."

"Yes-sir-ee." Wade was making no sense.

I caught up beside him. "Look, I'm really sorry about the money."

"Th-that's okay."

"You're not mad?"

"W-why?"

"Because you lost twenty dollars."

"N-no. N-not my m-money."

"Whose was it?"

"B-belongs to God."

I stepped ahead and faced him again. "What's that?"

"I-I gave the m-money to God."

"What are you talking about?" I glanced at Cathy, who shrugged, and her shrugging then turned into a shiver.

Wade pointed a curled hand at me. "S-something h-happened. Th-that's why."

"Why what?"

"Th-the race." He shuffled by me.

Cathy walked up to me and stopped.

"What are you talking about?" I asked.

"S-something h-happened. Yes-sir-ee."

I ran ahead of him again. "Tell me what this is about."

He looked at me and smiled.

"If you don't tell me, I'll tell your dad you gambled away money."

"He kn-knows." Wade continued on.

Cathy walked up to me.

"What are you talking about?"

"Yes-sir-ee."

I ran ahead and faced him one more time. "If you don't tell me right now, I'll stomp your face."

Wade smiled at me. He figured I didn't mean it. He was right.

"Maybe I should count to ten, then stomp your face."

He laughed; then I laughed too. We laughed and couldn't stop for half a minute. It felt good to be alive.

"S-something h-happened," he finally said. "I-I can see it in your f-face."

"Your dad knows about this?"

He nodded. "I's in the h-hospital. I wanted to give

this m-money to God and His w-work. I-I didn't know where to g-give it. I told Dad I wanted to help M-Matt. H-he said p-pray. So I d-did."

Cathy came up to me and took hold of my arm. I felt her trembling from the cold. The snow fell silently, heavily.

"I came h-home and thought of a r-race. I asked D-Dad. He said if I p-prayed, it'd be okay. I-I didn't know why. N-now I do." He shuffled on toward town.

I looked at Cathy, who shrugged again.

"Yes-sir-ee. God's m-money. Yes-sir-ee. Well s-spent."

We watched Wade shuffle toward Church Street, then followed him. Cathy still held my arm as we walked, and I did not mind. She continued to tremble and shiver, but I did not mind that either.

Why couldn't he be somebody else's neighbor? Then again, maybe I should give thanks he is my neighbor. Maybe I want to be like you, Wade.

"Maybe I do."

"Do what?" she asked.

"Oh, nothing. We need to get you home. You're freezing."

"And you're not?"

"No."

"Something did happen on the road, didn't it?"

"Yes."

"Can you tell me?" she asked. She now clung to my arm and brushed against me as we walked. I took shorter steps to keep pace with her, for it felt very nice to have her against me.

"Maybe later," I said.

"Promise?"

"Promise."

Snow fell over Bethel all that afternoon and into the evening. By church time nearly three inches had fallen. We bundled up and walked to church in the pure, silent snow. Mrs. Metzge had calmed down about her missing costumes. There was no pageant, but instead the children stood in front of the church and sang carols. People filled the church in spite of the weather, and the McLeans were there too. However the Parkers were not. Cathy sat down in the back row with me. I did not mind.

Candles lit the church, and the light made everybody feel warm. We sat and listened to the carols and watched the children sing at the front of the church. Wade sat near the front with his folks while Debbie stood up front with the other children. For the final song, the children sang "Silent Night," and the entire church joined in the singing.

Christmas arrived three days early in that eventful year. It arrived on a dirt road located approximately one mile southwest of Bethel—an unusual place for Christmas to arrive, but I suppose no more unusual than a stable in Bethlehem.

I had made a deal with God; I would leave Him alone and He would leave me alone. I'd fully intended to keep my end of the bargain. He never had any intention of keeping such a promise, and for that I will be forever thankful.

JERRY B. JENKINS CHRISTIAN WRITERS GUILD

Let Us Teach You to Write

"Join me in the experience of a lifetime, communicating the truths of God through the written word. We can help you master your craft and fulfill your call."
— Jerry B. Jenkins, author of the Left Behind series

You've been told you have a way with words. And you've wondered what it would be like to use your God-given gifts to touch hearts. Capture imaginations. Even win souls.

Now it's time to pen the next chapter of *your* story: the part where you work to establish a rewarding writing career.

We offer mentor-guided correspondence courses for adults and youth designed to develop the writer within.

With a pace of just two lessons a month, you'll have time to make real progress within the demands of family, work, or school. Wherever you are in your journey as a writer, we can help you develop your gift and take your skills to the next level. Let us teach you to write.

CHRISTIAN WRITERS GUILD BENEFITS

- *Apprentice* Course (adults)
- *Journeyman* Course (adults)
- *Pages* Course (ages 9 – 12)
- *Squires* Course (ages 13 and up)

- Annual Writers Conference
- Professional Critique Service
- Writing Contests
- Monthly Newsletter

"I am very excited about this course. My mentor is extremely helpful, and I have already begun to see how I can become a published writer."
— Tiffany Colter, *Apprentice*

"There is no way someone could get this type of encouragement, information, and education anywhere else — all from a Christ-centered perspective."
— Wesley King, *Annual Member*

Contact Us Today for More Information

CONTACTUS@CHRISTIANWRITERSGUILD.COM
(866) 495-5177 • WWW.CHRISTIANWRITERSGUILD.COM

CP003